Sonoran Shadows

A Novel of Suspense

Pat Walch

ISBN Paperback: 978-1-64873-549-3

Printed in the United States of America
Published by: Writer's Publishing House
Prescott, Az 86301

Cover and Interior Design by Writers Publishing House

Dedication

For Bruce…

who walked alongside of Sam and I

through every step to the last page, yet had to leave us

before the fat lady got to sing her song…R.I.P.

Acknowledgement

Thanks go out to my loyal and patient friends and my fellow writers in our Writer's Cramp group in Arizona; and old friends, family, and schoolmates back in Idaho for your hours of listening, reading, encouragement and input. Now you can have all the parts at once to see how it really ends.

1

I'd been restless all evening. But that wasn't unusual. Desert nights can be that way when you're alone. Weeks get longer; the house gets bigger and bigger. Six months since Trevor had passed, and I'd learned it doesn't get any easier as the months go by. Nothing on TV except last season's reruns and old movies. Jet was already curled up and asleep on his rug at my feet, and I decided sleep would be best for me, too. I rounded the corner to the bedroom and flipped on the light.

It had to be you . . . It had to be you . . . I wandered around and finally . . .

Icy fingers grabbed my heart. What the hell? What the

HELL? Frank Sinatra was singing *our* song! Trevor's and mine. But where? I sucked in a deep breath, streaked across the room, jerked the curtain back, and stared into the blackness of the night. A motor roared to life; bits of gravel spat against the fence as tires spun down the desert wash. The red glow of taillights flashed on, bounced up the bank onto the desert floor, then disappeared over the rise.

Jet's toenails clicked down the hall tile, then slid around the corner. His deep German Shepherd growl rumbled from his throat as he trotted to my side at the window. I reached to pat his head. "It's okay Jet. Whoever it was, they're gone now." I sat down on the bed, petted him with one hand while the other pushed against my chest to ease the pounding, to settle myself down. Why would someone be playing that song? Music, I hadn't heard since our friend Deb sang it at Trevor's memorial service.

Forcing a shrug, I scratched under Jet's chin. "Probably just kids making out . . . didn't notice the house up here. It's okay. Go back to your bed." He rolled those big browns up at me, and then meandered out the bedroom door, casting a quick glance back before he disappeared. He'd been a one-man dog before I came along, but eventually he'd accepted me as part of his world and we'd grown close over the last five years we've had together.

And now I guess we both realized it was just the two of us to watch out for each other.

It didn't take long for me to strip off my clothes and pull on one of Trev's old T-shirts and snuggle under the covers, willing sleep to come but afraid it wouldn't. I left my lamp on to discourage their return. Then smiled. Hell. They probably hadn't even slowed down by now the way they shot out of here. Yet, knots in my stomach pulled tighter as the seconds ticked away. Could it have been an innocent mistake that they parked so close to the house? A disc jockey's random choice of song?

Frank's song rattled around in my head until I must have finally cried myself to sleep. My lamp was still on when I awoke a little before five. I glanced around the room to the shelves

beside the TV, the king-sized glass snifter filled with weathered seashells and tiny sand dollars we'd picked up on the beach at Baja's San Felipe. Light reflected from carved niches on the onyx chess set we lugged back to Tucson from a gift store near the Mayan ruins of Chichen Itza. I sat up and blinked back tears as the unfairness of it all ripped through me, grabbed the open water bottle from my nightstand and hurled it across the room. Water spattered, pawns and other chess pieces scattered to the floor as I stared— wide-eyed, heart pounding.

"Jesus . . . where did that come from?" I said aloud, surprising myself and apparently Jet, who raced through the door again. I shook my head, trying to clear my thoughts. But they came too easily . . .

We'd been working our way through the never-ending U.S. Customs line for departing passengers at the Cancun airport when Trevor asked, "What were you thinking, Babe?" It was his turn to lug the heavy macramé tote. "I'll bet this chessboard weighs at least 25 pounds—not even counting the game pieces and all those pages of newspaper you wrapped 'em in. Couldn't you have settled for Mexican *dominos*?" he teased.

Tears streamed down my face as I replaced the pawns, bishops, and knights to the shelf. The black king was the only casualty. The cross was broken off the top of his crown. I was embarrassed to think I had lost control, yet felt a strange relief—like a burden had been lifted from my shoulders—as I set his highness back on his throne. I spotted the broken cross and laid it on the shelf to deal with later. Jet stayed out of the way, watching my cleanup. "Well, that's done." As I wiped my tears away, he sneaked a little closer, then on over and sat next to my leg. "What's the matter, boy? You wonder what's going on?" I patted his head. He looked up and leaned against my knee. All was good, again.

I dried drops of water from the terra-cotta sign next to the shelf. It brought instant memories of the peppery smell of tacos, the calls of street vendors in Nogales the day we'd picked it up. Bold black letters surrounded by flowers in bright blues, yellows, and greens— distinctive of Mexico's Talavera pottery— read: *Today is the First Day of the Rest of Your Life.* It had been hanging there, a part of our home for at least four years; yet I realized I hadn't actually read it since the day we'd hung it, hadn't given it a glance since the bottom dropped out of our lives.

My gaze still stuck to the sign, words seemed to come from nowhere. "It's time to get on with your life, Sam. Nothing will bring Trevor back. And nothing will lessen your feelings for him or take away your memories. But it's time to get off your butt and start living again."

It was me. My own voice. Talking to me. Was I going nuts?

Jet raised his head a little and turned it to the side, eyes wide open.

Nuts? . . . Maybe?

"Come on, Jet, let's go make some coffee." He jumped

up and we padded on together to the kitchen. Glad the coffee was all set to go; I punched the brew button on the way to the patio. The sun was about to peek over Pusch Ridge to take away the coolness of the morning air. The tang of the desert creosote caught my breath. But last night's mysterious music crept back into my thoughts. Should I call Bud, tell him what happened?

Not able to resist the scent of brewing coffee, I whistled Jet back inside, stole a cup of Joe, and headed down the hall to try to wash those thoughts down the drain. By the time I'd showered, dried my hair, and thrown on my favorite cut-off jeans and a denim shirt, my right brain had convinced the left one that I did need to call Bud. My cell phone blinked 5:27. Whoa . . . it was way too early to call Bud on a Saturday morning. The sign grabbed me again. *Today is the First Day of the Rest of Your Life.* How am I going to get myself out of this rut?

I peeked into Trevor's office, his sanctuary—a room forgotten as his cancer progressed. He'd kept it neat, almost too neat. Slipping down onto his chair, I opened the drawer and pulled out a thick pad. Across the top, it read - Speedway Lumber—Better Building Ideas. Just what I needed. I wrote <u>Saturday, September 10</u> across the upper part and underlined it, then numbered one through three along its left side. Surely, I could come up with at least three new ideas to get me started.

I stared at the unused monitor. Trevor's whole workday had revolved around his computer. Me? I'd never joined the techie generation past what was required for school; opting to have one of the girls in the secretarial pool type up my reports while doing investigative work at Colgan and Meredith Law Offices after I moved to Tucson. What a surprise to find myself wondering if it was too late to get into a computer class down at the U. My heartbeat shifted into high gear as to the right of number one, I wrote: Call UA for info.

My fingers glided along the smooth surface of the desk. Rosa kept it clean and polished for me just as she had for Trevor, nothing out of place. As I vowed to keep it that way, I hoped I could make good on that promise. Always a messy person on the job, it wasn't unusual for me to leave a project strung across my desk to tackle the next morning; or work on too many things at once, piling papers on top of papers, files on top of files. I couldn't do that to Trevor's office. It was time to put to use the things I'd learned from him.

2. Buy an organizer.

I guess it was a day for signs. *A Clean Desk is the Sign of a Blank Mind* stared down at me from the wall across from the desk—my office-warming gift for Trevor the day he moved his office into our new home. Laughing as we hung the plaque, I'd said, "Let this be your new motto, Hon. You need to kick back and let some of your work keep until tomorrow."

No more tomorrows for Trevor, and right now I wasn't so sure I was looking forward to any more myself. For months I'd felt like I was at the back of a cave, not even searching for a way out. Content to sit inside, shivering at its dampness, enveloped in the dark. Could I pull myself out? I realized that the answers wouldn't all come today. And probably not tomorrow. But I was off to a good start, wasn't I?

I opened another desk drawer and there was our recipe folder, torn corners of magazine pages and file cards sticking out—all the recipes we'd planned to transfer into his computer. Hell, we'd even mused about editing our own cookbook someday.

Hmm . . . someday. Maybe that would be a good project for me to get started on, a little bit of Trevor that I could pass on to family and friends. How we loved to cook. He had his favorites, I mine. And then there were those we'd discovered together. We'd often laughed about how we each enjoyed reading a cookbook the way most people enjoy a novel.

3. Start sorting recipes.

Rising from the desk, I grabbed my empty cup and headed

through the door just as the telephone rang. I grabbed the receiver halfway down the hall. "Hello."

It had to be you . . . CLICK.

I slammed the receiver down and jabbed Bud's number—to hell with the time. He answered with a sleepy hello and I began rattling, "Bud. It's Sam. Can you come over? Strange things are happening here."

"What's up? Are you okay?"

"I'm fine, but a little shook up. Just need you to come over when you can. Please. I'll explain when you get here."

Bud Holloway has been a good friend and companion. We met when I did investigative work in the attorney offices when I first moved to Tucson. Several times he and I ended up working on the same case either in the office or the courtroom. Our friendship grew from there. A detective on Tucson's police force, Bud's the survivor of a disastrous 'she got the gold mine and he got the shaft' divorce. He isn't in the market for another and we both felt safe in our friendship.

Some may think Bud and I are more than friends, and I'll admit I'd thought at times throughout our friendship that someday there may be something else, but for almost ten years our status had gone unchanged—before and after Trevor. Like the Three Musketeers, we'd spent many hours exploring the mountain ranges of the Sonoran Desert, sampling the fare at a new restaurant in town, or just having a beer beside our pool. And somewhere along the line, Bud became the brother Trevor never had. After Trev's cancer was discovered, Bud was always there to help with whatever was needed. And now, as we both fought to come to grips with Trevor's death, Bud tried his best to help me get my life back together.

Jet and I had huddled on the couch in the great room ever since the call. The electronic gate swung open and Bud's Toyota truck pulled up to the back patio. Jet jumped up and scrambled ahead of me, letting out a welcoming woof as I snatched the door open. Bud's eyebrows were raised, his face ashen as his six-foot-two frame pushed through the door to scoop me into a hug.

"What's going on?" He whispered into my ear, then pushed back to look me in the face.

A lock of his rusty blond hair drooped down onto his forehead. He finger-combed it back. He was wearing faded Levis and a light blue T-shirt—the 'Tucson's Finest' logo stretched across his chest shouted out proof of his regular workouts at the gym, the sleeves short enough to reveal a tiny strip of white showing above biceps bronzed by hours in the sun. His left tennis shoe bore the telltale black marks of shifting gears on his vintage ATV and Harley. "Come on, Sam," he said. "Let's have it. What the hell's going on?"

"Sit," I pointed at the kitchen table. Poured a cup for him and refilled mine. He sat across from me, drumming his fingers until I began.

"Well . . . last night as I went to bed, someone was playing loud music from the wash. You know the song. I sang the first few words. Trevor's favorite song by Frank Sinatra. How he loved Frank. It started when I flipped on the light to go to bed. They tore off down the wash when I pulled back the curtain. I figured it was just some kids out for a little necking, the song a coincidence. But, the more I thought about it, kids wouldn't be listening to that.

"I went to bed feeling sorry for myself and woke up the same way. Laid there looking around the room at things that brought back memories. Memories and tears. Finally, I decided it was time for me to climb out of the doldrums of losing Trevor and start focusing on all the good times we had together. So, I tinkered in his office awhile and then got a call. Nobody said a word when I answered. Just the music. That song playing again. That's when I called you."

Bud leaned forward, grabbed my hands in his, looked into my eyes, but no words came.

"Why would anybody do this to me, Bud?"

"Can't think of an answer." His lips pursed, head swayed from side to side. "As to why or who. But I want to hear more about this car last night. Exactly where was the car? Could you see it to get any description?"

"Down in the wash, below our fence. There was no moon last night, dark as hell out there when I let Jet out to pee before I locked up. I went to bed around midnight. By the time I got the drape pulled back, it was just a red blur of taillights. And it was loud. I think it was a truck, a pick up."

"How about the call, did your cell register a number?"

I shook my head. "Naw, it was on the house phone and I don't have caller ID, just the answering machine."

"That's okay; I can get a printout of your calls. Now, let's go take a look."

We walked out the back gate, and then angled over to the edge of the wash. Bud discovered wide tire tracks a hundred yards or so from our house that led down the opposite bank into the floor of the wash. They pulled across the sand, followed along below our fence at the wash edge and stopped right under my bedroom window.

"This wasn't any innocent mistake." Bud frowned and shook his head. "With no moon, they couldn't have driven this far through the desert and down into the wash without using lights. No doubt about it. They played that song for you to hear. That call this morning cinched that."

"I just can't believe somebody I know would do this." Tears popped from my eyes again.

Bud reached to brush them away. "Me neither. Maybe we'll find an answer when I check your phone records. In the meantime, don't answer any calls on your house phone. Let the machine take a message—you can call back, as needed. And, check your screen to make sure you know who's calling before you answer your cell. If not, let voice mail pick it up, too."

"Jesus . . . now, you've got me really spooked." I raised my eyebrows. "Or is that just cop-speak coming out?"

"It's the *detective* telling you to be careful. Even though you're somewhat isolated up here on the hill, you've got a good security system. And Jet is added insurance. But make sure your doors are locked. Keep the alarm set. One thing is sure." He chewed on his bottom lip. "If this is someone's idea of a joke, he'll soon find out it's not so damned funny.

"I'm on duty this weekend, what with Senator McManus and her team in town. Are you going to be okay here alone? They're having a rally in Old Town today and it's hard to say how long I'll be tied up. Why don't you see if Debbie can come over and hang out with you?"

"Oh, don't be silly. Jet and I can make it fine. But we'll keep the doors locked and won't answer the phones. And you, mister are going to sit right here while I fix you some breakfast. I'm starved and I know you aren't on duty this early, or you wouldn't have still been asleep when I called. Just having you here to talk has chased away my jitters. Thanks so much for coming over. Enchiladas and scrambled eggs sound good?"

"Now you're talking. Always time for Rosa's cooking. She still leaving surprises for you when she cleans on Fridays?"

"Always. She's got me so spoiled. She'd do all the cooking for me if I'd let her."

"Well, I don't check in 'til nine, the brass isn't due until ten. I've got my cop clothes in the car." His hands placed quotes around the 'cop' as he winked. "Tell me what I can do to help.

Just point me in the right direction.”

“You can grab some placemats and set up the counter, please.” I opened a drawer full of linens. “Except for the plates. I’ll heat them in the oven with the enchiladas, then dish everything up from the stove.”

I slipped the enchiladas into the oven, sliced jalapeno cheese bread for toast, and had just begun to grate cheese when we heard a whinny from the corral.

“Sounds like someone else is hungry,” Bud said as he slid off his stool, the counter now set and ready.

“Good job for you. Breakfast should be ready by the time you toss ‘em some hay.”

“On it. Come on, Jet,” he called, and the two of them were out the door.

Breakfast tasted so good we hardly spoke. The spicy flavors of Rosa’s enchiladas and bread were tempered a little by the cheesy eggs and fresh guacamole I stirred up. We cleaned up every morsel, and Bud helped with the dishes.

“Give Rosa my regards,” he said on his way to the door. “By the way, if she’s ever looking for more work, you let me know."

"I'm not ready to give her up!" I stuck out my tongue. "Besides, she doesn't have to work since she and Manny married, and he's retired now. But she loves this house and I think she has as many memories of Trevor as I do. You just need to come over more often."

"I'm all for that. Remember. Keep the doors locked and don't answer the phone. We have to treat this as a serious thing until we get to the bottom of it. Give me a call if anything else happens and please . . . please . . . stay inside today. The horses are good for all day. I'll check in by phone as soon as I'm off duty. Again, don't hesitate to call me. I can be here in minutes. We have a good crew on today; everyone's happy for the overtime."

He jumped in his truck, checked the lock after passing through the gate, and with a beep he sped away.

2

The Watchers

Two camo-clad figures leaned against a dusty black pickup on a rocky slope below Pusch Ridge, their elbows rested on the hood to support the weight of the high-powered binoculars held to their eyes. Both watched the white Toyota Tundra make its way down the lane from the hilltop estate and onto the highway.

"I'm surprised he left so quickly," said the taller, slender one. "Let's hope she'll be alone again tonight."

He grabbed a cooler from the back of the truck, pulled out two cans of Budweiser, popped the tops, and handed one to the other. The short one tore open a grease-spotted McDonald's sack and divvied up the contents onto the hood. They munched on almost-cold Egg McMuffins and hash browns chased with the ice-cold beer as the sun continued its rise above the Santa Catalina Mountain range. Both knew their work was done for now.

"We'll give her another shot tonight," the slender one said as he wadded his wrappers into a ball and tossed them out into the rocky landscape. He started the powerful Dodge Ram engine with a roar and pulled back onto the overgrown desert roadway to begin their slow descent down the mountain.

3

Thank God for the Tucson Pro Am and our local Channel 5 for broadcasting it or I would have gone mad that day. Not to mention that a local pro—my brother-in-law—was tied for 3rd place when I tuned in. Jon Morrison, manager at Tucson's Quail Hollow Country Club, is married to Trevor's sister, Teri. But I couldn't concentrate. Kept hearing music, then turned the TV down to see if that song was playing somewhere again. Fortunately, it never was.

After Jon finished the day at six under par, I fixed myself a stiff vodka tonic and stretched out on the couch to watch the rest of the players finish up. Jet hunkered on the floor next to me. I guess I fell asleep—probably both of us. Next thing I knew I heard music playing again. But this time it was my cell playing the lively notes of the *Can Can*. Bud was checking in.

"Hi there," I said. "All's quiet on the home front. How was your day?" I hoped my earlier pissy mood wasn't transmitting across the airwaves.

"About what you'd expect playing nursemaid to a bunch of politicians. Just peachy. So, no more music? No more calls?"

"Back to normal. Not another peep all day. Maybe it *was* just a sick prank."

"Let's hope that's it. Want me to drop by?"

"I don't' think there's need for that—didn't you say you were on duty again tomorrow guarding the big shots? Go home and get some rest. We'll be fine. And, thanks again for the quick response this morning. It was just what I needed." I crossed my fingers, hoping he didn't read between the lines.

"It's all part of the service, ma'am. Serve and protect. Now, you get some sleep tonight. And, remember, doors locked, no calls that you don't recognize."

"Yes, sir. Goodnight. By the way . . . last I saw, Jon's tied for third place in the Pro Am. Six under."

"Super. I forgot all about the that. If you talk to him, give him my best. And you . . . sleep tight."

I stared at my cell, unable to fathom it was already after six, and dragged myself off the couch. My stomach growled; yet nothing sounded good as I wandered into the kitchen and let Jet out the patio door. I filled his water and food dishes and stepped out momentarily for a look around the back lot, knowing he would have been barking if any strangers were around. We often went out this time of evening for a walk-about to give Koko and Diablo a carrot or apple along with their hay. One by one their heads popped up over the top rail in hopes of an incoming treat. Sorry, not tonight, kids.

It was the pits being a prisoner in my own house. Finally deciding to make a chef salad and call it an early night, I gathered up the salad fixings and soon sat at the table picking at pieces of ham, boiled egg, and cheese bits nestled among fresh greens slathered with my own homemade 1000 Island dressing. It tasted pretty darned good, and I was surprised to find my plate clean at the end of the newsreel covering highlights of the tournament. Go, Jon.

The dishwasher loaded and cranking away, I headed down the hall to my bedroom. A dip in the hot tub sounded so good, but I'd promised Bud I'd stay inside. My glance around the room reminded me of another promise I'd made earlier. I strolled to my roll top desk, plopped down on the chair and raised the lid. Without a second thought, I pulled my journal from its niche, caressed its worn leather cover, then reached to touch the four others in the bookcase alongside the desk. All were identical except for the year stamped in gold on the spine, my special gift under the tree each year from Trevor. I'd kept a journal since my teenage days, but had been unable to write for many months now.

My hands trembled a bit as I opened to the bookmark: January 3. It had been most of a year since I'd written. But what had there been to write about? How I missed him? Hated the thought of losing him? "Let it out," everyone advised. But that never worked. It only brought tears, the torn stubs of scribbled-on journal pages now evidence of my fits of anger, the shock of his being taken away.

We were so happy. We had the proverbial tiger by the tail. Bull by the horns. Whatever it is they say when things are perfect. Then one day he walked into the kitchen from his routine checkup with the news. We made the most of our last year and a half together. At first, we traveled to the places we'd always meant to visit. Then, as his cancer progressed, we simply held each other . . . a lot.

I picked up my pen.

Saturday, September 10, 8:30pm

My dear Trev,

Today I began a new chapter of my life. Yes, it's about time, you say? Last night something happened to make me realize that no matter how much I miss you, it's time for my self-pity to stop, for Sam to come back to life, to live for the both of us. Time to live up to my promise to you to continue on, to live with and enjoy the memories we made together. Not be saddened by them. To savor every minute we shared. Though we didn't think our time would be so short, we did make the most of the few years we had together, didn't we?

It took Frank singing our song to make me realize that life *is* too short—no matter how many years you have—when you are with the one you love, your soul mate. And we must be satisfied with knowing that we made the most of it. So, my dear, though I didn't know it then, I now realize why you wanted me to promise to carry on for the both of us. And I know that had it been me in your shoes, I would have asked that very same promise from you. And you would have unselfishly agreed because you would have known that is what I wanted for you.

Today was the first day of the rest of my life and I promise to live each day to its fullest . . . for us both.   I love you, S.

I was drained when I stepped from the shower. I had washed away not only the tears that were flowing when I got in, but also the self-pity I'd been carrying around on my shoulders for months. This had been an exhausting day, but an enlightening one. One I wouldn't soon forget. Still feeling the magic of my journal chat with Trevor, I slipped into his familiar worn T-shirt just before ten, hopped into bed, and dropped off to sleep almost as quickly as my head hit the pillow.

I awoke with a start.

It had to be you . . .

Shit!

Grabbing my phone, I hit the speed dial for Bud, turned on the lights, and listened again to the powerful engine's roar, the tires spinning down the wash.

"Bud, it's happening again."

"Are you OK?"

"Yes, same as last night. They're gone."

"I'm on my way."

This time Jet skidded through the doorway, his fierce bark said he knew exactly what these bastards were doing to me. "It's all right, Jet . . . they're gone again." I patted the edge of the bed and he jumped up beside me. I slid my arm around his neck and hugged him to me, felt the beating of his heart racing to keep up with mine. His eyes were on the sliding door, his continuous low growl breaking the otherwise silence of the room. His head jerked my way as I opened the drawer beside the bed, reached in to touch the checkered grip of the Colt .38 Special. "We're okay, boy. Bud will be here soon." His growl silenced, he angled his head across my lap, his eyes no longer focused on the sliding door or the open drawer, they looked up squarely into mine.

Bud arrived at 1:32, exactly 16 minutes after my call, record time for the 14-mile drive from his home on the opposite side of Tucson. It seemed like hours since that vehicle took off swishing down the wash, since I had pushed the speed dial.

The three of us searched the house and grounds together, but didn't expect nor really want to find anyone. He ran his police-issue million candlepower beam up and down the wash, seeing nothing but deep, wide tracks where the mystery vehicle had fishtailed away again. None of us got much sleep that night. We talked until four, then—hoping to at least get some sleep—I retired to my room, Bud to a guest room off the kitchen, and Jet chose his bed by the patio door.

4

The Watchers

This time dressed in black; the two figures watched the last of the lights blink off in the hillside home below. The tall one growled, "It's about damned time for lights out. We'll let her stew a little more now. See what happens after a day or two."

"Maybe she'll be spooked enough to just take a little vacation to get away from it all," said the stocky one. "Maybe run home to Mamma."

"Oh, she'll go . . . one way or the other. It's all up to her. Now, let's get out of here."

5

Sunday morning is usually just another day for me. But to wake up and smell coffee wasn't the usual around here. Then, I remembered Bud was here in the guest room. I threw on some clothes and joined the boys in the kitchen. The morning newspaper and all the ads were scattered on the table looking thoroughly read. Jet lay at Bud's feet, his tail thumping the floor.

"Good morning," said Bud. "I was hoping you'd be able to sleep in."

I poured a cup of coffee, put some sweet rolls on a plate, and joined them. "This is sleeping in for me." Giving his shorts, T-shirt, and flip-flops the once-over, I added: "You must've found someone to take your place today."

"Ya think?" He swallowed his first bite of strawberry-filled Danish. "Like I said yesterday, there are lotsa guys anxious to get overtime hours and this is pretty easy duty. Anything special on our agenda today?"

I shook my head. "But I'd rather not spend it in the house all day again, if you please."

"My thoughts exactly. I checked the wash again this morning and found nothing new. No cigarettes, no footprints, nothing that wasn't there yesterday except more tracks. How about a quad ride? Maybe we can find traces of the old stage route we've missed. One of my friends from Pima County Sheriff's Office will watch things around here while we're gone. He'll be out on the lane."

"That sounds absolutely wonderful. Weatherman says we should get up into the 80s today. Think the bikes will start? It's been ages since they've been out of the garage. Go check it out and I'll make sandwiches to take along."

"Let's go, Jet." He filled up his coffee, grabbed another roll, and they scrambled out the door. I allowed myself five minutes to indulge in my maple bar and coffee, then took my cup to the counter to get to work.

The Butterfield Stagecoach Line ran through Tucson on its way to San Francisco from 1857-61. What's left of one of their stations where they stopped for supplies and a fresh team remains right here on our ten acres. The three of us had searched, but found only a few ruts of the old road where the stages raced—perhaps at times running from marauding Apaches, maybe masked robbers. Who knows how many of those old stories were based on truth, how many had grown as they passed down through the years?

Tuna sandwiches were soon made and packed in a cooler along with a couple of cold beers and bottles of water for each of us. My Honda Rubicon was already running as I entered the garage, Bud was just unhooking the charger from Trev's Yamaha Kodiak. It wasn't long until the quads were gassed, the gear loaded, and we were on our way through the gate.

"No, not this time," I called to Jet, as he tried to follow. "Someone's got to stay here and hold down the fort." He stopped, barked once, and trotted over to lay on his old saddle blanket alongside the gate to wait for our return.

We thought we'd tried all the old roads and trails that crisscrossed our surrounding Sonoran Desert but Bud managed to find a trail on Trevor's GPS that wasn't marked with the telltale "breadcrumbs" of previously explored routes. About an hour out he pointed up a hill off to the west. "That looks like the remains of old mine diggings. Probably a good place for lunch."

"Last one there has to do dishes." I jammed my thumb against the throttle. Bud pulled alongside just as we topped the hill and found ourselves staring at three deep shafts gouged into the ground—tough work for miners in the days when they were digging mostly by pick and shovel. The shaft openings lacked the familiar wire fence now required by the Bureau of Land Management to keep animals and today's curious desert travelers safely out of harm's way. There was no evidence that anyone had been at this mine in many years.

Scavenging through the piles of tailings didn't give a clue to what those hardy souls were looking for. We kicked through their trash dump area; nothing there but rusted tin cans and broken bottles, a few shards of crockery cups and plates, and the curled leather soles of work boots worn smooth by craggy rocks the miners climbed in their struggle to find treasure.

We spotted familiar triangular mounds of rocks that miners used to mark the corners of their claims and walked over to the nearest one. What looked like a bit of rust down between two rocks caught my eye. I reached down, and pulled out a mud-crusted bottle. Probably once filled with a miner's whisky, it now held only a small rolled paper, brown around its edges. The rusted lid wouldn't budge. I handed it to Bud. He twisted until it broke loose, removed the lid, and handed the bottle back to me.

"Here goes. Hope this old paper holds together. I'm gonna try to get it out." I carefully squeezed my pinkie down the bottle's skinny neck.

Bud's breath warmed my cheek as he leaned in closer to watch over my shoulder. "Don't get your hopes up that it's an old claim paper. Doesn't look like it's been in the hot sun very long."

Holding my breath, I turned the bottle on its side and gently shook the paper down the narrow neck until I was able to hook a corner and slip it out with the end of my finger. It crackled but didn't tear as I opened it far enough to read a few words. "Lazey Daisy Mine. Filed by John F. March, May 4, 1936."

Bud whistled. "Do you realize that's almost 90 years old and still readable. Look. The embossing of the seal is like new." He brushed his finger tip across the raised nubs spelling out: State of Arizona. "Amazing."

We gingerly refolded and replaced the paper, screwed on the lid, and hid the bottle back under the rocks for some other lucky explorer to find, hoping they too would replace it with the respect due the miners who spent their time and energies to file and work this claim so long ago. I noted the claim's information on a pad and tucked it back inside my quad box before I forgot it.

"It'll be fun to see if we can learn anything about John March and the Lazey Daisy," I said as I pulled out our lunch cooler. "Maybe at the library?"

"Sounds good, but hey . . . I'm starved. Let's eat." Bud opened the cooler. "I'll set the table." He snickered a little as he tore open the sack that held our sandwiches and smoothed it out on the rear rack of my quad next to two camp chairs he'd already unfolded.

"And a fine table it is." I opened two frosty Pacificos, handed one across to him, grabbed a sack of potato chips, and we sat down.

"Cheers," he said, reaching over to clink my bottle of brew.

"A toast to a beautiful day. Just what I needed after that damned music. Thanks for suggesting this ride. I've been such a drag and have needed something to kick my butt out of the house for months. This has been a perfect start."

"You definitely needed to get away from those jerks. But somethin' else is going on in that pretty little head of yours. Spill it."

"Ya know, after that music the first night, I was so down. And . . .and I fell apart, Bud. Threw a water bottle at the wall.

Knocked things all over. A regular tantrum. Then, as I cleaned up the mess, I read that sign on our bedroom wall. *Today is the first day of the rest of your life*. Well . . . I made a vow to try to get the old Sam back, like Trevor asked. I made a list of things to get me started, did a little sorting in the office, even thought I might start using Trevor's computer to make that cookbook he and I talked about. Then that damned call came . . . the music again." I shrugged. "And you know the rest."

He reached across, took my hand, squeezed. "You've been through a lot all right, but it sounds like you're on the right track." A hint of a smile crossed his face. "And, it seems I recall Trevor teasing that you didn't know much about computers. Maybe you should check on a course at the U. Software and computers change pretty fast these days. How long has it been?"

"I'm way ahead of you there. I'm going to call them tomorrow to see what classes they may have available. If I don't chicken out, that is. It all sounded pretty good when I was planning it out yesterday morning . . . before the call. And now I'm not feeling quite so sure."

"No worries. It'll be good for you. You've been a lady of leisure far too long."

We finished our sandwiches, packed up our trash, and

headed on down the trail. We followed several faint ruts, only to be led to a box canyon, a cave, or another old mine. No lost stagecoach road. The sun and the miles were beginning to wear on us. It was time to go back home.

Jet met us at the gate and escorted us back to the garage to put the quads away. We all walked up to the pool deck, welcoming the shade that's always there that time of day.

"I'm ready for a margarita," Bud said, as he pulled out a chair. "Does Rosa still keep a pitcher for you?"

"Si, Senor," I nodded, and grabbed the pitcher and glasses from the bar fridge.

Rosa had been Trev's cook and housekeeper before we were married, and then, we all shared the cook part. She still came once a week to clean, and cooked up a batch of enchiladas or some other Mexican dish for me. Though I don't really need her, I couldn't bear to part with her after his death. Besides, I enjoyed the pampering and certainly could afford it. I had no idea how well I could afford it until Mike Colgan did the attorney thing with me after Trevor had passed.

"Here you go," I said, handing the chunky hand-blown glass to Bud. "I took a pan of Chile Rellenos out of the freezer this morning, so we'll have an easy dinner."

"Good. I've got a big day tomorrow and have some notes to make before our early briefing in the morning; they're keeping us pretty busy these days since the budget cuts. When someone retires, they just pile more work on the rest of us rather than hiring a replacement. Want to run over to my place with me to pick up a few clothes before dinner? I'm not going to leave you here alone at night until we get this thing figured out."

We drained our margaritas and climbed into his pickup for the round trip to his house. Jet rode in the back. Bud pulled over at the Pima County cruiser parked on the lane to let his friend know we'd be right back and then release him from duty. Jet roamed from one side of the truck to the other all the way to Bud's house, happy to be riding in the fresh air again. He'd been Trevor's sidekick on his days at work and I knew he missed it, too.

We chatted more about my plans on the trip over, after we got home, and all through dinner. Bud announced his plans to meet with the Pima County Sheriff to report the happenings of the last two days and assured me he'd hang here with me as long as needed. We both felt better about it all once we'd aired our thoughts.

We tuned in to watch the news as we cleaned up the dishes and were excited to learn that brother-in-law Jon had hung in to move up and take Second place in the Open.

"Hooray, Jon! I'm so proud and happy for him," I said, "though I hate to tell him we didn't watch it."

"You know what? They don't need to know. And, about that college course. No chickening out." He leaned over and gave me a peck on the top of my head before he retired to his room.

As I headed for mine, I wondered if we might find out more about John March and the Lazey Daisy. I went back into the office, grabbed my scratch pad and the telephone book. I found the number for the registration office at the University of Arizona and added it to my list for tomorrow morning. I flipped off the light and felt a smile spread across my face. This had been a really good day. A new beginning.

6

When I rolled over to look at the clock the next morning, I was surprised to see it was almost eight. Lollygagging just a bit, all at once my brain de-clogged and I remembered my plan to call the University this morning. Bud would never let me live it down if I didn't at least try.

There was a note leaning against the pepper mill on the kitchen counter. . .

'Good morning - Hope you are able to sleep in. Please don't go outside of the fence today unless you are in the car, stay on the roadways if you do. I'll file the necessary papers and give you a call. I'm sending someone out this morning to check for tire casting. They will be in official vehicles. I doubt they will need to come inside the fence. If so, I'll call to let you know. If you need anything—ANYTHING—call me on my cell.

P.S. Coffee's made. Take a break.

See ya later, Bud.'

A rumble rose from the pit of my stomach at the thought of coffee. As I poured a cup, I realized I was famished, too. I scrambled eggs and cheese, onions and jalapenos together, toasted raisin bread, then carried it all out by the pool to enjoy my breakfast. Bud said to stay inside the fence, not the house. I wasn't about to let these creeps get me down—but I didn't let Jet out of my sight.

Back inside, I checked my list and called the U for information; ended up with an appointment for 1:30 that afternoon. Though I didn't expect results so soon, I knew it was a good thing or I might have chickened out.

I felt a bit out of place walking down the hall at the administration building. Was I ready for this—going back to school after eighteen years? Jeez, had it really been that long? Afraid so.

My car beckoned. I was about to spin around and run when a voice said, "May I help you? You look a little lost."

Surprised, I turned to look into the impish blue eyes of a young man who almost ran into me as he raced down the hall. His reddish blond hair a little rumpled, he wore faded jeans and a fire-engine red T-shirt—a witch's face and hat peeked out of a huge hoagie bun displayed across the front. It was all I could do not to laugh. "Sand Witches" was lettered above the bun; 'They're Terror-ific' in smaller lettering underneath. I'd read about Sand Witches when they opened right on campus a couple of years ago. Two sisters with a zany idea to open a lunch place with ingredients freshly made in-house. Who would've thought today's students would even care about homemade buns and meats and dressings? I've heard it's almost impossible to get even close to the door at lunch time on school days, and here in front of me was the picture of today's typical student, broadcasting their popularity.

"I'm looking for the registrar's office," I said.

"Follow me. I pass there to get into my next class. We were swamped at lunch hour today." He pointed at his shirt. "Uh . . . Are you a new student here?"

"Yes. Here to sign up for some computer classes. Hoping they have some beginning classes at night."

"They do. In fact, you're talking to one of the teachers of Computer Basics. Jeremy Sharpe—with an e—at your service," he said and extended his hand. His grin was contagious.

My own face melted into a gigantic smile as we shook hands. "Samantha Beale," I said. "Also, with an e. I have to say you're not exactly what I expected or remember of the teachers from my school days. Nor my picture of the computer nerd we hear so much about today. Nice to meet you, Jeremy."

"Yeah, I've always had a knack with computers and one of my teachers recommended me for the teaching job knowing I'm working my way through school. Sorry, but I've got to run. Here's the office. I'll probably see you around. Most of the night classes are in the same basic area. Hopefully you'll end up in my class. I get paid per student." He winked, opened the door for me, then off to class.

The perky little clerk walked up behind the counter and smiled. "Hi there, what can we do for you?"

Just slightly over five feet tall, she looked about fifteen, dwarfed by the chest-high counter that divided her desk area from where I stood. She wore a blue and white striped T-shirt tucked behind the bib of her denim overalls. Her brown hair was loosely gathered into one large braid down her back. She looked like Daisy Mae from the vintage cartoon strip rather than Cassie as her name badge read. I looked down at my modest tan slacks, matching short sleeved knit blouse, Easy Spirit suede mules. Jeez, am I really ready for this? Butterflies returned to flutter in my stomach; moisture seeped onto my palms.

"Well, Cassie, I'm Samantha Beale here for a 1:30 appointment."

"Then you'll be seeing Mrs. Marks," Cassie said, "and I believe she's all set for you. I'll be just a sec." As she turned and walked toward an open door, I noticed her overalls ended in frayed cut-offs about six or eight inches above her knees, pink panties peeked through a thread-bare spot on the lower side of her left cheek. Oh, Boy. I was not ready!

A tall, slender woman wearing a white silk blouse tucked into a calf-length faded denim skirt appeared at the open doorway. Her black hair was neatly pulled back and tied by a Navajo print scarf at the nape of her neck, exposing a rather classic and handsome face of a Native American. Her high but delicate cheekbones pointed the way to small silver loops in her ears. She neither wore nor needed any makeup and her smile had already begun to shoo away my butterflies. Now this was more like it. My idea of a teacher.

"Hello, Samantha," she said striding through the opening in the counter. "I'm Sandy Marks. Please come in." She held out her hand. A firm handshake from both sides told me we had something in common. I've always thought you can tell a lot from a person's handshake. It can show self-confidence or wariness, dominance or fright. Sandy was not lacking in self-confidence.

She led the way to her office. The sign on the door read Sandra Marks, Dean of Women. Yes, definitely not lacking in self-confidence. She closed the door and waved me into a brown leather chair across from her massive desk. Though she was not a small woman, the desk almost dwarfed her as she sat behind it. I could see why she must love it, though. Made from a dark, reddish-black wood, it had to be authentic in its aged look. The petroglyph designs carved into the front of the desk defined its Native American heritage.

As she turned to open a file drawer, I scanned the shelves along the wall: filled with textbooks, biographies, and novels; interspersed with Southwest treasures, each no doubt with its own history, its own memory. A basket, handmade from pine needles, intricately woven with zigzags, diamonds, and other classic native designs. A brightly costumed Navajo Kachina doll. A totem bear carved from the beautiful blue lapis gemstone.

"Do you mind?" I rose to get a closer look at the lapis piece.

"Be my guest," she said. "It's my favorite, made by my grandfather. He gave that to me when I was a little girl."

"Those fine lines running through the stone must be gold," I said. "I understand it's quite often found in lapis."

"According to Grandpapa, greedy prospectors smashed the lapis to get to the gold until they discovered it was worth far more to leave it in its natural state for art and jewelry."

"A fantastic piece. You are lucky to have such a beautiful treasure in both the artwork and in the legacy of your grandfather. Does he still carve?"

"Only when he finds a special stone," she said. "He's become quite choosy in his old age." She laughed and her eyes spoke volumes of love as she looked at the little bear.

"But I'm taking too much of your valuable time," I said. "We'd better get down to business. I'd like to set up a class or two to learn more about using computers. Back a few years, I was a semi-decent typist, but I'm afraid my late husband was the computer expert in our family. I'd hate to see all his nice equipment go to waste. And, since I'm not quite ready to go back to being a co-ed, night classes would work best for me—probably other folks more my age."

"That sounds great, Samantha. I hope you don't mind my calling . . ."

"Please call me Sam. I haven't been called Samantha since I was in trouble back in my real school days."

"Okay, Sam, but only if you'll call me Sandy. We have a

pretty complete schedule of basic classes set up at night, both on campus and at our extension facility out on Skyline, near Oracle Road." She glanced down at the open file. "It looks like you live out in that area, so we'll first want to check on their availability. We offer mostly intro computer classes out there, today starts their second week of class for the quarter. Then you may want to follow up with some specialized classes here on campus, taught by our own professors. Most of the basic off-campus classes are handled by student teachers."

"Yes, I just met one of them on my way in. A nice young man, Jeremy."

"Ah. That would be Jeremy Sharpe," Sandy said, nodding. "A very bright student, but I'm afraid he's rather errant in his attendance. Jeremy's working his way through school and sometimes spreads himself a bit thin. You'd do well to have him as your instructor, if he's got an opening. He knows his stuff."

"When I called this morning, they asked me to bring a list of my software. I've no idea how to find that. Never used a computer growing up, except an old Macintosh at my mom's office. I'm afraid I was more into horses and boys in those days. The only software I've really used—and then only simple typing well over five years ago—was Microsoft Word. For now, I think we'd better stick with the basics and see where that takes us."

"So, I assume you don't use the internet and email? Are you interested in that?"

"Are you kidding? I'm planning to type some recipes and maybe an occasional letter. That's it for now."

Sandy guided me through the class list and soon had me enrolled in Computer Basics and Windows for four weeks, then progressing to Intro to the Internet and Microsoft Word for the next five. I pulled myself out of the chair and looked at the nine-week schedule with pursed lips and raised eyebrows. "Thanks for your help, Sandy. I hope I can handle all of this."

"You'll love it once you get into it," she said as we walked to the outer office. "You can find information about anything on the internet, and email is such fun. Beats writing letters." She extended her hand once again, and said, "Good luck. Remember, Sam, my door is always open."

A bell rang as I left the office and students poured into the hall from all directions. I felt like a sandwich—and old sandwich—worming my way out of the building. I envied their enthusiasm, their youth, yet I felt surprisingly good. In a way, I was just like them. I was on my way to a new life. I had actually done it; I could cross Number One off my list.

My head buzzed with questions and doubts as I pulled

through the parking lot. A cobalt blue Camaro caught my eye in the corner of the lot; its T-top opened to the sun. Maybe I should trade off this stodgy old Toyota 4Runner and get myself one of those.

The familiar tones of the *Can Can* announced an incoming call on my cell. Bud's number was on the screen. "Hi, how's it going?"

"Hi yourself. I just signed up for my classes at the university and am on my way home. What's up?"

"You did it . . . good job. I filed the reports on the weekend incidents and have arranged for the county to increase their patrols in the area for the next few nights. The sheriff and I agree the repetition takes it out of the prank category, and we'd like to come over this afternoon to brainstorm a little with you. Maybe we can come up with some answers or ideas as to who or why. Are you okay with that? Being just outside the city line, you're actually in his jurisdiction."

"Sure. Any time after 3:30 should be good for me."

"Let's plan on four. That was good with Schaeffer from Pima County."

"Your guys were out in the wash looking at the tracks just before noon. Come up with anything? Or were they really your guys? You said I'm not in your jurisdiction?"

"No, they were my guys all right. Doing a favor since they had the time. We got it done before I notified Pima. Told the sheriff we had it covered and already sent off to the lab. He was okay with it; we work pretty well together. The boys said there wasn't really a definitive track to work with. Too much sand, too much spin. They did get a partial tread cast where the vehicle came down into the wash. It was pretty dry but they're hoping they'll get something out of it."

"Okay. See you at four, unless I hear from you."

Office Warehouse was on North Oracle, right on my way home. It was twenty after two when I marched through the doors, confident I was about to mark Number Two from my list. I found a whole aisle of organizers, ranging from pocket size to three-ring-binder size, in all colors. I swear there were hundreds of them to choose from: two pages a day, a page a week, down to one page a month.

Finally, with a Day-Timer stowed in my bag, I opened the car door to toss it in when I noticed a blue Camaro parked on the far edge of the lot. The same car from the U campus. Were they following me? Whoa, Sam. Get a hold of yourself. How many blue Camaros do you suppose there are in a city of almost a million people? Besides, the one on campus had an open top—T-top in fact. Chill out. You're freaking out. But then, as I exited the parking lot, I decided it could be the same car when I saw the distinguishing lines of the now closed T-top.

Heading north on Oracle, I searched the rear-view mirror for that familiar blue car and darted to the right into the shopping center on the corner at Magee. I sat in my car for at least ten minutes, watching northbound traffic and all the cars pulling into the shopping center parking lot. No blue Camaro. Okay. Settle down. It's safe to go home. What's with this talking to myself? And answering?

I pulled back onto Oracle which becomes SR77 to follow the contour of the Santa Catalina Mountains along my right. I was so focused on my rear-view mirror; I almost missed my turn on Santiago Way. Once off 77, I breathed deeply willing my heart to slow, relieved no one was following. I think I even relaxed a bit as I turned onto La Montana Drive, our lane. How glad I was that Trevor had installed a pretty sophisticated security system when we built the house. And then added the remote-controlled gate after learning about his cancer. It seemed he was still looking out for me, but I was definitely spooked at the so-called coincidences that seem to be popping up. And, damned if I could figure out from whom or why.

Jet roused from his bed with a bark just before the gate buzzer sounded at 3:50 p.m. Bud's voice summoned me to the intercom: "Hi Sam, Sheriff Schaeffer from Pima County and I are here."

"Come on up." I pushed the button to trip the gate, wondering why Bud hadn't used the remote I'd given him. Then guessing he didn't want to give the sheriff the wrong idea, I followed Jet to the front door to welcome them.

"Sam, meet Sheriff Gary Schaeffer. Sheriff . . . my good friend Sam Beale."

"A pleasure Mrs. Beale." As we shook hands, he continued. "I'm sorry we're not here under better circumstances. I'd like to get right down to business so we don't take up too much of your time."

"Of course, Sheriff, thank you for coming." I led them into the great room, gestured toward the two leather chairs across the coffee table from the couch. "Please sit."

Tall and fortyish, Schaeffer carried the look of a cowboy in his tan uniform. His low-slung gun belt circled a trim waist. He wore some kind of snakeskin boots and a brown Stetson hat. Made you wonder if his horse was tied up at the gate. He pulled a small spiral notebook from his breast pocket as he sat, opened it to a page marked with a red tag, and scanned it for a couple of seconds.

"I understand you lost your husband about six months ago. Please accept my condolences. I apologize for having to bring all this up again, I know it's gotta be hard for you, ma'am. Have you had any similar or other suspicious events since his passing? Or before?"

"None at all."

"Can you think of any reason why someone would want to do this to harass you?"

"No." I shook my head.

"How about your husband? Any enemies that you know of, anyone who might want to punish you for their bad feelings toward him?"

"Enemies? Gosh, no. Trevor was a contractor, built this subdivision, our home, as well as many others in town. Santiago Homes has a great reputation, you can ask anyone."

"Yes, I see a lot of those signs around. Now, who would have known about this song . . . uh . . ." He thumbed to the next page of his notebook. "*It had to be you*" being special to you and your late husband?"

"Certainly no one who would have any reason to use it against us. We had it played at the celebration of his life. But, I can't imagine any of our attendees doing this awful thing."

"Please excuse me if I get too personal, Mrs. Beale, but how about an ex-wife or girlfriend?"

"No marriages, and no serious exes or break-ups that I've heard of."

"Trevor was pretty much of a workaholic before he met Sam," said Bud. "He didn't have time for romance until Sam came along and swept him off his feet."

"Well, I'm not so sure about that," I said.

"I know his attorney was his best friend at ASU and I believe they went to high school together, too," Bud said. "I'll contact Mike and see what I can find out."

"Wait a minute," I said. "There was something funny happened today. I was at the U and as I left, I noticed a blue Camaro with a T-top in the parking lot. I stopped at Office Warehouse on my way home, the one on Oracle, and saw the same car in the lot there as I pulled out."

"Did you get the license number?" Bud said, scooting forward in his chair.

"No, I didn't think to look, but I just saw it from the front so there probably wouldn't have been a plate anyway."

"Then how did you know it was the same car? Did you see the driver?" asked Schaeffer.

"No, there was no driver in it either time, but it was exactly the same cobalt blue color and I didn't notice it in the Office Warehouse lot when I arrived. It was backed in right by the exit when I left."

"Any other identifying marks on the car?" asked Bud.

"No. No dents or anything that I noticed. I took a good look at the car in the campus lot and fantasized about getting one for myself. I'm sure it was the same car."

"We'll alert our patrols to keep on the lookout for it, although I'm fairly sure it wouldn't be the vehicle that was out here in your wash. From the description you've given Bud here of their getaway, a car built that low to the ground would probably still be stuck right there in the wash if it tried to roar out in a big hurry. I'd like to go look around the scene. Okay if we go on out there?"

"Sure. If you don't need me, I'll stay here. It's giving me the creeps to go out there thinking someone is doing this on purpose. Take Jet out with you, please, Bud, he's due. I'll wait on the patio."

I barely had time to squeeze lemons, make lemonade and get iced mugs filled and passed around the table when they walked up to rejoin me.

"Thanks, Mrs. Beale," said Schaeffer. He drank his down over half way. "That hits the spot. Here's my card with my direct number in case you need to reach me. And, I've written a number on the back that will get you the quickest response team at any time—day or night. Don't hesitate to use it. Have you thought of anything else you want to add before we finish up? Any questions for Bud or me?"

"No, but I want to thank you for watching the place a little closer for me. Here's my home and cell numbers. If your men need to contact me about anything they question—even during the night—please tell them to do so. I'll be keeping my cell phone with me at all times and right by my bed at night. I certainly want to do anything I can to help. Bud has probably already told you about my alarm system, and Jet will alert me to anything unusual, as well."

"Thanks again for the lemonade. It was mighty good." He drained his mug, stood, and gave Jet a pat. "We hope to get to the bottom of this soon to avoid any further disturbances for you. In the meantime, ma'am, I'd feel better if you had someone with you here at night."

"I'll stay here again tonight, Sheriff, and we'll have someone stay here with her until we catch this guy. Thanks for the extra support from your team."

"That sounds, good, Bud. You have a good night, now. And try not to worry. My men will be watching." He tipped his hat.

Bud followed the sheriff to the car.

7

The Watchers

The long-range binoculars, too far away to be seen by the naked eye, were trained on the two lawmen.

"Looks like the gang's all here. City and County," said the tall one.

The seed had surely been planted . . . how long would it take to grow? How long before she would be glad to leave her fancy-schmancy El Rancho de Santiago?

8

Bud returned to the patio, his brows pinched, his lips formed a straight line. "I've been thinking about the song, Sam. Who would know besides your good friends? Was there anyone at the service that you didn't know?"

"Don't have any idea," I said, staring off into space. "It's still pretty much a blur. There should be some photos in the packet of stuff the Friends Chapel brought to me following their services. Come on. Let's see if we can find them."

I hadn't looked at the photos at all. Why would I? Yet, I remembered putting that packet on the desk in the office when it was delivered. Rosa probably tucked it away somewhere. I turned into the office and looked on the book shelf. There it was. A zippered album, bound in rich leather, with "In Memoriam" embossed in gold script along the spine. We found the guest book, cards attached to pictures of floral arrangements, and grabbed the photos taken of the gravesite service and crowd.

I scanned the faces, handing each photo over to Bud to study, and then read through the names in the Guest Book. Most were good friends or those who worked with Trevor, many of whom had visited him during the last few months when he wasn't able to stray far from the house or hospital. Maybe Clint can identify those few neither Bud nor I recognized? Clint Campbell was Trevor's foreman and partner in Santiago Homes. He had taken on the full responsibility of running the business for most of the last year.

"Who's this lone woman standing back under the tree here," asked Bud. "She's in several photos, though always in the background."

I studied the photo. "Hmmm. I didn't even notice her. Let me get a magnifying glass." After a careful inspection with the glass, neither of us recognized nor remembered the strange woman under the tree.

"Could she have been an old girlfriend?" Bud asked. "I know you told the sheriff you didn't know of any; and even so, it would be a big stretch for jealousy to be motive enough to haunt you like this."

Trevor hadn't been married before. As far as I knew, not even close to it. He'd been so wrapped up in his business; it seemed like he had little time for a personal life at all. He'd never mentioned any old loves and neither had I in our little more than

57

five years together. "No, it's got me stumped. I'll take these we don't recognize and show them to Teri and Jon, and Clint tomorrow. One of them should know those that we don't." I packed the unidentified photos in a manila envelope to deal with tomorrow.

Teri and husband, Jon Morrison, lived on the northeast side of Tucson, near Sabino Canyon. Their two kids, Sara and Josh, often gave me a chance to play "mom" while giving Jon and Teri a treat to be alone on some of his golf trips. Rosa loves to spoil the kids with her bean and cheese burritos when they stayed over. The kids hadn't been over since Trevor had become ill.

"How about a margarita while I put the Chile Rellenos in the oven? We're both due for a little relaxing."

"You're on," said Bud. "First, I've got to get out of this monkey suit and feed the horses."

"Oh man, I'm surprised they haven't been letting us know they're hungry. Grab the 'maggies' on your way back and I'll get dinner on its way."

He soon appeared at the kitchen counter with two frosty margaritas on the rocks. No more suit, no more tie, looking indeed relaxed in cut-off jeans and a bright green T-shirt and a stock of hay stuck in his hair. "Here's to a speedy resolution of the case," he said raising his glass.

"I'll drink to that," I said as we clinked. "These guys picked a helluva time to start harassing me, if that's really what this is. When I said I was going to make some changes in my life this is not what I had in mind!"

"Trevor would be proud of you," Bud said, watching me from a counter stool, as I cut lettuce, onions, and tomatoes to go with Rosa's refried beans, rice, and chilies.

"He made me promise to go on, you know. Living life for the both of us, not to shrivel up and die with him. It took me a while to remember that promise and what it meant to him. What it meant to me. No matter how hard it gets, Bud . . . I'm here for him."

"And I'm here for you. We're gonna get these guys, Sam. We're gonna get 'em for all of us."

My throat felt clogged, tears wanted out. I pushed back the tears and shoved out the words "Let's eat."

We talked through dinner, me sharing my excitement over my new adventure at the UA, Bud trying to convince me that I needed someone to stay here with me until we got to the bottom of this stalking. Or whatever the hell it was. I could think it nothing but a sick, sick joke, yet had absolutely no idea why anyone—much less who—would want to do this. Could it possibly be as we'd first thought? A couple of teenagers? Had I seen that blue Camaro somewhere else besides the school and office store? I searched my memory, tried to tie someone, somewhere with that wonderful blue car. How could I forget that car?

"I'm sorry, Bud. Guess I was off in la-la land. What did you say?"

"Do you think Rosa would want to stay with you for a few nights, just to keep more of a presence in the house, keep you company?" Bud asked as I rinsed and put the last plate in the dishwasher.

"You're trying to duck out on me already?" I laughed, trying to lighten my mood, and led the way into the great room.

"It's not that at all—but I'm afraid you're stuck with me until we think of someone else, I'm not leaving you here alone until this is over."

"I wouldn't think of asking Rosa to stay now that Manny's home all of the time. I'm lucky to have her here as much as I do. Let's see how it goes.

"I don't want to alarm my folks unnecessarily, but if this doesn't get cleared up soon, I'll see if I can talk Dad into coming down. He keeps saying he's going to surprise me for a visit some of these days. He'd probably jump at the chance to find a mystery along with it. But let's wait a few days and see what happens. I know a pretty good detective who can probably get it figured out."

"Your dad's a good idea. And I'd like to get to know him. Heard so much about him, but I get the idea he's pretty much of an Idaho guy and not interested in the desert. Let's not get in a hurry to call in the troops; I'm free as the breeze this month so far, so no worries. And with extra clothes here, it's easy to just shower here and take off right to work in the mornings if that's okay?"

"Of course. *Mi casa es su casa.* Can't you read the sign?" I said it jokingly, then surprised myself when the next words seemed to stick deep in my throat. "Bud, I . . . I really appreciate your being here for me. You've been my rock this past year. I don't know how I can ever repay you."

"That's what friends are for." He grabbed my hands and pulled me from the couch. "Now you get on to bed. This has been one bitch of a day for you and you need a good night's sleep. I'll be here, so don't you worry your little head a bit. You've got Tucson's finest plus Pima County Sheriff's posse watching after you."

I gave him a hug, flashed a smile and headed down the hall. "Goodnight, my friend." And blew him a kiss.

"Sleep tight," he called.

After I passed the office door, I stopped and turned back. At the desk, I picked up the To Do list, grabbed a Sharpie and made a big line through: 1. Call UA for info; and 2. Buy an Organizer. Boy did that feel good.

I opened up the sack from Office Warehouse and pulled out my new organizer. "I'll leave you for tomorrow." I laid it on the desk, and trotted off to bed.

9

I hadn't expected to sleep well, but here it was almost 8:30 Tuesday morning when I opened my eyes. Knowing Bud would be gone to work already, I grabbed my robe and slippers and padded for the kitchen hoping that first cup of coffee was there waiting for me as it was yesterday. But found an empty pot still sitting in the coffee maker. He must have been in a real hurry this morning. Maybe he got an early call. Then I remembered he fixed the coffee while I cleaned up the dishes, so it should be all set. I jabbed the button.

"Ummm, does that smell good," Bud's voice boomed down the hall.

I almost dropped my cup as I pulled it from the rack.

"Well, good *afternoon*, Detective." I laughed. My eyes angled toward the clock, its smiling chili pepper hands pointing directly to 8:30.

He struck a handsome pose in his gray pin-striped suit, light blue shirt, red tie with little alligators traipsing around on it.

Still damp from the shower, his hair was combed and parted neatly in place.

"And here I've been listening to stories of late nights and early morning investigations all these years. Who do you think you're kidding, Holloway?"

"It does make a difference when I can sleep at the scene of the crime," he said. "Cuts the hell out of my travel time. Is that coffee down far enough to steal a cup?"

"Guess you've earned one." I poured and handed him the cup. "How'd you sleep? Any disturbances? I was dead to the world all night. Don't think I ever moved."

"Not a peep. Jet and I were up walking around a couple of times. Where in the heck is he this morning?"

"Oh, I just let him out."

"Well, I checked in with Gary this morning. His patrols saw nothing out of the ordinary during the night. Looks like you just got out of bed, Missy." He looked at his watch. "I'm clear for an hour or so. Why don't you go take a shower and I'll rustle up some omelets to use up those leftovers from last night if that's okay with you. I'll give you 20 minutes."

"Wow. And he cooks too. Now that's an offer I can't refuse." I scooted for the shower.

The phone began to ring as I threw on some jeans and a peasant blouse. I grabbed it, taking care of the short call on my way to the kitchen. Bud was just pulling Rosa's handmade tortillas from the warming oven and we sat down to eat.

"God, how do you keep so slim with food like this around all the time," he asked. "If I stick around here much longer, I'm not only going to put on a few pounds, I may start speaking Spanish."

"That's why Rosa only comes in once a week. I'm a sucker for her cooking . . . hell, what am I talking about? I'm crazy for ANY Mexican food. But hers is the best."

"What's on your plan for today? Anything important on the phone?" Bud asked.

"I'm running those photos over to Jon and Teri for a look-see, then on to the office to see if Clint recognizes anyone we still don't know. And some grocery shopping so you won't have to be signing up for Spanish classes." I winked.

"That was the U on the phone to let me know there is an opening in their Beginning Computer class at their off-campus facility this evening. It's right down at Ina and Oracle. That sounds really good to me. I met the young man who teaches the class when I was on my way to the Registrar's Office yesterday, and hoped I might be able to get him. He seems pretty easy-going. Man, teachers sure have changed."

"Just a minute. You shouldn't be out running around alone at night. I'll take you there and keep an eye on things around here . . . hey, wipe that look off your face. I won't take no for an answer. Besides, it will give me some time to run home and take care of a few things while you're safely in class."

"I don't need a full-time babysitter. I do appreciate your being here during the night, but I want you to promise me you won't go putting off anything that you need to do. I'm sure I can get Jon and Teri . . . or Debbie . . . to come over. Anytime."

"It's all settled then. What time is your class?"

"It runs from seven to nine. I want to be there about fifteen minutes early to get settled in. I'm still a little uneasy about this back-to-school stuff."

Bud took his last bite and stood. "I gotta go. I cooked—you're on for dishes. See you here by six. We can grab a burger on the way and get you there in plenty of time. It's nice they have a class so close.

"Be careful today. And, call me if you even think you see that Camaro again . . . or anything else that looks fishy." He gave me a thumbs-up and was out the door.

As quickly as he was out, the door opened again. "And I'm buying," he said, a big smile on his face as he pushed the inside button to lock the door and closed it.

The dishes finally in the dishwasher, I grabbed my purse, stuck in the packet of photos, and was on my way. I programmed the address for tonight's class into my GPS to pinpoint its location on my way into town. I found myself looking at every car as I pulled onto Oracle. Did I expect the blue Camaro to be sitting there, just waiting for me? Was it just a coincidence to see two identical cars yesterday? After all, Tucson's getting to be a big city. Nevertheless, I vowed to heed Bud's warning, and kept my eyes peeled.

"Turn left on Ina, destination on right." I nearly jumped out of my seat belt. "Gertie! You're going to make me pee my pants some of these days," Sure enough, there on the right as I turned the corner where Ina changes to Skyline, I spotted the University logo on the big sign at the entrance to the Saguaro Shopping Center. "Thanks, Gertie. Good job." Doesn't everyone talk to their GPS?

Last night I had called Teri, to say I'd be over around ten this morning. I pulled into their circular drive, amazed to see their snug little family of four all represented at my first glance: the Arizona style courtyard ablaze with marigolds, petunias, and Mexican Bird of Paradise bushes; huge terra-cotta pots overflowed with barrel and prickly pear cactus plants—all proof of Teri's green thumb. Jon's Rolls Royce-looking golf cart was parked near the roadway, ready to go to work. Eight-year-old Sara's pink bike leaned against the garage door. Josh, at ten, was a skateboard enthusiast. His Bart Simpson patterned board safely rested upside down a few feet off the sidewalk leading up to the front door.

My timing was good. The kids were already at school, both Teri and Jon were at home. After hugs and apologies for it being so long since we'd visited, I explained the happenings of the last couple of days and spread the photos out, pointing to those faces neither Bud nor I had been able to put names to. Jon was able to identify a couple of guys who played golf with Trevor.

"How about this woman right here?" I handed them the magnifying glass I had tucked into the envelope.

Jon and Teri took a good look and shook their heads.

"I thought it might be someone you would remember from school, Teri. Perhaps an old girlfriend of Trev's?"

"She doesn't look like anyone I remember from school," said Teri. "And I never really knew any of his girlfriends after I moved away from home."

Jon said, "The more I look at her, the more she seems familiar, but I just can't place her."

"Maybe it's someone who works in a store or restaurant or office we frequent?" said Teri. "Or someone Trevor and Clint built a home for." She shrugged, then shook her head. "But why would anyone do such a thing? And surely not a woman?"

"Clint's my next stop." I gathered up the photos. "And, I'd better be on my way. Clint said he would wait in the office until I got there. He's so busy these days trying to do everything on his own, I don't want to keep him waiting.

"It's so good to see you both." I grabbed their hands. "Nice job taking second place in the Open, Jon. And Bud sends congrats, too. Let's get together for some laughs once this mess is over."

"If we can help in any way," Jon said, "you give us a call. Anytime Bud isn't available, you can stay over here or we'll come there. You're not staying out there alone."

"Thanks. Hopefully we'll find out it's just some crazy kids not thinking about the consequences," I said. "Otherwise, I can't imagine who or why. I'll keep you posted."

More hugs and I was quickly off the grounds of the golf club; lucky to be in-between rush hours for downtown traffic. I made it to Clint's office in seventeen minutes, and back on my way home in another fifteen.

We'd looked at the photos and Clint picked out a few more people he knew from on the job: some buyers, a few sub-contractors. But the mystery woman was still a mystery. Who could she be? I wasn't sure if it was the thought that maybe she had something to do with this harassment thing, or if the green monster of jealousy was simply rearing its nasty head. Maybe she was just another acquaintance, another mourner. But why didn't those closest to Trevor recognize her? Why had she stood back away from the crowd?

Home already? It was one of those times that you wonder how you possibly made it there—with your mind a thousand miles away. Did I stop at all the right places? Apparently, my automatic pilot had taken over, for here I was pulling through my gate, safe and sound. I stopped to run back to the mailbox.

I'd better get myself together. And what about the blue Camaro? Hopefully, my auto-pilot was watching out for that, as well, for I didn't remember a thing. They could have been following right behind me and I probably wouldn't have known it.

Jet met me at the door, followed me to the office. I dropped the mail on the desk, took the photos out of my purse and sat down. "Did ya miss me, Jet?" I gave him a few pats, then pulled the mystery woman's photo out of the packet and put the rest back into the album jacket. I laid hers aside for now and began to sort through the mail. A power bill from Arizona Public Service, bill from MasterCard, then a flat brown envelope. It was addressed with a blunt marker, in a scrawl that looked much like a kid's printing. Maybe something from Sara? Funny, there was no return address. I slit the end open and discovered a silver CD, no label or writing on it. A brand-new blank CD? I reached in to pull it out, and then stopped before my fingers reached its edge, dropping the whole envelope on the desk. Should I wait for Bud? Could this be from the same guys? What did it mean?

I speed dialed Bud's cell. "Hi Sam, what's up?"

"You're probably going to think I'm paranoid, but I just got home and was sorting the mail. There's a plain looking manila envelope with a CD in it."

"Did you open it?"

"I opened the end of the envelope, but didn't . . ."

"Don't touch it. I'll be right there," he said. "I'm down on Orange Grove following up on an overnight burglary at Hastings. Should be there within ten minutes."

I got up and left the office so I wouldn't be tempted to peek a little more at the envelope and its contents. I went to the kitchen and started a fresh pot of coffee. Jet and I waited in the great room for Bud.

I'd barely gotten a sip when I heard the gate swing open, checked out the window to see Bud's unmarked tan Ford Victoria come to a quick stop. He hurried up the walkway at the back of the house; we met him at the patio door.

"Let's take a look at that mail," he said.

"In the office." I led the way.

He grabbed Trevor's pen from its holder on the desktop, and lifted the envelope to check the other side. "Looks like a kid's printing. Postmarked yesterday here in Tucson. Nothing significant about the stamp . . . everyone's using the Forever stamps these days." He pulled latex gloves from his pocket, slipped them on his hands, and removed the disk.

I turned on the monitor and hit the switch on the computer. Nothing happened. Bud checked the cables and power strip. Everything seemed to be plugged in. "Damn, I don't know what's wrong with this," I said. "I switched it on yesterday and it came right up."

"That's okay," Bud said. "I've got my laptop in the car. It's got a CD drive in it."

He was back in a flash, sat the laptop on the desk just as the Windows 10 logo flashed on his screen. I felt each beat of my heart drumming in my neck as we waited for the computer to boot up. Bud inserted the CD and clicked on the play button. "Here we go."

"I've wondered around and finally found . . . somebody who…"

I tried to keep the tears back, but couldn't. It felt like I took a kick right in the stomach. Someone was definitely targeting me for this nasty . . . God. I still don't know what to call it. Bud shut the music off and wrapped his arms around me, burying my face against his chest.

"Go ahead, let it out. You're due. I'll listen to this whole thing down at the station. There may be some sort of recorded message on it, but you don't need to hear it. That's what I'm here for."

My sobs shook me to the bone. I tried to get hold of myself, but decided to let it take its course. Finally, there were no more tears. I looked up at Bud, seeing the hurt in his eyes, knowing he was bleeding for me. And the front of his shirt was sopping. "Thanks, again, for being here, I guess this whole thing just finally hit home. Someone is actually doing this intentionally. It's not a joke or some teenage prank like we thought. Or maybe hoped? Bud, I can't let them soil my memory of Trevor and what we had together."

"That's our Sam." He gently pushed me away and lifted my chin with his index finger, still wrapped in green latex. "Trevor would definitely be proud of you," he said, leaning down and looking me straight in the eye.

"Now, here's what we've got to do. You need to go in and lie down, get some rest, and let me go do my job. I'll lock all the doors when I go. Same rules on the phones. I'll call you on the cell as soon as I listen to the rest of this disk to let you know if there is anything new.

"Right now, we don't have any idea what this is about. I want you to try again to think of anything that may have triggered bad feelings toward you, Trevor, or the both of you. I'm going to contact Clint to see if there were any business deals that may have gone bad—something that you wouldn't have known about. We've got our work cut out for us, Sam. And we've got to work together on this. Give me a call if you come up with anything new or need me for anything.

"I don't think I'll be able to sleep. I'd planned on checking out the computer to list the software and info I may need for my class tonight, but unless we can figure out what's wrong here, I guess that's impossible."

His eyes widened in disbelief. "You don't plan on going to class tonight, do you?"

"I'm damned if I'm going to let these SOBs do exactly what they want to do—take over my life. No matter what their reasons are, they aren't going to keep me from the rest of my life. Not now, not ever."

"It sounds like you have your mind made up. But, do me one favor . . . don't leave the house the rest of the day. And keep Jet with you. I'll try to knock off early and be back as soon as I can. We need to talk some more before you go to that class tonight. If you're still determined to go."

I followed him down the hall, clicking the lock as he walked through the back door. He turned and said, "Set the exterior alarms when I leave. And don't forget . . . hamburgers are on me tonight." A wink and he was out the door.

10

The walls were closing in on me as I moped around the house, needing to light somewhere, not knowing where. Searching for some clue that would lead to answers. To something. Jet watched me curiously, his eyes following my steps. I stopped to caress the roughly woven wool of the Navajo rug hanging next to the fireplace, my thoughts zipped back to the day Trevor bought it from a beach vendor at Rocky Point where we wound up on our first real date. And since then, that's where we went when we got a hankering for the sea, for the salt air, and a stroll along the beach to renew our shared passion for Mexico—its food and its people.

Trevor was a regular in our office; everything was all business when our paths first crossed. I was receptionist at Colgan and Meredith then; he, just about the best-looking client to ever walk through the door. But that was before I'd grown interested in investigation and been advanced to assistant for Michael Colgan, the litigator in our office.

At first Mike gave me easy paperwork jobs: tracing missing persons, property transfers, and a few divorce cases. Mike and Trevor had been friends since their days at Arizona State. Mike helped set up the paperwork for Trevor's construction business way back when both were getting started; and because of their friendship, continued to serve as Trev's personal and business attorney through the years.

About six years ago Trevor and Mike were spinning their wheels tracing the owners of some seemingly abandoned property north of town that Trevor wanted to develop into a subdivision. It was rumored to be tied up in red tape to preserve the historic value of the stage stop ruins that remained on the parcel. Mike turned it over to me. I tracked down the owners and was called in to report my findings to the two of them.

"How the hell did you do it?" Trevor asked, his left eyebrow arched in a question, right eye squinted a little crookedly.

"You know," I said. "I believe women have a little more patience than you men and that was all it took. I searched layers and layers of documents to finally learn it was owned by a Hiram Duncan. And, the rumor was right. He's a very rich man and determined to maintain the historic value of the old stage stop. When I couldn't get an appointment with Mr. Duncan, I found out he is a big supporter of the Sierra Club and wangled a chance meeting at a fundraiser.

"I promised him the integrity of the stage stop would not be compromised: what's left of the buildings would remain a lasting shrine of the old west that was so much a part of the history of this area and it would continue to be private property—not to be commercially developed. I must have hit him at the right time. He believed my story. He confided that he feared his family would ignore his wishes after he died and sell it to the highest bidder—to hell with the stage stop, to hell with history. He planned to give it to the State before that happened.

"If you want the property, you'll have to agree to his terms to keep the buildings on that one spot. It's all right here in my report. I've made copies of everything." I handed Trevor and Mike each a file full of documents.

"That stage piece is only a small part of the property." Trevor nodded, his lips pursed as he thumbed through the file. "I've heard a few things about old man Duncan. I'll figure out a way to do it. Good work. Sam? Is that right . . . Sam?"

I nodded and smiled.

"You deserve a bonus for bagging this property for me."

"Not necessary. It's what I get paid for."

"Then, why don't we all go have some lunch, my treat?" he said looking at his watch. "We can discuss the details so I know exactly what I'm in for. Hiram Duncan's known to be a shrewd old duffer. We don't want to screw it up now. I need all the facts and welcome your advice on how to handle the old man.

"Do you like Mexican food? All this talk of business makes me hungry."

Mike pushed back from the conference table and held up his hands as he rose. "Don't count me in. I have another appointment for lunch." He picked up his file, adding as he gave me a thumbs-up, "Great job, Sam. Maybe you do deserve a bonus."

Intrigued by the prospect of some time with this great looking client, even if it was just a lunch, I smiled and said, "Lunch it is . . . and I love Mexican."

And, the rest, so they say, is history.

My stomach cut loose with a little growl. I snapped back to reality, looked at the clock to see that it was almost two. I made half a peanut butter sandwich, grabbed a peach yogurt, and headed for the patio. I stopped just inside the back door to turn off the alarm and scoop some food into Jet's dish. "How about some lunch for you, too, fella." And shut the door.

The patio bar is perfect for a mid-day snack. The palm thatched roof hangs out far enough to shade the stools at any time during the day. But, since I hadn't had a chance to read the paper this morning, I made a quick run to the delivery box by the gate, grabbed a club soda from the bar fridge and turned on some country music, then plopped myself on a chaise lounge to relax with my paper and lunch.

My attention went straight to photos of Jason Day, Rory McIlroy, and Justin Thomas warming up for the PGA golf tournament getting underway at Dove Mountain Country Club, just a few miles away. I was sorry I missed watching Jon on Sunday, but was proud that he had taken Second Place in the Pro Am. Maybe he could get me a couple of passes for this week's events. These were the times I missed Trevor the most. We so enjoyed playing golf and watching the tournaments on TV and always tried to go in person when they were in Tucson or Phoenix.

I woofed down the sandwich. My eyelids were drooping. I blinked them back to focus on the page. The sun was working its magic. I was beginning to relax, lowered the back of the lounger and stretched out, keeping my head in the afternoon shade of the table's umbrella.

11

The Watchers

Back up on Pusch Ridge, the two watched as the Beale woman ate her lunch.

"She doesn't look too frazzled to me," said the stocky woman, as she looked across the pickup bed at the slender man. "How are we going to get her out of there?"

"Don't worry; I think she'll change her mind if my little surprise works out."

"What the hell have you done now? You know we promised there'd be no harm to her. If your brother's plan didn't work, we'd wait for him to get here."

"Who said anything about harm? Just wait . . . we've barely started. If you can't take the heat,

you can stay home and do whatever it is that you do. Shut up and quit your whining. You're the one who wanted to be a part of this. And by the way. He's my step brother."

The rattlesnake slithered across the gravel drive and onto the pebbled finish of the patio at the hillside estate. The day was hot; the snake was on the move. It sensed the coolness of the water in the pool nearby, slid toward its edge, and dipped its head close to the surface. He drew back in a quick coil, raised his head and swung it from side to side, hoping to sense the heat of prey as he also searched for respite from the sun's rays. The eight buttons at the end of its tail angled upward as he began to glide across the patio to the nearest shade—his destination directly under the lounger where Sam lay sleeping.

12

I sensed rather than felt something touch my hand, and began to flex my fingers.

"Don't move, Sam, we've got a rattler here," Bud whispered.

My eyes sprang open, and focused on Bud. He was standing close by, holding my walking stick, which was no doubt what I had felt on my hand. My heart fought to leap from my chest, but I couldn't move. I'd been in Arizona long enough to know snakes can react quickly and unpredictably. I had no idea where the snake might be, what he was doing. But did know I was going to pee my pants if I didn't get out of here soon. Had to hold it—any movement or alien smell could have triggered the snake to strike. I ached to turn my head to look, but trusted Bud to do the right thing. He was a native to Arizona's mountains and desert as well as the dangers of its city streets. I had to trust his judgment.

"I'm trying to keep his attention on me, so don't move a muscle. I'm drawing my gun just in case, but hope if I keep threatening with this stick he'll head off back toward the desert and we'll be rid of him. I'll try to warn you if I'm going to shoot, but may not have time."

"I'll trust you to do whatever you need to. Don't worry about hitting anything around the pool as long as it's not me. Just don't take too long. I'm so scared I could start shaking this whole lounge any second."

Bud inched the tip of the stick closer to my lounge. Where the hell was this snake? I strained my eyes downward to focus on the pool. A slight breeze had come up, dancing the sun's rays across the surface ripples. My eyes wandered over the pool deck, to the bar, strained to see the clock above the mirror. Almost five. I'd slept for at least two hours. I should've felt rested. Yeah, right. As rested as you can when you expect at any second to feel the prick of a rattler's fangs—maybe in your backside, maybe somewhere more vital.

"I think he's on the move now," Bud whispered. "He's decided this stick is bigger than he is and doesn't want to fight. He's out from under your chair and headed toward the gravel. In another few seconds we'll have you out of there safe and sound."

From the corner of my eye, I could now see the front part of the snake, moving warily across the patio, his tail must still be under me. Bud moved closer to the lounge, keeping the end of the stick between him and the snake, encouraging it away from me.

Once the snake was fully in my line of sight and away from my chair, Bud reached for my arm and said, "Okay, you can get up slowly and I'll steady you."

Maybe not so slowly, but I was up and out of that chair before he finished his sentence. Our eyes remained glued on the snake until it disappeared down the drive behind the patio and under the back gate, toward the wash.

"Wow, that was close," I said. "Too close. No more naps on the deck, especially without Jet here."

"Why wasn't Jet out here with you? You should always keep him with you, especially when you aren't locked inside. And what about staying in the house did you not understand?"

I don't think I'd ever heard Bud raise his voice that way. My hands were shaking, my stomach flip flopping, but knew I was in the wrong and couldn't feel sorry for myself.

"I forgot to fill Jet's dish this morning, so I gave him some lunch when I came outside to eat mine. I didn't plan on going to sleep, but that sun felt really good and I guess I dozed off. I know better than that." And now I knew that I needed to change the subject.

"If you're going to buy me that burger you promised, we'd better get a move on. I've got to get myself ready for class."

"You're not . . ." Bud stopped, then slowly shook his head. He leaned my walking stick back against the end of the bar, and grabbed a beer from the fridge. "I'll be ready to go at six," he said as he popped the top and headed inside.

My stomach still in an uproar from the snake encounter, I hoped the computer class would get my mind focused on something besides these crazy things that were happening lately. After all, it wasn't that big a deal to have a rattler in the yard. It's Arizona for God's sake—not an unusual sight here in the desert. They don't like us any more than we like them and certainly don't seek us out. Even so, I'd had just about enough for this week, thank you very much, but wasn't going to let Bud know it was getting me down.

I stopped by Trevor's office to try again with the computer, thinking it might have been a simple thing we overlooked or a power glitch when we tried earlier. Not a peep, just dark screen. What could have happened to this?

Was there a black cloud hanging over my head these days? Haunting music at night, receiving the CD by mail, computer not working, and now waking up with a rattlesnake under my chair. What would be next? I was beginning to think this new leaf I'd turned over wasn't so great after all. What is it they say? Be careful what you wish for?

We stopped by In and Out Burgers for two Double Doubles and fries on our way to my class. Our earlier excitement with the snake hadn't done a thing to quell our appetites. We devoured every bite. All double meat, double cheese, special sauce, lettuce, tomato, and the thick slice of onion.

UA's off-campus classroom building could have been a dentist's office except for the red, white, and blue GO WILDCATS banner strung above the doorway about halfway down the strip mall. Bud dropped me off at 6:40 with a promise to be back at nine sharp.

I followed the Basic Computer signs to my classroom, hoping it was basic enough for the likes of me. I peeked in. There was Jeremy, the student teacher, at his laptop. His hair was neatly parted and plastered down with hair gel, he wore a maroon polo. Much more the teacher image than the rushed student I met yesterday. His desk faced three rows of empty tables—no people yet. Just a monitor at each chair, five in each row. Cables sprouted from their backs and crawled like roots reaching down and across the floor.

My feet seemed glued to the threshold. Did I really want to go in?

Jeremy looked up and rose from his chair. "Oh, Mrs. Beale. I saw your name on my new student list. Welcome."

I'd been had. "Hello again," I said, forcing my feet on through the doorway.

He met me halfway, his hand extended "Glad you came in early." We shook.

"This is only our second week. We can quickly go over and catch you up on what the class has already covered. You probably already know it anyway."

"Please call me Sam. I've used computers for simple office typing, but I'm afraid I've forgotten most of that in the past few years of not working. My home computer wouldn't turn on today so I didn't bring the software information the school office said you'd need. I hope you don't require too much homework. I may be flunking already."

"Okay, Sam it is. We are all pretty informal around here. I've asked the class to call me Jeremy. I'm really just a fellow student, picking up a few extra well-needed bucks moonlighting."

He guided me to a computer station and went through a few troubleshooting steps while starting the computer, explained what they had covered last week, and gave me printed review material to take home for catch up. The other students were in place by then and we were off.

During a mid-class break, I found many of the twelve other students had been left behind in much the same technological boat as me—they were here to get their oars in the water to get into sync with the world. Some younger, some older, and some with a chip on their shoulder. Like the young woman to my left who pitched daggers my way each time Jeremy stopped by to check on me. The last half of the class flew by.

I packed up my notes and study papers and stopped by Jeremy's desk on the way out. "Great class," I said. "I wonder if you would be interested in making a house call to check out my computer. Or, if you can recommend a repairman? I'm afraid I've already tried everything that we talked about at the beginning of tonight's class. You sound very well qualified to troubleshoot it. I'd pay the going rate for a service call."

"Glad to see what I can do. As I said, I'm always looking to make a few extra bucks," he said. "I don't have any classes tomorrow morning. If that works for you, please set a time and tell me where."

We decided on 9:30 to avoid rush-hour traffic, since he lived near the University and would have to travel from the busy downtown area. I gave him directions and my cell phone number in case he ran into any difficulties.

"Thanks so much, Jeremy, see you in the morning." I started toward the door.

"Uh oh. Teacher keeping you after school on your first night?" Bud's smiling face appeared around the door jamb.

"Hey, Bud. Oh, I'm sorry. I really didn't forget about you. Bud Holloway, meet Jeremy Sharpe, my new teacher and just-hired computer diagnostician. He's agreed to come out tomorrow to check out the problem with the computer. Bud's my good friend and chauffeur tonight, Jeremy. He was at my house when I tried to boot it up."

Bud nodded and reached to shake Jeremy's hand. "It was deader than a doornail, I can vouch for that." They shook and exchanged pleasantries.

"Let's not keep Jeremy here any longer," I said, slinging my tote over my shoulder. "Plus, I've got some reading and homework to catch up on. Jeremy, give me a call if you have any trouble finding my place in the morning."

"Oh, Sam. Here's my cell number in case something comes up and you need to cancel from your end." Jeremy handed me a card and we were gone.

"Uh huh . . . Sam, is it?" Bud chided as we stepped outside. "A bit young for you, maybe?"

I turned, slugged him in the shoulder, and ran to the other side of his car. Laughter barreled from both of us as we opened the doors and jumped inside. The pent-up emotions of the long day rushed out. It was just what we needed.

13

The Watchers

The woman and cop didn't notice the blue Camaro sitting in the shadows of the now closed Banner Auto Repair just across on the corner at Ina, the lone figure watching them get into the unmarked Victoria. Their minds no doubt occupied with idle chatter about the class, about plans for tomorrow, about anything except the things that had been happening to upset their lives . . . like unwelcome rattlesnakes and midnight music.

The woman driver had hoped this scheme would work to scare the Beale woman off, get her to run away from the strange and threatening happenings. How much more can she take? How

much longer until they have to up the ante? The
days are slipping away.

14

Bud was up and gone, the coffee waiting when I swished into the kitchen in my robe and slippers. I poured a cup and called Jet to follow me to the deck—which, by the way, I scanned carefully before stepping a foot outside or sitting down at the table. No unwelcome visitors in sight. What a beautiful morning, I hoped these 80-degree days would never end and I hoped my life would soon settle down and quit being weird. I'd missed my morning swims that used to start my day. Hadn't done my laps for ages and decided it was time to resurrect some of my old habits to see how they fit with the new ones. Jet jumped up to follow as I dashed back into the house to put on my suit.

"What's the matter, Jet; think I'm going to run away? You know things aren't right around here, don't you?" I stroked his head. "Trust me; I'm just as anxious as you to get things settled back down."

After a labored eight laps of the pool, I gave up. They didn't come as easy as I'd hoped. I figured another cup of coffee and a twenty-minute dip in the hot tub should ward off any kinks that may want to develop in those unused muscles. After almost a half hour in the tub and a quick rinse under the patio shower, I was ready to face the day.

I donned a pair of Hawaiian print shorts and a tank top and sat at my desk. As I pulled my journal from its cubby hole, thoughts drifted to Trevor and how we each had enjoyed our own quiet time once we'd had morning coffee together. He in his office mapping out his day and me right here at my desk writing whatever popped into my head that morning.

I read through my words from Saturday, then just sat there wondering what I would write today. The intercom buzz broke my reverie. I raced to the panel, glancing to the clock on my way—9:25. The intercom button brought Jeremy's smiling face to the screen. I keyed the mike, pushed the button to open the gate, and said, "Good morning, Jeremy. Welcome. Pull on up to the sidewalk, the computer is near the front door."

He was opening the door of his yellow Volkswagen bug as I bounced through the courtyard.

"Wow, these are some digs." He whistled; his eyes roved the grounds, stopping on the corral area, horses still munching on hay Bud had pitched. "I was beginning to think I had taken a wrong turn and then spotted this house sitting up here all by itself. Then I really wondered if this was the right place when I saw that sign that read: El Rancho de Santiago. Thought maybe this was home to some Mexican land baron or someone famous. You aren't someone I will be embarrassed that I didn't recognize, are you?"

"Hardly. Just someone lucky to be married to a homebuilder whose company is Santiago Homes, hence the name on the sign. Trevor and I thought it better to retain some privacy by not putting our name on it."

"A good thought, especially in today's world," said Jeremy. "Now let's take a look at the computer to see if Doc Sharpe can work his magic."

I liked this guy, felt comfortable with him right from the start that day at the school. If Trevor and I had a son . . . well, what can I say? I guess I'd picture him to be like Jeremy when he grew up.

"Let's get started," I said, leading the way. Jet greeted us at the front door. "Jeremy, meet Jet, my roommate. He'll have to give you the sniff test before he lets you in. He's pretty protective of me, but a real teddy bear once he knows you're okay."

Jet's nose gave the leg of Jeremy's Levis a quick once over, then raised to meet the hand that Jeremy—a little tentatively—reached out to him. "It looks like you passed the test. Here's the office," I said, turning on the light. "Make yourself comfortable. How about a cup of coffee? I was just going to make a fresh pot.”

“That would be great. I had some studying to do last night for a test this afternoon, and I’m afraid I got up a little too late to have more than one on the run this morning. Black, for me, please.”

“It only takes a few minutes. Call me if you have any questions. I’ll be straight down the hall in the kitchen.” My finger pointed the way.

I was pouring the coffee when Jeremy came through the doorway. “Well, I’m afraid I have bad news. It looks like I won’t be able to mystify you with my talents. Your hard drive has crashed. It’s toast.”

“Oh no, I hope I didn’t do something to ruin it. What causes that?”

“You never know. Sometimes it’s a power spike, a virus received over the internet, or it could be just old age. That’s a pretty vintage computer, I’d say, at least five to ten years. That’s a long time for a computer these days. I hope you have it backed up.”

“There’s nothing on it that belongs to me, it’s my late husband’s business stuff which should all be backed up at the office. He had a laptop he used as well as this one.

“How about some churros with your coffee? They are

homemade and delicious. Rosa, my housekeeper, keeps them stocked in my freezer. Here, I'll take this tray if you'll grab that carafe. Let's go outside and enjoy this beautiful morning while we talk about what I need to do. Keep a sharp eye out. We had a rattlesnake out here yesterday; I think maybe the pool brings them in sometimes for a drink. Come on out, Jet, you can help keep watch."

"What a gorgeous view," said Jeremy as we sat down. "You can see for miles from here. The mountains, the desert floor . . . all so beautiful." He pointed to the corral area. "That stable looks like it's been around for a long time. Was this an old homestead?"

"Actually, an old stage stop. The Butterfield Stage provided a winter mail and passenger run through here from 1859 through 1861 when the pony express replaced the mail service. They came right through this property, stopped here to pick up fresh mules or horses and give the passengers a rest; then headed to Picacho and straight up through Maricopa over Butterfield Pass, named for the stage line. From there on to Yuma and San Francisco. There was too much snow to use the northern routes during the winter months.

"See our barn and loafing shed out there? Those walls and rafters were all that was left of the buildings from the stage stop. We kept the old corral posts and rails that were sturdy enough, tried to match them as well as we could to finish our corral. Trevor put a shallow shelf in the original well to make a feeding trough for the horses. So, we are sitting on a little bit of history here."

"Quite a bit, I'd say. I'm studying some of Arizona's history myself, focusing on stories about train and stage robberies, and researching some of the tales of what happened to treasures said to have been found and lost by miners through the years. There may really be some gold in them thar hills," he said, pointing northwest to the Tortolita Mountains.

"Sounds fascinating." I smiled, nodding. "Bud and I were out in the desert yesterday and found the remains of an old claim, Lazey Daisy Mine. Papers were filed in March, 1936, in surprisingly good shape in an old brown whisky bottle. But let's talk about my computer. Can it be fixed?"

"I could replace the hard drive for you, but with the improvements that have been made during the last few years; I'd recommend you buy a new computer. Today's software takes up so much hard drive space. You really need to upgrade. Five years ago, two gigabytes would do anything you wanted; today an average laptop has at least five hundred."

He laughed as my eyebrows shot up. "You don't even know what a gigabyte is, do you?"

"Gigabyte, mosquito bite . . . they both sound bad to me! I plan on doing only simple typing with it, hoping to work on a family cookbook. And I'm also taking an internet class to learn about email. Could you help me choose a new one that would work for me?"

"I'd be glad to help you if we could wait until this weekend. I need to get my test taken today, and I work lunch hour most weekdays at Sand Witches. How about Saturday morning? That's my first day off. Maybe I can squeeze in a little research to find a simple software package for that cookbook you're talking about, if you don't already have one."

"Saturday will be fine, and no—I don't have cookbook software. Hadn't given it a thought. I'd love your help with that. Sounds like you keep a busy schedule, so let's get you packed up and out of here. I really appreciate your coming out this morning. Oh, will you have time to help me install the new computer if we find one on Saturday? You can keep track of your time and add this morning's to the shopping and installing time on Saturday— or I can pay you today, whichever you'd prefer."

"Just pay me on Saturday. Is it okay if I have another one of these churros before I leave? They're delicious."

"Help yourself. I'll give Rosa your compliments." We finished our coffee, and while Jeremy gathered up his tools in the office, I packed up a half dozen churros for him to take home.

On the way down the walk, Jeremy pointed to the veranda on the second story of the garage, above the doors. "That looks like an apartment up there, is that where Rosa lives?"

"No, she and her husband live down off Skyline. She just comes in once a week. Trevor was thinking more about resale value when he added that apartment to the plans. It's only been used a few times, and just as a guest cottage. It's pretty compact, has a nice view out the front.

"By the way, Jeremy, what do I owe you for today?"

"I usually charge fifty dollars for a house call," he said. "But I don't usually get my breakfast." He raised the sack of churros. "Thanks for these and the coffee."

"I'll put fifty on your bill," I said. "And, good luck on your test today."

"Thanks, Sam. Have a great day. See ya Saturday." He jumped into the VW and drove through the gate.

Back in the house, I stopped to close the gate and lingered at the console. It seemed quiet, too quiet. I thought of the laughter and freshness of youth Jeremy had brought into the house this morning. A house that yearned for laughter. And what else, I wondered, to make it back into the home it used to be. As I walked to the small entertainment center in the master suite, I realized I was looking forward to Saturday and the adventure it might bring. I flipped through the CDs until Jimmy Buffet's smiling face beckoned. I slid *License To Chill* into the player, then stepped to the roll top to pick up where I left off— seemingly hours ago— to write in my journal.

"License to chill . . . and I believe I will." I sang along and wrote the words. "Yes, I believe I will," I repeated and wrote on:

Wednesday, September 14, 11:15am

License to chill . . . and I believe I will.

What is it about this Jeremy that makes me feel alive again? Maybe he's the son we never had? Has he been sent to rescue me? Rescue me from the malicious pranks of the last few days . . . or rescue me from myself?

Things are happening I don't understand. You know what they say: 'when it rains, it pours.' Well, it's dumping!

All I know is something snapped inside me when I looked at that sign the other day. It was like a neon light flashing, drawing me to it, opening my eyes. I wish it was the first day of yours, too, Trev. I know that can't be. But, you ARE still here beside me, in my heart. I hope I can burst this black cloud that's hanging over

our beautiful home and carry on with those dreams
we made together.

I closed the journal and rubbed the cover as Mr. Buffet finished his song and started into the next. I held the journal to my chest, happy to have broken my writing slump, to be able to think and write these words without remorse, but with promise that life does go on. I made a vow of renewed determination to make good on my words. This time there were no tears, only a feeling of strength that I would get through this madness.

I wandered into the office, settled in the chair, and stared at the computer. Wished it was working, wanted to do some of the exercises in the work papers Jeremy had sent home with me.

My list beckoned from the desk: 3. Start sorting recipes.
Anxious to get going, I grabbed our recipe file from the drawer, almost ran to the pantry. Sure enough, there on the shelf right above my collection of cookbooks sat my wooden recipe box. I stretched up to grab it, blew a puff of dust off its rounded top and carried it to the table to begin.

Still at the table, I was elbow deep in recipe cards and notes when I heard Bud's car pull in. It was twenty after five. I had lost myself in this project, spent the whole afternoon picking out our all-time favorites and some great recipes shared by our friends. I knew they would all love to be included in the cookbook, when—not if—I get it done. It was off to a good start. I wasn't sure just where to go from here, but darned anxious to get that new computer set up and start typing up these recipes.

"Looks like you've had a busy afternoon," said Bud as he came through from the patio. "What's all this? It looks like recipes, but I can't believe you are actually cooking dinner?"

"Don't sound so surprised, smart ass," I said, flipping him the finger. "Just for that remark, I think I'll let you cook tonight. As a matter of fact, I thawed a couple of steaks today and I just ran across a forgotten recipe for Debbie's delicious Crab Caesar Salad. I have a can of that good lump crab from Costco, so you are on the barbecue to cook the steaks while I make the salad. Okay? I don't have that EQUAL OPPORTUNITY KITCHEN sign over there for nothing." I laughed and pointed above the door.

"Sounds like you've lightened up some today," Bud said. "I'm sorry I didn't call to let you know, but the results came back from our lab this afternoon. They weren't able to pick up a thing off that envelope or CD. The perp must have worn gloves."

"Would you believe I've been so wrapped up in these recipes, I hadn't even given it a thought?"

"So, what's the occasion, planning a party?"

"No, just sorting out recipes for my cookbook project."

"I forgot about that. Sounds like fun. I'll be happy to help you choose since I've been the guinea pig for many of the Beale concoctions. I'm going to change into some shorts and relax a little before you put me back to work. It's been a long day. How'd you come out with Jeremy and the computer?"

"I'll grab us a couple of brews and meet you on the patio. Tell you then. I'm ready for a break, too."

"Sounds great. I'll just be a few minutes," he called out, and I heard his door shut.

Maybe it was the steaks that were cooked to a T. Or the combination with the crab salad. I'd forgotten what a great recipe it was. Or perhaps the bottle of Pinot Noir we emptied. But, for the first time this week, Bud and I were able to relax and enjoy a perfect evening under the stars. We laughed a little and probably cried a little more. But bottom line, I hoped maybe we'd gotten rid of our frustrations and fears of the past few days.

As I got into bed that night, my thoughts did stray a little. Not to bad things that were happening, but to how lucky I was to have a good friend like Bud staying right here in my guest room for support, and to the prospects of my new friend, Jeremy. For the second time today there had been laughter in this house. I closed my eyes and looked forward to tomorrow.

15

Saturday was finally here!

Thursday and Friday had flown by while I gleaned through our collection of cookbooks for the recipes Trevor and I had sampled and proclaimed to be keepers. I was building quite a stack of cards and a pile of books with pages marked by brightly colored tabs. I was having fun with the sorting and planning stages and hoped the fun would continue when the typing began. Did I mention that typing had never been my long suit?

Jeremy was also the teacher for my Thursday night class, Intro to the Internet. I was one happy camper to know I wouldn't have to get used to a second teacher. Jeremy was so easy going— just what I needed.

I was truly keeping myself busy, with neither time nor reason to worry about anything other than what was happening at the moment. Best of all, I'd had no more experiences with the pranks as we called them. I hadn't been off the premises except with my chauffeur when he took me to class. Nowhere to see or worry about blue Camaros. I was beginning to believe that maybe it *was* just some teenager's idea of a sick joke, paired with my overactive imagination. Something we could laugh about next week.

I was on my way to meet Jeremy at Office Warehouse to see what he called the good selection of computers he wanted me to consider. He had researched the pricing from several stores. Office Warehouse had agreed they would match any competitors' prices, and Jeremy said they would be the handiest to my home for needed supplies or computer help. God, had it only been five days since I bought my organizer there? Seemed like a month, so much had happened.

I turned into the parking lot, pulled up beside Jeremy's bug, and our shopping spree began. After looking at six different computers, we ended up spending far less than I had anticipated, purchasing one that Jeremy promised would take care of anything I could possibly want to do. Plus, he surprised me with simple-to-use software for my cookbook project, *Cookbooks Made Easy*, compliments of his friends at Office Warehouse as a thank-you for my business.

We stopped at KFC for a quick lunch on the way back. Once home we pulled out the old computer and Jeremy jumped right in and had my new HP up and running in no time. Left to my own resources, I would still have been trying to decipher the unpacking directions. He walked me through the basics of the computer's start-up and operation, then reviewed my homework assignments to complete the exercises in the materials from the classes I'd missed.

"Bring these with you to class next Tuesday, with your questions," he said.

"Don't worry. I'm so excited to get going on this, I can hardly stand it." I looked at my watch. "But it will have to wait until tomorrow. Can you believe it's almost five o'clock? We've had a busy day. If you have no plans, you're in for a real treat. I know you enjoyed Rosa's churros the other day. Do you like enchiladas? And some of her special margaritas? You're invited to stay for dinner; Bud should be here any time."

"That sounds super, but I don't want to butt in. Sounds like you already have company coming."

"Oh, Bud's not company, he's part of the family, like one of my brothers. A great friend to both Trevor and me over the years. And Rosa made plenty yesterday, knowing what was planned for today. Her shredded pork is to die for. I won't take no for an answer."

"What's going on in here?" Bud's voice boomed down the hallway. "I had hoped to get here early enough to pick up some hints on how to get more out of my computer."

"You're too late for that," I said, "but just in time for margaritas. We were on our way to the patio."

"I can handle that," Bud said. "How about you, Jeremy?"

"Si, amigos!" Jeremy grinned from ear to ear as he shook Bud's hand.

"You guys go on out. Bud, please get the pitcher and limes out of the refrigerator. Show Jeremy where we keep those on-the-rocks glasses. I'll grab the salt and be right out as soon as I check the message on the answering machine. We've been so busy all day; I just noticed it blinking a minute ago."

"Sounds like we've got our orders, Jeremy," Bud said as they hurried out the patio door.

I pushed the button on the answering machine, a strange voice echoed in my ear, "Sooo, Samaanthaaa, diiiid youuu en-jooy yeeerr vizzz-zit wiiiith Meesteer Raaaattlesnaaake?"

"No!" I screamed, clamping my hands over my ears.

Bud shot through the door, Jeremy a couple of steps behind, Jet almost got caught in the screen door as it pulled shut. "What is it? Are you okay?"

"H-h . . . Hit the replay." I spit the words out, pointing to the machine. My hands were shaking; I leaned on the counter to steady myself.

Bud started the message again: "Sooo, Samaanthaaa, diiiid youuu en-jooy yeeerr vizzz-zit wiiiith Meesteer

Raaaattlesnaaake?" Bud jammed his finger on the OFF button and looked at me, pain dripping from his eyes as he pulled me into a bear hug. Jeremy's mouth gaped open, his raised eyebrows frozen in wonder.

"Duh . . . does this mean what I think it means, Bud? I . . . tha . . . that snake didn't just wander in off the desert, did it?" I couldn't believe my own thoughts. "Jesus. I could be in the hospital—or worse—if you hadn't gotten here when you did the other day."

Bud opened the machine to reveal the tape. He grabbed a plastic bag from the drawer, covered his hand with the bag, pulled the tape inside, then zipped it up. The detective was taking over. His lips squeezed tightly together, a frown scrunched his face. Jeremy's eyes were open so wide, I was afraid he was going to bolt at any minute and they might fall right out onto the floor.

I shook my head and said, "Let's break out those margaritas and see where we are with this whole mess. Jeremy, I guess we owe you an explanation. Do you think you are ready for this?"

"I . . . . guess so." he said. "Especially if it includes a margarita." He tried to joke, but the fear in his eyes told us he had grasped the severity of the moment.

"I think we could all definitely use one about now," Bud said, putting his hand in the middle of my back and guiding me toward the door. He grabbed the salt on his way out, took the glasses from the freezer and began rubbing the rims with lime. Jeremy dipped them into the salt and filled the glasses with ice and the margarita mixture.

"Think we should spill the beans before dinner, Sam?" Bud asked as he handed out frosty glasses all around.

"Why don't you fill in some of the blanks for him while I go put some cold water on my face and see if I can settle myself down. Come on, Jet, I may need a little help. Cheers, guys, we won't be long."

I threw down a couple of aspirins, took a quick shower, and picked out jeans and a fresh T-shirt with a big red chili pepper on the front. It read: Bite Me—in bold green script. It matched my mood, damn it. They weren't going to get the best of Sam Beale. I could take it so long as people didn't start getting hurt. But I had to admit, this snake incident had me more than a little worried, but I put on a smile as I came out the screen door with my empty glass raised. "Anybody else ready for a refill?"

"I'm afraid we're ahead of you, Sam," Jeremy said. "Nice shirt. Wow, I gotta say, you are a bit of a feisty pepper yourself—taking all this weird stuff into your stride like you have. Out here by yourself so much of the time. You're lucky you have a cop for a good friend." He raised his glass to Bud.

"I'm a little old to need a babysitter, but I'm afraid I may have to take some drastic measures if we don't get to the bottom of this soon. Glad to see we didn't scare you off, Jeremy. I wasn't sure you'd still be here when I came back out."

"Oh, he's very interested in solving mysteries. In fact, came up with a great idea to give us a hand with things around here. Jeremy's in the market for an apartment, Sam. They are tearing down his building to make way for one of those new high-rise condos that are popping up everywhere in the downtown area. He's been holding out until the last minute to take advantage of the low rent he's had for the last couple of years. I hinted I might know of a vacant efficiency apartment: nice view, super landlady, good security, only possible drawback is right now it appears to be haunted or jinxed. So, I think he could probably swing a pretty good negotiation on the rent. What do you think?"

"I think you're maybe squeezing him into a corner here, Bud, don't you? Putting my best friend on the spot is one thing, but I'm afraid trying to pull poor Jeremy into this thing is well another."

"Hell no," said Bud. "We were afraid we were railroading *you* into our idea. Just do us a favor and think about it. It gives Jeremy a great place to live at a decent price, helps provide security for you to have someone else here on the premises, and gives me a chance for a day off once in a while, as well. Can you think of a better deal? And, he's ready to take it sight unseen."

We discussed the logistics of it over dinner. I put up a good argument, but they convinced me it was a good plan all the way around.

"I'll see if Rosa is available to come over on Monday to help clean and open up the apartment. We furnished it when we did the house, so moving in shouldn't be too much of a job."

Jeremy agreed to come over to help with the clean-up and bring his things over a few at a time in his bug. I insisted on taking no rent, settling instead for his help with my computer training and projects around the property. Everyone was happy with the new arrangement.

"I don't have much, really," Jeremy said. "Mostly my computer stuff and books. My apartment came with furniture and I have to admit I don't do much cooking at home, so not much in the kitchen department. That's the good thing about working in food service. You get to eat free so it works well with my budget and lack of cooking ability."

"Any kitchen things you need and linens are already in the cupboards. Trevor insisted we get mostly all new stuff for the house when we moved in here, so you'll have our old cookware and dishes and mostly hand-me-down furniture. It's a mixture of his, mine, and ours. Not fancy, but functional. We moved

Trevor's big old desk and bookcase from his downtown office into the living room up there. It should give you a great place for your studies. It's not something we want to move again if we don't have to, it weighs a ton. I think you'll be very comfortable."

"And you can't beat the price if you can handle these strange activities we've been having," Bud added.

"I'm sure I'm going to like roughing it out here." Jeremy laughed, looking around. "Thanks, you guys. I'd better get going. Sounds like I've got a big day tomorrow getting packed up and ready to move. See you Monday."

As we watched Jeremy's taillights fade down the lane, Bud turned and said, "Well, that's the best thing that's happened all week. I think that kid's going to be just the ticket for you around here. Not just to provide extra security, but to give you something else you've needed very badly over the last year and more, Sam. Laughter, vitality, and maybe even a little fun. Not to mention teaching you how to use that new toy of yours. I really believe you're headed in the right direction. Now you get going in the direction of bed and let me do my job."

I scooted off down the hall to my bedroom, excited about having Jeremy coming to live here. Too excited to sleep as I thought about the events of the past few days.

I rolled up the top on my desk and pulled my journal from its roost. I needed to talk about it, and have always found my journal a place to let out my feelings and thoughts, a relief that poured out with the words as they found themselves to the pages . . .

Saturday, Sept 17, 9:30pm

I decided it was time to make a change. Little did I know the changes that were about to occur were not within my control. What I thought was a dream, then the beginning of a sick joke that someone is playing on me appears to have been an attempt to harm or kill me. That's right . . . the rattlesnake we had on the patio now seems to have been put there. Can you believe it? Does that mean someone actually came into the yard and turned it loose? If so, how could they have done that without Jet barking . . . or could I have just slept right through it? Or, could it be that someone was watching me from a distance and just witnessed the whole thing? I'm afraid I'm getting paranoid. But who wouldn't?

So many positive things have happened this week and I must keep myself thinking of those. Not dwell on the bad, but not drop my guard either. Bud says to let him do his job. That's not easy when things seem to be getting worse every day. I'm excited about Jeremy being here, but don't want to put someone else in harm's way. I honestly think I am really helping him out in the process. He seems very anxious to move in.

Thank God for Bud. As he says, it *is* his job. And I know he's good at it.

16

The Detective

Bud wandered around the house, checking that the slider and kitchen doors were locked, then on to the front. He stopped on his way back through the great room to rest his knee on the window seat beside the fireplace; Jet already in his bed, turned up his head.

"You've got a good instinct with people, Jet," Bud kneeled down and patted Jet's head. "What do you think about Jeremy coming to live with you? I know, you can't help but like the kid, but it kinda bugs me that he came into the picture around here just about the same time this all started." Jet raised his head and looked Bud in the eye. "I just hope we're doing the right thing about him, I want to believe in him, but I want you to help keep a sharp watch for me. Think you can do that?

"Good talk, Jet, back to sleep." He scratched the top of Jet's head, then stood up to stare out the window. His eyes searched around the garage, across to the corrals, studied the shadows in the loafing shed. He wondered just how safe Sam and Jeremy would be without him.

Tomorrow he'd check the security system to make sure everything was working properly, as well as walk the perimeter fence again to look a little closer. He would call Sheriff Schaeffer to update him on the new incidents, asking him to continue the extra patrols on a 24/7 basis.

He would catch this bastard, but how? When would they stop the threats that are driving Sam up the wall? And why at a time when she's just beginning to accept her tragic loss?

17

Sunday started early for me. Six a.m. It was time to try for my ten laps today. I stopped to put the coffee on and headed toward the pool. "Come on Jet. Let's go check out the patio." He was more than happy to oblige and beat me to the door. Once out he circled around the pool like he knew what I was asking. I was on the seventh lap when Bud poked his head out the door.

"Good morning, early bird. Here's some coffee for you," he said, setting a steaming cup on the bar. "I'm on my way over to the house to check on things and pick up some grubbies. I figure I'm in line to help you get started on that apartment today so I may as well get dressed for it. Anything I can pick up along the way?"

"I'm thinking of ribs for dinner today. There's no wind so it should be a good day to barbecue. If that sounds good to you, I'll get some out of the freezer. Thought I'd make some baked beans. Would you pick up some salad fixings and anything else you see that sounds good to go with ribs. I will definitely appreciate your help. No need to hurry back. We've got all day and I'm in a lazy mood."

"Sounds great. Call me if you think of anything else. I walked out to the gate and saw a sheriff's patrol car down on the lane. So, things should be fine here while I'm gone. I'll check in with him on my way by. You know how to reach them if needed. Keep Jet out here with you. And don't . . ."

"Yes, Bud. I know the drill. I'm sorry about the other day when I left him in the house to eat. Believe me. I learned my lesson that day."

I felt exhilarated but tired as I climbed from the pool, and glad I hadn't gone for fifteen laps. I toweled off, grabbed my coffee and sat down at the table to map out my day. I was anxious to call Rosa to tell her the good news about Jeremy and the apartment, and solicit her help for Monday. It was time to tell her what's been going on around here. I had told her we'd had a prowler in the wash the one night to explain Bud's using the guest room in the house, but didn't share the news about the haunting music. I told her about my new goals and adventures with the university and signing up for the computer classes, but saw no need to alarm her if we were able to get a quick fix on the situation. But the ante was going up, and I didn't want someone to get hurt. Rosa would need to take extra precautions along with the rest of us.

Rosa insisted on bringing her husband, Manny, over after church to help with the apartment. I argued that Bud would be here and we could handle it just fine, but knew she was much more concerned to learn all of the details of our problems than the needs of the apartment. What could I say?

"Sure, come on over. And plan to stay for dinner. We should all be ready for some barbecued ribs when we finish up this afternoon." We agreed she should bring some flan, their traditional Sunday dessert.

I took more ribs out to thaw and went to get showered and dressed for the day. As I zipped my shorts, I gazed around the bedroom, admiring the handiwork of Manny Flores and smiled at the thought of seeing him again.

Trevor and I met Manny on one of our many trips to Aqua Prieta, the Mexican town just across the border from Douglas, Arizona. A regular maestro with wood, Manny had crafted a good share of our furniture and woodwork in the house. We had shared many a tequila and taco with him as we brought new ideas and fabrics to discuss with him before our final decisions were made on each piece. We listened to his stories of his father and his grandfather before him and the pieces they had crafted through the years.

We brought Manny to Tucson once the house was framed to give him its feel. Each door, closet, and cabinet was handmade by Manny, many onsite. As the building neared the finish line, our furniture was trucked up to Tucson in trips of Manny's own rickety old Ford. That was when Manny met Rosa and what appeared to be love at first sight. I'm not so sure it wasn't his handiwork she fell in love with, as it didn't take her long to put him to work in their own home once they married.

Each of our bedrooms includes a structural adobe fireplace in one corner; molded niches provide the perfect display for Native American artifacts. Manny's carved folding doors open onto closets with more niches and tiled shelves inside. A dressing table, sporting one horizontal row of drawers, hangs suspended against the wall alongside the bed. Heavy chains reach from the ceiling to anchor each side of the polished hardwood top.

Manny's fingers have become twisted through the years, but his love of each unique piece remains far greater than the pain or discomforts of his arthritis. On his last load of furnishings from south of the border, Manny surprised us with something we hadn't ordered, hadn't planned. A three-foot-high Mayan idol signifying peace, carved from Ironwood, a deep brown hardwood streaked in blood red wisps and swirls. Manny's face came back so clearly now, tears of love in his eyes. "Let this bring *pas* to your new *casa, mis amigos.*" Trevor lovingly christened it "Manito" that day and we placed him on a tiled pedestal amid the lush greens of the entry garden where he greets our guests and reigns as guardian of our house. We had agreed the courtyard needed something, but hadn't known exactly what until that day. Manito was perfect—the finishing touch to our new home.

Manny was now retired, but not idle. His fingers are still busy carving smaller figurines of animals and Native American and Mayan idols, sandwiched between household projects to keep Rosa happy. He's become quite well known, selling his work at local resort gift shops and galleries in the Tucson area.

I wasn't up to any more surprises, so waited for Bud to return to open up the apartment. In the meantime, I whipped up some baked beans to be put into the oven later, and gathered up cleaning supplies and fresh linens. Bud's timing was great. I had just cleaned up my kitchen mess when he popped in. I told him we were having help with the cleanup and company for the ribs. He was delighted with both. By the time Rosa and Manny got here, Bud and I had opened up the apartment, had fresh air sifting through the Spanish iron grating outside the windows, and the furniture moved away from the walls.

"There's really not that much to be done," I said. "I noticed there's no TV in here. If you guys will bring the one out from the office, we can leave it on the table and let Jeremy choose where to put it when he gets here tomorrow. Bring the satellite receiver, too, please."

By the time Bud packed in the TV—and Manny the receiver and remote—Rosa and I had the appliances wiped down, furniture dusted, floors damp mopped, and were on our way to put clean linens in place. "We'll slide the furniture back and should be all set for Jeremy to move in his stuff," Bud said.

"It will be so nice to have someone using this beautiful apartment," Rosa said, looking around the room. "I've always thought it a shame there ees nobody here to eenjoy it. And, Senora Sam, I am so happy to know you will have your new friend, Jeremy, here to share your time and chores. Now, let's go talk about these loco things that have been happening and see what Manny and me can do to help weeth them."

I looked over at Bud as he winked and said, "Is anybody hungry besides me? Why don't we light the barbecue and have a cold drink while dinner cooks. Talk always goes down better with *cervesa*, I'm told."

"*Muy bueno*." Manny said. "My stomach ees empty, too."

Bud's ribs were fall-off-the-bone good. The BBQ sauce recipe he'd stolen from Trevor a couple of years ago tasted a little spicier than usual, but—wouldn't you know—Manny and Rosa added more hot sauce. It was a wonderful evening reminiscing around the table on the patio, topped off with Rosa's authentic flan: creamy on the inside, crusty and rich and caramel-ly on the top.

Rosa and Manny hadn't been to our home for a meal in well over a year. Though we had new issues to worry about, they seemed trivial compared to those we'd all struggled through over the last two years. It was good to laugh with Rosa and Manny again. It was good to be able to enjoy the company of friends, to joke and talk of both the past and the future, to forget for now about the troubles we were facing. Hell, it was good to be alive again.

18

The Watchers

The black Dodge pickup worked its way slowly up Pusch Ridge. "Look, there's an extra car there today," the man said, pulling to their spot. They unloaded chairs and binoculars, made themselves comfortable.

"God damn it." The slender guy pulled his glasses away, turned to his companion. "Rather than packing up, it looks like she's bringing someone else in."

"Oh, that's her cleaning lady's car, and that must be her husband. Think they're going to move into the apartment? Maybe she's going away and she'll leave them house-sitting."

"Well, that's wishful thinking. Those two don't look like they'd be much of a challenge if that were true. If not, we'll keep hammering at her. She's bound to break soon."

He stepped away from the bed of the truck, flicked his cigarette off into the brush, and kicked a rock into the side of their cooler. "Whatever it is could sure as hell delay things. It's not as damned easy as we thought. Better call Jimmie tonight and give him an update."

"It can wait until tomorrow. Since we're here and we have sandwiches, let's stay and watch the sun go down just in case someone shows up to give us an idea as to what we can expect."

"I sure as hell hope they're not fixin' that garage up for a security guard," he said, shaking his head. "That's all we need."

He jumped up. "What I really need is a beer. You want one?"

"Yeah, and grab the sandwiches too."

Four beers later and a few minutes before 10, things were still going strong around the patio firepit at the Beale house.

"Do these people never quit?" she yawned stood up, and threw up her hands. *"Let's get the hell out of here, I've had enough."*

19

My cell phone was playing its tune. I sprang from bed and started toward my dresser, then realized it sounded a bit farther away. Where had I left it last night? It quit. I looked at the clock on my nightstand. 7:30. Seven-thirty? I couldn't believe it. How had I slept so late again?

Then I remembered: we'd talked until almost midnight. It started to get chilly about eight, so we lit a fire in the pit and gathered around it, intent on trying to figure out the who and why of our strange events. Who was targeting me? Rosa could not identify the mystery woman, nor could she confirm any important women in Trevor's life for the almost 12 years she had worked for him. Oh, he'd had plenty of dates all right, she'd said, but no one took his attention away from his business. Santiago Homes was definitely number one to Trevor. That was until Sam came along. So, Rosa said.

I finally found the phone lying on the desk in the office. God, I must have been tired. Or maybe too many *cervesas*? No, I remembered having only two, maybe three beers through the whole evening. And jabbering like a bunch of magpies. I guess we all just needed to talk, to get it out. Our thoughts had too long been pent up, afraid to be let out. To conjure up each other's memories, grief, loneliness. Why is it we stay mute during times of grief—like if we don't say anything it will go away? It *doesn't* go away. We must talk about it, talk about our lost loved ones, let folks know it's okay to tell stories. Okay to speak of them. They are dead but not forgotten. Never forgotten. Talking is how we control and overcome grief and can enjoy sharing our memories with others.

I checked the missed calls expecting to find Bud's name. There was a voice mail from Jeremy: "I've got the car loaded and am on my way out. Hope I'm not too early. I'm bringing coffee and donuts. Please call and let me know you're okay."

I called Jeremy on my way to the kitchen, found coffee in the pot and a note from Bud propped up on my cup. It read:

"Hi, Sam, Another early meeting - Monday morning. I'm going to update Pima County and my reports at the office with the latest. Let me know if there's anything new, or if you and Jeremy need any help with the move-in. If not, I'll see you after work, B."

I felt pretty special standing there in my PJs: messages from two wonderful guys worrying about me, going out of their way to make sure I'm okay. What a lucky gal. I'd consider myself anything but lucky if I didn't get dressed before Jeremy showed up with a carload of his belongings and found his new landlady still running around in pajamas.

I raced down the hall and dressed in plenty of time to hear the buzz from the gate. I started to hit the open button, but caught myself. Even though I was expecting Jeremy, I still needed to confirm who was waiting at the gate. I hit the video switch and there he was, his grin sprang right through the wires and transferred to my face. I triggered the mike, "Anyone with donuts can come on in," and switched the gate open.

He pulled his VW over to the garage and walked on up to the front door carrying a tray with two cups and a sack from Dunkin Donuts, his big smile still plastered on his face. Jet beat me to the door, but never uttered a sound once he saw Jeremy through the security door. I patted Jet's head and said, "Good Boy, shall we let him in? He has donuts."

"A peace offering for my new landlady," Jeremy said, holding out the sack. "Hope I got the right kind. I picked some that looked sorta like Rosa's churros just to be safe, but there are maple and chocolate ones too."

"Never met a donut I didn't like, so you are safe there. Let's dig in, I'm starved. How's the packing going?"

"My car is full of boxes. It'll probably take me a couple of more loads to get my computer equipment and books, but you know that's not saying much with a Volkswagen. There's not a lot of space for boxes in there."

"Yummy donut. Coffee, too," I said, licking my lips. "Thanks. This hits the spot. We got the apartment mostly ready for you to move in. Had lots of help yesterday. Rosa and Manny came over and it didn't take long with the four of us. I've got the whole day set aside to help get you settled. We can take my 4Runner and probably get everything in one load if you'd like, save you a trip or two?"

"Wish you had called me; I would have gladly come over to help and loved to have had a chance to meet Rosa. I had most of it packed up yesterday morning. I'd love to get it all done with one more load if you're sure you have time," he said, taking the last bite from his donut. "The boxes are sitting just inside the door so I had a clear way to sweep and mop my way out. It shouldn't take long to load 'em up."

"Sounds good to me. Grab your coffee. Let's go introduce you to your new home. I'll give you time to get your things settled, then we can make a run to pick up the rest of your stuff whenever you're ready."

"Wow, it's perfect," Jeremy shouted as the door swung open.

About 800 square feet, the living, dining, and kitchen consisted of one large room and a small half-bath which filled the space above the two-car side of the garage. Six steps led up to the bedroom, bath, and a small studio occupying the space on the higher, RV side.

"I thought it would be," I said, "especially you being a bachelor. There's plenty of room—please feel free to use it however it works best for you.

"The upstairs studio is small, but may be a great place to study if you don't want to spread out down here on the counter or desk. This was Trevor's work desk from his old office, so I'm afraid it's had more than a few scrapes and gouges from belt buckles and tool belts when he and Clint went over their plans.

"Give me a shout when you're ready to go or if you have questions or need anything in the meantime. There's an intercom downstairs just inside the garage door. Just push HOUSE and I should be able to hear your beep."

Jeremy didn't even hear me—he was still taking it all in. He'd opened the French doors and walked out onto the terrace above the driveway. "This has to be a killer view of the sunsets.

I can hardly wait." He turned and motioned me out with a jerk of his head. "I'll set up my tripod out here. I do a little work for *Arizona Highways*. I can see a cover photo here." He framed the scene he was casting with his outstretched hands. "Catching the corner of the house next to that huge saguaro as the sun slowly sinks into the West."

"How many jobs do you have?"

He laughed. "I'm planning to be a freelance writer. My focus right now is history or travel pieces for *AH,* and I do some things for *Sunset* from time to time. Anything that helps get me through school. I love writing and the research that goes along with it."

"That sounds interesting," I said. "Is that how you got started with computer work?"

He was still surveying the grounds from his perch, arms now crossed. "It's more like computers is how I got started writing. I grew up with computers. Didn't get into the games like most kids and many adults do. I surfed. I learned I could travel online to anywhere I wanted to go. Be an expert without ever leaving home. Now, I want to surf for real: feel the sand and waves between my toes."

"A great goal," I nodded. "And I'll bet you'll make it." I tossed him his keys and we walked back into the room. "Once we get you all moved in, I'll give you the codes for the alarm and the gate opener, and we can go over any questions about the satellite TV or other electronics. Listen to me…teach you about electronics? Ha. Can I help you put any of this away?"

"No thanks. In fact, I'd like to wait until we get it all out here, then I can work on finding the right place for everything all at once. Any time you are ready to go—the sooner, the better for me. I can't wait to get moved in." He rubbed his palms together. "This place is going to be perfect. For everything. Thank you . . . thank you. I'll be down in a minute."

We left at five minutes before eleven o'clock to make the run over to Jeremy's. I understood why he was impressed with his new digs. His whole apartment would've fit inside half of our main room, but it had obviously been fine for a student watching his budget. And, he was only a couple of blocks from the U and his job. A great set-up for a starving student, but not much on entertaining.

We headed back up our lane at 12:45, the SUV loaded with computer gadgets, books, hanging clothes, and a small box of kitchen wares—a very small box. Jeremy had not been exaggerating when he said he seldom cooked at home. I could already feel the mother instinct coming through, thinking about some of my favorite dishes I rediscovered in the recipe sorting, anxious to try some of them out on Jeremy. It will be fun to have someone like him to share meals with on a regular basis. And, I had a feeling Jeremy was going to appreciate some good home cooked meals for a change.

We noticed a rectangular package, about the size of a 12 pack of Pepsi, leaning against the mailbox when we approached the gate. Jeremy bounded out to pick it up. A hand reached into my chest and squeezed around my heart as I saw the familiar scrawl on the plain brown wrapper. And no return address. And no postage.

"Wait." I screamed it out. Jeremy froze in mid-stride, his face a mishmash of confusion and fear as it turned my way.

"Let me call Bud," I said. "I . . . I'm not expecting anything. And the writing on that package looks a lot like the one I received last week with the CD." I fished my cell from my purse and hit the speed dial.

"Oh man. I'm sorry, Sam." Jeremy's pursed lips now mirrored disappointment in himself as he got back into the car. "I guess I was so wrapped up in my own excitement, I didn't think. I've got to get my head around this."

I felt like a bee was buzzing from one side of my stomach to the other as I waited for Bud's answer.

"Holloway."

Tears sprang from my eyes as I described the package to him.

"You did the right thing to call me. I'm on my way." He told us to go back down the hill and wait at the beginning of our lane until he got there.

Silence hung inside the car as the minutes stretched by. I felt like we were cast in a movie playing in slow motion. Sheriff Schaeffer's unmarked Avalanche got there first. We got out of the car to meet him as he pulled alongside.

"Glad to see you are okay, Sam. Bud caught me on my way back to the office from lunch, so I was pretty close. He and I got together this morning to catch up, and we had planned to meet with you later this afternoon. Looks like our schedule got moved up a bit. This may be nothing, but then . . ." A siren whined in the distance, getting closer, then stopped.

"That should be Bud now," the sheriff said. "Probably just turned off the highway."

We filled the time introducing Jeremy and Sheriff Schaeffer and retelling our story as Bud's Victoria raced up the road and slid to a stop. Shortly behind him, an unmarked black van arrived. Bud had followed normal procedures and notified the HAZMAT team, better known around the department as the Bomb Squad, according to Bud's tales. He explained that while the likelihood of it being a bomb was slim, protocol required taking every precaution offered to avoid any risk to people or property. Boy, was that a mouthful!

Jeremy and I stayed at the bottom of the hill as the others caravanned up to our gate. Bud kept us posted via cell phone as the team went through their paces to scan and open the package once they determined it was not booby trapped.

We could wait no longer. Though we had no clearance, we drove on up and parked behind the official vehicles. Everyone was crowded around a metal table, staring at the open package.

I felt a little foolish as I glimpsed what appeared to be a bouquet of flowers wrapped loosely in black tissue paper. My embarrassment morphed to disappointment as I drew close enough to see the red and purple flowers had died in transit. Then to terror when I read the choppy note lettered from cuts of newspaper print:

RoSes are DEAD, viOlets are toO, WHo wiLL BE next, maybe it's YOU

My legs felt like stems of the dried roses in the package as I swayed toward Jeremy. His arms flew up to stop my fall, the sheriff jumped to catch me around the waist as I crumpled toward the ground. My mouth felt stuffed with cotton. I tried to speak, but could think of nothing to say.

20

Up until now it had seemed like a dream, but when you get a no-questions-asked death threat, you have to sit up and take notice. Or maybe you have to fall apart. Pick me.

I wanted to run and hide. Hide where the bad guys couldn't find me. Hide from the mail and hide from the phone. They were getting inside of my head and I knew that was exactly where they wanted to be. I knew—but couldn't stop them. I kept thinking—*this is the first day of the rest of your life, Sam.* But then . . . it could also be your last.

Bud and Jeremy managed to get me into the car and up to the house. I was numb, feeling sorry for myself, scared. You name it, I had it. Or did it have me? I was a basket case. I hugged and thanked the guys, begged off with a headache and headed for the sanctuary of my bedroom. I just needed some space . . . some Sam time. I had to get myself pulled together, and I needed to do it fast. Otherwise, they would win. THEY would WIN. And I couldn't let that happen. Someone had to have a real hard-on

139

against me to come up with these threats and I needed to get to the bottom of it. Before things got any worse.

The needles of hot water stung my body. They needed to sting to wash away the slime that oozed over me and slid into my brain. I wanted it gone. My skin finally felt the prickle of cooling water. A cleansing raced through my mind and seeped out of my pores. I was whole again; I had exorcised the slimy bastards for now. It was time to fight.

I almost tripped over Jet as I came out of the bedroom door. "Sorry about that, guy. Come on, let's go find the fellas."

We walked toward voices coming from the patio. Bud, Jeremy and Sheriff Schaeffer were sitting around the table. They were drinking a beer, but their faces said this was no party.

Bud looked up as I opened the door. "Here she comes now. Let's see what she thinks."

The Sheriff jumped up. "Mrs. Beale." He stepped toward me, extending his hand. "I'm going to get right to it. I think it's time we took more drastic measures to ensure your safety. I'd like to put you in protective custody until we get this thing wrapped up." He was still gripping my hand, his eyes riveted on mine. The easy-going cowboy of his last visit was gone.

"Exactly what do you mean by protective custody, Sheriff?" I asked and retrieved my hand from his grasp. I sank into the chair Jeremy had pulled out for me. "I won't leave my home. Damn it. I think that's exactly what they want. Though I still can't figure out why."

"But these threats are getting worse by the day," the sheriff said. "And I . . ." He sat back down, collecting his thoughts before answering. "I don't know how much longer you will be safe staying here. It's my job to protect you. Our job." He nodded toward Bud. "I'd like to get you away from here, into a safe house.

"My gut tells me you're right about someone wanting to get you out of your house. We've been sitting here for the last hour trying to figure out who or why. If we make a show of your leaving, we may be able to trap them into making their play."

Until now, Bud and Jeremy had let the Sheriff handle things. "Their play?" A mist of spit followed Bud's words. "Is that what you county boys call these threats, Sheriff?"

"Whoa, boys," I said. "Take it easy. We've been okay so far. Shaken up . . . yes. But no harm, no foul. We have good security here, a good alarm system. I can even hire a security guard if you feel that's necessary. I don't want my home invaded by these dirt bags."

"Thanks, Sam," Bud said, giving his jaw a glancing slap. "I needed that. Sorry, Sheriff. That was uncalled for."

"No worries, Bud. I know emotions are running high. I've really appreciated your help with this investigation and want us to keep working together to bring it to a safe and speedy conclusion. I'll welcome your ideas. Got any?"

Bud gnawed on his bottom lip, looked over at me. "How about your dad, Sam? You and I talked about maybe having him come down. I think with Jeremy here part time and your dad here, we could have a pretty good security team. How about it Sheriff?"

"I'd still rather we get Sam clear away from here."

"You don't know Sam as well as I do. She can be awfully stubborn at times. And, she's a pretty damned good shot if needed. I think a little target practice may be in order, though. I imagine it's been a while since she's handled a gun.

"How about you, Jeremy? Done much shooting?"

"Wait another minute, you guys. Let's not rush into things." My hands sprang into action, palms forward, bouncing to emphasize my point. "I don't want to include Jeremy in any more plans. He's not even moved in yet and I don't want to put him in any danger here."

"If you think you're getting rid of me that easy, think again," Jeremy said. "We didn't sign a lease, but we made a deal. I'm not letting you welch out on me. Otherwise, I'm homeless." He shrugged his shoulders, stuck out his lower lip in a pout.

"And Bud. Yes, I do know how to handle a gun. You don't

grow up in Wyoming without learning to hunt to put food on the table for the winter. I haven't shot lately, so I'd like to be included in any refreshers you do with Sam."

Though I won the battle to stay at home, I gave in to the fellas on the rest of it. Bud and Jeremy finally talked the sheriff into going along with the plan—at least for the next few days—until things could be worked out to his satisfaction. After all, it *was* his jurisdiction.

Schaeffer wasn't too keen on the gun part of it, but agreed with Bud that we all needed to be ready if it came down to that. Bud promised to stay over at night as long as needed. Jeremy would continue my classes right here at home to avoid unnecessary travel at night. I would call Dad that evening to invite him down, and contact Clint tomorrow to arrange for additional outside security lights and motion sensors to be installed as soon as possible. Sheriff Schaeffer agreed to increase his patrols. The plan was set. For now.

I had always figured my dad wanted a boy, and he and Mom compromised by naming me Samantha so I could be Sam for short. I may as well have been a boy. Dad taught me everything he did as I was growing up. I could ride with the best of them, bag my own deer and pheasants come hunting season, and knew I had to clean every fish I kept to bring home for the frying pan.

I could change a tire when I was six years old and pound nails with only an occasional thwack on my thumb.

I guess he'd forgotten that I had probably been the biggest tomboy in Idaho when I called him that night and told him my story. I immediately reverted back to his little girl. And his little girl was in trouble.

"What the hell? Who would do these things, Honey?"

"That's what we've been trying to figure out, Dad. At first, we thought it was just some kids playing pranks, but the threats have become ruthless and are pointed directly at me. Do you remember our friend, Bud Holloway? You met him at the wedding. The detective? Well, Bud's been staying here at night this week, thinking we would get to the bottom of things by now. The county sheriff is running increased patrols and has suggested I move into a safe house. But, Dad, I can't do that. I can't let these people—whoever they are—run me out of my home. Bud's willing to stay indefinitely, but I can't ask him to do that.

"Can you come down? I've been trying for five years to get you back down here, but not under such drastic circumstances. Once we catch these SOBs maybe we can relax and enjoy a real visit."

"You bet I'll be down. As soon as I get someone lined up to take care of my stock."

"Oh Dad, I'm sure Betsy will be happy to take care of them. She'd do anything for you. Are you still pretending you don't know she's stuck on you?"

"Now you just keep your nose where it belongs, little lady. Betsy and I have been friends for years and friends will do most anything for friends. Don't you worry. I'll get someone to watch the place and see how fast I can get a flight out of Lewiston. I'll call you in the morning to let you know when I'll be there."

"OK, Dad. And, thanks. I really need you." I struggled to hide the quiver that plagued my words.

"You . . . you got any guns down there?" I knew he was trying to clear his own throat; the words were difficult for him as well. "It sounds like you'd better keep one handy. At least until I get there and can take care of things for you."

"Yes, I've still got the Colt you gave me when I graduated, and I've been keeping it close these days. And the gun cabinet is still loaded with Trevor's small arsenal. You think we're covered in case we have a siege to worry about?" I hoped my try at a joke would hide the tear sliding down my cheek.

"If there is anything I can do to help with your travel plans, you let me know, Dad. I need to keep busy. Talk to you tomorrow. I love you."

Monday, September 19, 10pm

Things are escalating; there is no question about the threat that came in the mail today. Someone has threatened my life. Just as I'm trying to get my life back, someone wants to take it away. I'll be so happy to have Dad here with me, and I'm worried about Jeremy. He shouldn't be exposed to this crap, yet it seems he wants to be a part of it. Should I let him be the macho man, or should I send him packing? I'll see what Dad has to say.

As much as I like Jeremy, sometimes I think his coming into our lives the way he has this last week could be more than a coincidence. Could he possibly be a part of this whole thing? No, I can't believe that. Though I thought I could sense doubt on the sheriff's part at first, but once he got acquainted with Jeremy, he seemed to agree with the whole plan to include him.

I've got to trust my instinct on this one . . . and that instinct says he's a good guy. And we are damned lucky he stepped into our

lives. I hate myself for thinking like this.
Time to quit . . .

As I pulled back the covers, I forced my brain to think about the things that needed done tomorrow. Sure, Bud had already gone to bed; I slipped across the hall into the office and clicked on the desk light. Tomorrow's page awaited. I wrote:

Call Clint - security
Call Debbie - board horses

21

Tuesday's sun was streaming through the curtains on the bedroom slider when I awoke. I slipped into my swimming suit, grabbed a cover-up and headed for the kitchen. Bud was already gone, but Jet met me at the doorway. Reaching down, I ruffled his head, grabbed a cup of coffee and we were out the patio door.

Another glorious Arizona morning. So far, the fall had been unusually warm, expected high today: eighty-four degrees. Wispy, cotton candy clouds scattered high across an otherwise clear sky. I settled onto a lounge beside the pool, set my coffee on the table. Jet flopped onto the concrete next to me.

My mind went into a spin. Were we doing the right thing—or rather: things? I thought through the conversations of last night, the animosities of the sheriff, Bud jumping to my defense, Jeremy pledging his support, and now Dad on his way to Arizona. How lucky I was to have them in my corner. And, how happy we would all be once this was over and things were back to normal.

To normal? That snapped me back. My coffee had probably gotten ice cold while I was in la-la land. I tipped my cup to my lips and found it empty. I had just taken another trip on automatic pilot.

I jumped into the pool. Icicles sliced through my body, then warmth inched its way up as I stroked toward the shallow end. In my rhythm as I reached the turn, I finished my ten laps and climbed up the steps. Jet greeted me with a cold nose on my leg. Shaking the water from my hair, I splashed him as much as possible and said "Does that feel as good to you as it did to me?" I patted his back, rubbing the water in. "It's about time you had a bath, anyway, my man. We'll get to that later today. Right now, I've got to get some clothes on and get into gear."

I wrapped a towel around me and was half way through the kitchen when my cell rang. Careful not to slip as I hurried down the hall, I grabbed the phone from my night stand just as it went silent. "Dammit." *Missed Call* flashed on the screen. Dad's number. I punched it to return the call.

"Hello . . . that you Sam?"

"Hi, Dad. Sorry. I got to the phone just as it quit. What have you found out?"

"I was lucky to get the last seat on a Horizon flight out of Lewiston to Boise tomorrow morning and connected on down to

Tucson on Southwest. I'll arrive at 2:17. How's that? Does it work for you?"

"God, you have no idea how fantastic that sounds." My heart was already doing flip-flops just thinking about it.

"I'm anxious to see you, too, Honey. Can you pick me up?"

"I'll be there with bells on."

"You can forget the bells. Oh, Betsy said to say hi. She's going to take care of the horses and will probably have old Spud spoiled rotten by the time I get home. He gets along great with her new Lab retriever. We'll be expecting puppies some of these days the way those two carry on."

"Give her my best and my thanks for taking such good care of you guys up there. Have a good trip, Dad. I'll see you at the airport."

It was a little after ten when I called Clint to set up an appointment for work on the security system. I'd put it off, arguing with myself about how much I should tell him. He hadn't pried the day I stopped by with the photos from the funeral and I wasn't sure what Bud might have told him when they visited later. At any rate, I needed Clint's expertise and advice, so briefly explained we were trying to discourage any further incidents and let it go at that. He promised to review our system plans and get back to me

A-sap with his recommendation, an estimate, and an appointment with Desert Security.

I crossed Call Clint from my list. Next up was Board Horses. My friend Debbie McCoy works for El Commodore Stables just a few miles away, off Oracle Road. The telephone rang and rang. I was about ready to hang up when Debbie answered, a little out of breath, "El Commodore Stables."

"Hi Debbie, it's Sam. Sounds like I've caught you at a busy time."

"Well, things have been busy around here ever since I talked the boss into boarding horses and giving riding lessons in addition to offering our trail rides. And, much better for me as I get a piece of the action. What's up with you? We need to do lunch some of these days, girl. It's been way too long."

"Lunch sounds wonderful, but I'll have to take a rain check for now. My dad's coming down tomorrow and we've made plans to get out and show him some more of Arizona. I wondered if you have room to take my horses for a short stay. We can do lunch after he goes back home."

"Sure, bring them over. We're still in our slower season for trail rides, and we keep most of our string off the resort property when we're not working them. I should be able to stable yours for as long as you need. Bring 'em on down. There's always someone here nine to five."

"Thanks, Debbie. I'll probably get them ready and have Dad help me bring them over later this week."

We chatted a little about things, and about nothing. She has a new guy she's seeing and will tell me about him when we have lunch. I shrugged off a shiver as I hung up. It went against my grain to lie to Debbie, but we wanted to keep this under wraps as much as possible. My brother always says: "Loose lips sink ships." Well, this was one ship I was determined to keep afloat—no matter what it took.

Debbie had been my best friend ever since we worked together at the office of Thane Marketing in Boise almost ten years ago. She and I kept our horses at my folks' acreage out near Kuna and got together as often as possible on the weekends to play golf or ride in the desert. Before long, the folks retired and moved to the mountains, taking my horse along with them. I met the man of my dreams and no longer saw much of Debbie except at work in those days.

Debbie had a hankerin' for year-round sun, never did like the snow and cold winter temperatures of Idaho. She moved to Arizona about the time Drew and I got married. We kept in touch, me mostly writing letters; Debbie was a phone person. She jumped around a little, working for a while at Nordstrom's in Phoenix until she landed a job at an advertising office, then moved on to Tucson to capture her dream of working with horses and maybe bulldogging a good-looking cowboy in the meantime. So far, the cowboy part hadn't happened, but she was always on the lookout.

When Drew and I split, and I got over my initial blues, I gathered up my stuff and moved to Tucson, shared a condo with Debbie for three years until Trevor and I married. Since then, our time together has been stretched out again, in fact, almost non-existent through Trevor's illness. She'd begged me to get together for lunch, but so far had received nothing but promises.

"So, am I evicted?" Bud called as the back door opened.

Engrossed in my computer homework, I hadn't even heard him pull in. So glad for the whole afternoon to catch up, I must have shut out everything else. Jeremy would be happy to see my homework caught up with the rest of the class. Just because we were doing it at home now, didn't mean he should cut me any slack.

"I'm afraid you're out of here. Dad gets in around two tomorrow. Can I take you out to dinner tonight? Debbie said their new chef at the Hilton makes a mouthwatering Swordfish Oscar. You game for a little seafood?"

"You know me. I never turn down good food or good company. Seems like the thing I remember about the El

Commadore was their bread pudding and that tangy, buttery rum sauce. I can almost taste it now. We gotta save room for that.

"But, don't you want to wait until your dad gets here for a night out?"

Shaking my head, I said, "Knowing Dad, he'll be ready for a relaxing night at home after fighting airports and schedules all day long."

"Besides, home's a much better place to fill him in on all the details of what's been going on around here," Bud said. "And I'm betting that's going to be the first thing on his agenda."

"You're right. I thought we'd do steaks tomorrow night. Something easy. Especially if I can talk you into cooking them. I know we just had them a few nights ago, but it makes a no-brainer after a busy day for us all."

"How can I refuse since you're treating me to a night out tonight? We should probably plan to have an early dinner. Your dad will no doubt be famished after flying most of the day. Those airports don't offer much for a meat and potatoes guy from Idaho."

"And Jeremy said he has class and needs to be on the road by 6:30. I'm hoping he'll have a chance to get a little acquainted with Dad before he has to leave."

"Barring anything unexpected, I'll plan to be here in plenty of time to get the steaks on well before six. Now, if we're going out to dinner tonight, yours truly has to get out of this tie and into the shower. That is, if no tie is okay with you and the Hilton?"

"Sure is. I'm wearing something comfy and casual. Debbie said they have a dinner for an in-house group of two hundred and fifty Wendy's managers in their western event area out by the stables tonight. So, the majority of the hotel guests will be out there, leaving the inside restaurant for us locals."

I chose a knee length white linen skirt with a print over-blouse; its yellow background spattered with red and brown Kokopelli stick figures. A silver Concho belt held the blouse in soft gathers around my waist. Red leather sandals with almost no heel kept me at a respectable walking height beside Bud.

I topped off a glass of Gewurztraminer for him as he walked into the kitchen, eyes roving me from head to toe. "You'd think we planned this," he said, his left hand pointing to the red polo shirt he wore tucked into his tan Dockers, his right snatched the stemmed glass from my fingers. "Thanks. You read my mind."

"You look quite handsome," I said, raising my glass. "In fact, I must say we make quite a striking pair. We should fit right in with the tourist scene, don't you think?"

We drank our wine and were off for a night on the town. "My car, you drive," I said, handing him the keys to the 4Runner. The gate opened as we walked across the driveway. Jeremy's VW braked and pulled in front of his assigned taller side of the garage.

"Do you think your VW will fit that side of the garage when it grows up?" Bud teased as Jeremy unfolded himself from the little car. I laughed. Jeremy stuck out his tongue.

"Looks like you guys are off for a fun night. I'll be heading out to my class shortly. Any special instructions before I go . . . besides making sure the alarms are set?"

"That's it. Except leave a light or two on upstairs while you're gone. We left some on in the house," said Bud. "To look like someone's home.

"Sam's taking me out to dinner before she kicks me out. We shouldn't be late. I've still got to pack up my things tonight. Her dad will be in tomorrow. Oh, don't be surprised to see a deputy sticking pretty close. I let the Sheriff know we'll all be out for a while."

"Can we bring you back a dessert? Their specialty is bread pudding with rum sauce."

"Sounds like a good nightcap. I'll save room. You guys have fun. And thanks."

Once at the El Commadore, we were surprised to find Juanita's restaurant for the last twenty-some years had been completely remodeled and now sported a whole new look: *Chimayo*—in orange neon letters suspended above a half wall sporting a painted scene of a quaint and definitely old Spanish adobe church.

"It's a National Historic Landmark named after a Roman Catholic sanctuary in Chimayo, New Mexico," said Maria, our hostess. "And famous as a pilgrimage site noted for its healing soils that rose from the ground since back to the early 1800s."

She handed us our menus and continued, "Chimayo features local area ingredients and chef's creative ideas to bring fresh and new flavors to our patrons, but I'm afraid we can't guarantee healing abilities.

Serena will be your server tonight. She will be happy to answer any questions you may have about our new menu."

Bud glanced over the wine list and took care of the ordering when Serena arrived. We stuck with our plan but enjoyed keeping the menus at the table to read more about Chimayo's new offerings for another time. We discovered we were lucky to have come down that evening. The swordfish was not on their regular menu—but a special entrée for that week only.

Debbie's recommendation was indeed a winner. The Swordfish Oscar was a work of art: swordfish steak crowned with crisscrossing king crab legs and asparagus spears, béarnaise sauce oozing across the top and down its sides, with delicate lemon buttered angel hair pasta at the side. We each capped off our meal with Mexican coffee to wash down our half of Chimayo's signature Peach Cobbler. Yes, we were disappointed to discover our coveted bread pudding no longer remained on the menu, but the first bite of the cobbler assured us we would not have to apologize to Jeremy for bringing a substitution.

It was a delicious meal, a relaxing evening, a perfect thank-you for my wonderful friend who had come to my rescue—had been my rock—and would soon be turning the reins over to my dad.

As we waddled out of the restaurant, I heard someone say, "Well, hello there, Sam."

I looked up to see Sandy Marks, from UA, coming out of the ladies' room directly across the hall, a Chimayo emblazoned "doggie" bag in her left hand, the other reaching for the arm of an older gentleman.

"Why Sandy, how nice to see you again." We met in the middle of the corridor. "I see you've been enjoying dinner here, too," I said, pointing to her bag. "It's hard to believe we didn't notice one another in the restaurant. Although with all the changes, I guess, it's really no surprise."

I introduced Sandy and Bud, and was happy to meet her grandfather, whose birthday they were celebrating. We moved into the lobby, chitchatted a little about the new restaurant and about Grandfather and his carvings. As our conversation began to lag a bit, I asked, "Do you live in this area?"

"Grandfather does. He's lived in the same place, just off the highway a little north of here, for at least fifty years, long before the rest of the city moved out to be his neighbors. I'm over close to the U, in one of the older historic areas.

"And I'd better be heading that way. By the time I get Grandfather home and myself on across town, it will be time to call it a day. It's been nice meeting you, Bud, and I'm so glad to see you again, Sam. Maybe we can get together sometime soon for lunch and go out to see Grandfather's carvings if you are still interested."

"You bet I am." We agreed to make contact soon and headed out to the parking lot.

22

I was already up, recipes scattered around the kitchen table, when Bud came out of the guest room. Hangers laden with clothes draped heavily across his shoulder. "Good morning, Sunshine," he said, "how's your day so far?"

"Starting off fine, but I'm sorry to be losing my favorite roommate. Here, let me get that door for you. Anything left in there I can help you carry out?"

"No, I'm good. I'm coming back in for a cup of coffee and I'll be on my way. Gonna stop by to update Schaeffer about your dad. He should be happy to hear he's flying in today."

Jet followed me to the patio door, slipping out with Bud. Jet had been nervous lately, no doubt trying to figure out what the extra activity was all about. His haven had been upset, as well as mine, and we both wanted to get back to a status quo. I wondered how long that would be—until we restored what we had become accustomed to—but felt deep down that our little humdrum life was not going to return anytime soon. Dad's arrival today would turn yet another new page for Jet and me.

I couldn't wait to see Dad. Not only because of the stability he would bring, but it had been five years since I'd seen him—at our wedding—and I'd missed him. Getting him away from the little Idaho ranch he and Mom bought after he'd had his fill of the city life, as he called it, was not an easy task these days. Easier for Mom: she and Dad divorced after a couple of years of living in the mountains and she returned to Boise, operated a travel agency until she met and married my new stepdad, Tom Shyler. She and Tom now live in Las Vegas. He is manager of the Monte Bello Resort and she loves every minute of the action of Vegas.

Dad still has Apache, my paint horse, and three others he's accumulated. I don't know why he still keeps four horses around, but when you have forty acres of pastureland rolling across the hills, I guess it doesn't much matter. They are his family. I doubt he could bear to give them up any more than ol' Spud, his Golden Lab.

Bud came back into the house for his last load of gear, picked up a cup of coffee to take along. "I'm running a little late," he said, leaned over and gave me a quick peck on the top of my head. "If you want me to take you to the airport to pick up your dad, just give me a call. I know you said you want to do it yourself, but if you change your mind let me know. Remember what the sheriff said."

"I'm sure Jet and I will be able to provide pick-up service for Dad. I'll see you between 5:30 and 6:00? I'm counting on you to grill steaks tonight."

"No problem. I'm looking forward to getting better acquainted with your dad, too. Why wasn't he here for Trevor's services? I forget."

"Pneumonia."

"Okay, I remember now. I should be here in plenty of time to get those steaks on. See ya tonight." He laughed, shaking his head. "We sound like a couple of old married people."

Jet was waiting to come in as Bud left for work. I refilled my coffee, filled Jet's water and food dishes and settled back to my job at hand. I had sorted the recipes into piles: meats, side dishes, desserts, pasta, and miscellaneous. I was sure I would be adding more as I went along, but this would be a good start.

Jeremy had installed *Cookbooks Made Easy* on my new computer and I was eager to try it out. I decided to dig right in. No sense in using practice materials to hone my long rusty typing skills when there was work to be done. I paper clipped the new piles together and inserted them into the file folder, stacked up scissors, paper clips, and my Post-its on top, then headed down the hall for the office when I heard the intercom buzzer. I stopped at the control station and pushed SPEAK: "Grand Central Station. All aboard."

"Top of the morning to you," Jeremy said. "Saw Bud leave, so figured you were up. I will be doing the same in a few minutes. Anything I can do for you this morning before I take off?"

"No, I'm fine, Jeremy. Thanks for asking. I'm about ready to begin typing some recipes on the new software, then Jet and I will pick up Dad this afternoon. Bud has promised to cook steaks for dinner. Hope you can join us so you can meet Dad."

"Love to. What time do you pick him up? Want me to grab something for dessert for my part of the dinner? Anything special for your dad? Or you?"

"Whatever you bring will be appreciated. I doubt my dad ever turned down a dessert in his life and I inherited that trait from him. You guys will get along great.

"And, thanks for sticking in here, Jeremy. This is definitely above and beyond the call of duty. You have another test today? How often do you have those things?"

"Too often, that's for sure. By the way, that peach cobbler was awesome. Thanks, again. You be careful today. And, give me a call if you run into any snags on your typing. If I don't answer, I'm taking the test. Later, Sam. Over and out."

I made it to the office, booted up the computer and clicked the cute little smiling cookbook icon. I was lost in the cooking world. *Cookbooks Made Easy* turned out to be a lot of trial and error—mostly error on my part. I broke the ice by typing a trial recipe for Swordfish Oscar based on our dinner discussion about the entree last night, with plans to try it soon while it was still fresh on our palate.

The phone brought me back to reality. It was 11:45. Jeremy was checking in and I hadn't even cleaned the guest room to get it ready for Dad's arrival. But looking at the stack of recipes that were turned upside down, I smiled as I realized I had completed all of the Meat section—typed and saved. It wasn't as easy as the software people made it sound, but I had muddled through all those from the file folder. There would be more to add when I started on the recipes flagged in the cookbooks, but for now, I relished this victory. I was on my way. And right then, I needed to get busy on Dad's bedroom before I had to be on my way to the airport.

I waited just outside the security barriers, sorry that I couldn't be there standing at the gate as Dad came out of the jet way. It was 2:48 and I still hadn't caught sight of him. I cupped my hand to my ear and strained to make out the announcements as they blared through invisible speakers. I couldn't understand a word. Not a word. Those damned terrorists. They've taken every speck of joy out of travel for both the traveler and the greeter.

Minutes dragged by. And then, there he was, his Stetson shining like a beacon in the midst of a herd of cattle now funneling through the security opening. All of a sudden, I was jumping up and down hoping he could see me in the crowd, then pushing my way through the throng. And finally, we were hugging like long lost lovers.

"Oh, Dad, I'm so glad you're here," I said. My heart was about to jump from my chest. I could feel my hands shaking as they patted his back, and then I was sobbing like a baby.

"Wait a minute there, Little Missy," Dad said in the familiar style of John Wayne in his western movies. He pushed me out to arms' length, spread his legs a little, feigned drawing his pistol and cocked his head as he said, "We'll circle the wagons and get these hombres rounded up in no time—pilgrim."

I burst out in laughter. "I love you, Dad." I brushed the tears away. "And, I've missed you. Let's get out of here and figure out what we need to do to stop these bastards."

We gathered up his worn and scratched leather duffel from the baggage claim and were soon on our way to join the other thousands of people fighting their way to get home before the official beginning of rush hour.

"My God, doesn't anyone work anymore?" Dad said, shaking his head.

"This is nothing. You should see it at 5:15. I'm glad I don't have to do this every day. Wait until we get home. You'll think you are back in Idaho with all them wide open spaces . . . pilgrim."

He laughed a little. "Don't try to steal my thunder, there, kid. I'm the star of this show."

We chatted all the way home catching up on the last five years. Everything, but the problems at hand. As we approached our gate, it all came rushing back. Do I open the mailbox . . . or not? Just then a patrol car pulled up behind us. A deputy stepped out, introduced himself, and asked to see my identification. Sheriff Schaeffer had made good on his promise to increase the watch on our place. Once Deputy McConnell had verified who we were, he opened the mailbox, retrieved the mail, handed it over, and—making sure there was nothing more he could do for us—was on his way.

I thumbed through the mail. "It's the first time I've ever been happy to see bills and junk mail, not to mention a patrolman walking up to our car. Nothing out of the ordinary here today. Hope that means the sheriff's increased security is working."

We spent what was left of the afternoon getting Dad settled.

Jeremy was the first to get home. I had already updated Dad about how he happened to be living in the garage apartment. He trooped in carrying a Costco blackberry pie and a good-sized container of Vanilla Bean ice cream. I introduced him to Dad whose eyes were about to pop from his head over the size of that pie.

"How'd your test go today?" I said.

"I think I aced it. That last minute studying last night worked wonders. Especially without the distractions of people and downtown traffic coming and going at all hours. I'm lovin' it here.

"I gotta run out to clean up before Bud gets here. Let me know what I can do to help with dinner besides all my labors over the dessert." He winked at Dad and was off out the patio door, yelling: "Nice to meet you, Hank," over his shoulder.

"I can see why you've taken to him so quickly," Dad said. "Now, what can I do to earn my keep?"

I was washing veggies for a salad and pointed him toward the sack of Idaho potatoes he'd brought tucked away in his bag. "Thought you'd never ask. Wash up some of those russets, please, and wrap them up to bake in the barbecue. Foil's right there in the center drawer. I'm spoiled having all this help. Bud's on the grill tonight."

"Sounds like you're getting these boys pretty well trained. I should have known. Hell, I may as well have stayed at home."

"You'll be sorry you said that—I'll give you a whole list of things that will keep you busy."

He stuck out his lower lip like a kid who'd just dropped his ice cream.

Jet's bark interrupted our banter as he came running through the kitchen. We heard gravel crunching in the driveway. "That'll be Bud," I said. "He's the only other one who has the code for the gate. He must have gotten off early. It's not even five o'clock."

I let Jet out to investigate, put the salad in the refrigerator, took out the steaks to season and bring to room temperature. Dad had finished the potatoes, so I sent him out to light the barbecue and get them started.

I looked around the kitchen and marveled at how excited I was to have activity here again. I enjoyed the meals Bud and I had shared this last week, but I especially loved cooking for a group. Everyone pitches in to do their part, turning it into not just a meal but an event. It was good to have things happening in the kitchen again. It had been too long.

"The cook's here," Bud said as he came through the door, Jet at his heels. "I stopped to say hi to your dad on the way in. I see you've put him to work already. What else can I do besides see who needs a beer and get this show on the road. I'm famished. No time for lunch today."

"Don't get in too much of a hurry, now. I barely took the steaks out. And the potatoes are just now going in. Jeremy's taking a shower. I'll bring out some snacks if you'll take care of who wants what for drinks."

I fudged a little on the snacks—stopped by Trader Joe's and picked up some cooked shrimp, cheese cubes, and antipasto items at their deli on the way from the airport. So, in a few minutes, I was joining the guys on the patio with a tray that looked like I'd worked for hours.

"Just in time," Jeremy said as the patio gate clanged to a close. "Man, that looks inviting." He pointed at the tray.

"She's worked all afternoon getting that ready," Dad said, winking at me. "Isn't she a wonder?"

"I'm beginning to *wonder* about you, Dad. He's pulling your leg, guys. Dig in. You can thank Joe's for our hors d'oeuvres."

We kept things on the light side through cocktails, letting Dad get acquainted with Bud and Jeremy. Once the steaks came off the grill, we started to eat and conversation turned to catching Dad up to date with the details of what was going on. As soon as dinner was over, Bud brought out photos of everything mounted in a loose-leaf binder, including what little we were able to get of tire prints in the wash from the first evening's threat to the package of dead flowers received on Monday. These were mixed in with copies of the reports filed with his own department, as well as Pima County.

"There's been nothing to establish a link with any incident or person who may be harboring some kind of a grudge against either Sam or Trevor," said Bud. "Sam and I went through the names and photos of people who attended Trevor's service and identified everyone with the exception of this woman." He handed the picture to Dad. "She was sort of in the background when this photo was taken, and we can't find anyone who recognizes her. Or tie her to any connection that could have brought bad feelings toward Trevor. And even then, it would be a real stretch for them to do something like this to Sam—after the fact. We are pretty much stymied." Bud threw up his arms, his lips pursed, mouth turned down at the corners.

"The best we can hope for at this point is to discourage any further threats to Sam or to draw them out in some way before things get worse. That's where you come in, Hank," Bud continued. "Between you, Jeremy, Sheriff Schaeffer's men, and myself, we figure we can keep someone with Sam at all times. I don't think they'll be quite so brave with reinforcements around. So far, their tactic has been fright or playing on her memories of Trevor. It's pretty much amateur stuff."

"I'm not so sure I'd put that little diamondback caper under the fright or amateur category," said Dad, pushing back from the table to accentuate his authority. "Sam was lucky that you showed up when you did, Bud. Or God knows what might have happened. I'd say there's no damned doubt that these guys mean business. And we'd better get our shit together to make something happen from our side instead of waiting around to see what they come up with next."

Jeremy hadn't said a word, just listened to both Bud and Dad. "Can I give my two cents worth, you guys? I guess I'm probably the least involved here—up until now, that is—but I think Bud's right. Steps have already been taken to make this place more fortified with Hank and me here every night and the increased patrols from the county. Hopefully, that will put an end to it. I think we should give it a chance."

I had to agree with Jeremy. "And I called Clint yesterday to have someone come out to increase the security lights and sensors on the property. Rob from Desert Security will be out tomorrow. If they have any way to watch us and see what's going on down here, they may have given up already. Though with the wide-open spaces around us, I'm not sure how easy that would be. Not many places to hide and watch.

"Unfortunately, in today's world, there are far too many ways to keep an eye on somebody, even in your neighborhood," said Bud. "Photographers have high power lenses; hunters can purchase high powered scopes that will zero in on their targets several miles away. Remember your call after the snake. They were watching. I think the best we can hope for is they will see the troops being brought in," he nodded toward Dad and Jeremy. "And the security beefed up. I'm hoping they won't like what they see and will decide to let it go.

"If not, we make a new plan. Likewise, that will give us a break while we regroup. Our best defense is to assume the offense. Fight back. As Sam says, don't let these bastards chase her out of here. Keep a sharp eye out at all times, but try to remain as cool as possible. Keep the sheriff and I alerted if you are leaving the premises or see anything unusual around here. What do you think?" His brows arched, his eyes focused first on me, then on to Jeremy and Dad.

"I'm in," said Jeremy. "Other than the evenings I have to teach, I'm all yours after day classes."

"I'm here as long as you need me," said Dad. "Betsy is taking care of the stock. I didn't dare tell her what was going on down here or she'd have packed her forty-five and come along. You know she thinks she's part of the family, Sam."

"And just when are you two going to make that official, Dad?"

He rolled his eyes and gave me one of his looks.

That was all it took. "Ok guys. Beginning tonight, it's business as usual to the outside eye. On the inside, though, we'll be eyes and ears alert and ready to protect our fortress." I raised my margarita. We all clinked glasses, and heads nodded all around.

"One for all and all for one," Bud added, a smirk rippled across his face as his eyes scanned once again. What had he started?

23

"Good morning, Dad," I said, as I sauntered into the kitchen.

The great room and kitchen separated the guest rooms from the wing with the master bedroom and office, so I hadn't even heard him get up this morning. I had slept well, and knew it was due to Dad's presence in the house, and possibly last night's celebrating. The sun was streaming through the windows. Jet looked up from his spot on the rug beside the patio door, right next to Dad's chair. He and Dad must have bonded. I poured a cup of coffee for myself.

"How long have you been up? I see you've put away almost a whole pot of coffee, and from the looks of the newspaper, already read it from front to back. Anything exciting in the news?" I busied myself starting another pot.

"Damned scary compared to the *Idaho County Tribune* where the closest thing we have to a crime wave is a hungry bear breaking into someone's porch freezer to steal some of last year's huckleberry crop. I don't know why you city folks would want to stick around here with the number of car thefts, break-ins, and out and out hold-ups and shootings that seem to happen in a normal day. It's no surprise someone is trying to pull this crap that's been going on right here at your house. And, I'm not so sure we aren't batting our heads against a wall trying to figure out why it's happening. Who says they even have to have a reason in this environment? It just seems like the thing these folks do. Just drive by someone's business and start shooting."

"Well, it's not as bad as you make it sound, Dad, for the number of people who live in the Phoenix and Tucson areas. Speaking of environment, let's go out to the patio and enjoy this wonderful morning. I hope you will be here long enough to learn why I love the desert so much. Besides, you and I are going to do a little wrangling this morning. We need to move the horses down to the El Commadore until things get back to normal around here. You remember my friend, Debbie. She's the manager of the stables there and is making room for Diablo and Koko as long as needed. We could even take a little ride through the hills if you'd like before we load them into the trailer for the move."

"Now, that sounds great. It's been a long time since we've been riding together."

"We may have to ride a little rough off of these horses. I'm afraid it's been quite a while since either has had a saddle on his back. Close to a year, probably more," I said.

Diablo and Koko were a little frisky, all right, but they soon settled down and seemed to be as happy as we were to be out on the trail. We rode down into the wash to look over where the car had been parked to play the music. I pointed out the property lines of our ten acres, the boundary houses that made up our Santiago West subdivision, and traced Santiago Way from the beginning of our private lane down to Oracle Road. Then rode in the foothills of the Santa Catalina Mountains at the base of Pusch Ridge on trails lined with prickly pear and cholla cactus, mesquite and palo verde trees. We stopped to have a sandwich and count the arms of a hundred-year-old saguaro.

"The saguaro is native only to the Sonoran Desert. Aren't they wonderful, Dad? They say they don't even sprout an arm until they're eighty years old or more. There was an old giant right along the freeway almost to the California border a few years ago, but it has since fallen down. Top heavy, I guess. It had over forty arms, seems like the guidebook said forty-seven. We tried to count them but came up with a different number each time."

"They are definitely quite a sight, especially up there where they climb up the slope of the mountain," he said, pointing to where cacti ended and sheer rock took over on the top of the ridge. "Almost as thick as pine trees up in our country—without as many needles, of course." He grinned and gave me a wink. He wasn't about to give up anything to the desert. Not yet, anyway.

"Oh, look," I shouted. "There're three big horn sheep—two ewes with a ram. Sometimes we get to see the babies, too. I'll bet you're surprised to see them here in the desert. You probably think they're only up home in your mountains."

"I guess they do stretch a long way, but clear from Alaska to Arizona? I *am* surprised. Let's see if I can get a shot of them." He pulled a camera from the bag hanging from his saddle horn. "Betsy will never believe this."

He moved closer to the saguaro to focus the sheep in the background, the giant cactus on the side of the photo, and clicked the shutter. "There," he said, checking the monitor on his camera. "Take a look." He handed it over.

I was flabbergasted to see my dad with an almost new digital Nikon, only a few scruff marks on the case that hung from the saddle horn. "Wow. When did you give up your old 35mm?"

He looked uncomfortable, as he had taken a sudden interest in the ground, eyes darting anywhere but at me. "Well, I got that for Christmas last year from Betsy," he said, rather sheepishly. "She had been giving me a bad time about having to wait so long to see my pictures, 'cause I never remembered to take them into town for developing. So, she got this for me."

"I didn't even know you have a computer? And printing your own pictures?"

"No ma'am, not me. I told Betsy I wasn't going to cave in and get one of them damned things. So, I just take the camera over to her and she prints my pictures out for me when I have some. It's been fun to be able to see them in this little window here as I snap them and play 'em back by pushing this button. See." He reached over to show me, then took another shot of the sheep.

"I'm proud of you, Dad. And now, I'm going to expect to receive a few pictures from you once in a while. How is Betsy, anyway?"

"She's just fine. Won't hardly let me alone. Keeps bringing me over pie or chili. Who knows what? Claims it's too hard to cook for just one, so she brings it over so it doesn't go to waste, she says. Trouble is it's going to my waist." He patted his stomach.

I smiled. His stomach was as flat as always. "Why don't you two just move in together and be done with it. You both know you have feelings for each other. Doug's been gone long enough, it's time you two gave in."

"Enough of that, young lady. I don't need your advice in that department. I think we'd better head for home."

"Well, hand me that camera and let me take a picture of you with Pusch Ridge in the background, then one with you looking back at our place from here."

"What the hell?" dad said as he tucked the camera back in its case. "Something white over by that rock." He walked in that direction, dodging between cactus and creosote. "Lazy no goods, it's a damned McDonald's sack. Some people just don't care." He stuffed it in his saddlebag.

That done, we mounted up and got back in time to get the horses brushed and loaded into the trailer for the short drive to the El Commodore Resort well before Debbie's shift was over. On our way, I coached Dad on the story I had given Debbie so he wouldn't spill the beans. Debbie was in a meeting, so we turned Koko and Diablo over to her assistant for stabling, and left my cell phone number if anyone needed to call. I heaved a sigh of relief as we pulled out of the driveway, the horses safely parked there until we cleared things up at home—and I didn't have to add anything further to the story I'd concocted yesterday for Debbie. Life was good.

A Desert Security truck was waiting for us at the gate, along with a Pima County Sheriff's car. "Hello, Mrs. Beale," said Deputy McConnell. "I understand you have an appointment with this gentleman."

"We are expecting Desert Security, but this is not our normal guy. Where's Rob?" I turned to the guy wearing Desert's uniform, 'Dennis' embroidered above his pocket. "Rob always does our work."

"He was in an accident yesterday, ma'am. A hit and run. Got busted up pretty bad. They sent me out to take care of your order."

"I checked his ID, Mrs. Beale. His name is Dennis Vance. Says he's been with Desert Security a few weeks, mostly in the shop. If you'd like to call the company, I'll be happy to wait here until you make your call."

"I'd like that, thanks, Deputy. I was looking for Rob, or at least someone who is familiar with our system. I'll only take a few minutes."

I walked on into the house and dialed Clint. No answer, so left a voice mail. This was a good example of why I hated to bother him. But these matters had always been handled by Trevor, and I trusted Clint to know what was best to do under our current circumstances. I looked up Desert Security, dialed, and asked for the manager.

"Alex Brooking. How may I help you, Mrs. Beale?"

"Hello Mr. Brooking. I was expecting Rob to work on our system today. Instead, your man, Dennis Vance, is here. You see, we've been having some vandalism, and decided to have some changes made to our system. I called to make sure Dennis was a legitimate employee and this wasn't another part of our ongoing problems."

"Yes. Dennis has only worked for us about six weeks, Mrs. Beale, but has proven himself to be very capable working with our security equipment in the shop. I believe he has a good understanding of your system. We went over it thoroughly here this morning.

"Rob suffered injuries in an accident yesterday and will be laid up for some time. We were forced to put Dennis out in the field a little earlier than we planned, but have every confidence in his work or we wouldn't have sent him out. I appreciate your concern and thank you for checking. Security is not something we want our customers to take for granted. You were smart to call us. If you do feel uncomfortable with Dennis, I'm sure we can schedule one of the other men to come out next week. What do you think?"

"I'm sure Dennis will do fine. It just caught me unawares not to see Rob. I hope you don't think me a ninny, Mr. Brooking. Thank you and please give Rob my best wishes for his speedy recovery."

"I will, thank you."

Dennis proved to be, as Mr. Brooking said, very capable of understanding our system and making the necessary changes we requested. Dad followed him around like a puppy, no doubt a nuisance, but Dennis didn't seem to mind. He showed both Dad and I how to operate the new remote for the additional lights and sensors he had installed, explaining that they could be turned off independently of the original system with this remote if it was deemed unnecessary to continue their use at any time. He'd finished and was on his way a little after five o'clock.

24

The Watchers

As the Desert Security truck pulled onto Oracle Road headed back to town, Dennis saw the familiar blue Camaro coming up behind, pulling into the lane beside him, its driver's face screwed up in a question. He smiled, nodded, and raised his hand to form an "O" with his thumb and index finger. The Camaro driver returned his smile and, with a thumbs-up, sped off down the street.

25

Thursday, September 22, 5pm

What a beautiful day! It feels so wonderful and safe to have Dad here. How long has it been since we rode horseback together? No time when he came down for the wedding, he was in such a hurry to get back to Idaho. It must have been the last time I was at the ranch just before I moved to Arizona. Right after I split up with Drew. I ran up to get away from it all.

How the years fly away. And now, here he is, coming to my rescue again. What makes us forget how much our family means? Why does it take a catastrophe of sorts to make us call on those we love for comfort, to bail us out?

Those were great days, in Elk City. Dad, Betsy, and I spent most days riding the trails in the mountains, along the American and Clearwater Rivers. It's gold country. Gold and big game hunting. As we rode it was not surprising to hear the splash of what you expected to be a fish jumping, only to discover a moose grousing to feed on tender weeds growing along the bottom of a pond just a few feet from the edge of the road. Or a doe with her spotted fawn moseying down for their morning drink along the other side of the river.

And it was so clear that Betsy is in love with him . . . the little smile she tried to hide as she looked at him, the pride in her eyes that lit them up when he said something to her. Though, I'm sure neither of them wants to tarnish the memory of her late husband—Dad's great friend, Doug.

Why does love hurt so much? It's easy to understand why neither Betsy nor Dad wants to admit their feelings for each other. Both have lost their mates, Dad's to divorce, hers to illness. The effects of Doug's illness and subsequent death took its toll on both of them.

I guess they're comfortable the way things are. To just enjoy their companionship. They can spend whatever time they want together, and be alone when they want. But it is damned tough when that special someone is no longer there to share those feelings, whatever the reason.

I'm glad Mom found Tom. It's funny how things work out. All those years together and now each has found something they had been missing for a long time. Probably didn't even realize they had problems until it was too late to "fix" them.

I hope Mom's keeping busy so she won't be wondering what's going on down here, why I haven't called. She's the last thing we need, for sure.

"Sam?" Dad's voice startled me. I'd been lost in my own little world.

"Come on in, Dad. I'm in the bedroom." I closed the journal as he stepped in. "Just taking a few minutes to write in my journal. How was your nap?"

"Darn good. But, I'm hungry. Why don't we run down to that Kentucky Fried Chicken place we passed on the way home and pick up some supper? No need for you to fix something. Besides, I don't get much chance to enjoy the Colonel's cookin' up in the hills. And this has been a pretty busy time for you. Sounds like you could use a night off."

I looked at my watch. "I didn't realize it was getting so late. Jeremy should be home. Let's check to see if he wants to join us for a bite before he goes to class. It's getting close to six o'clock already."

Jeremy joined us for dinner. We brought back the Colonel's Feast, complete with chocolate chip cake for dessert—which we saved for later since the time came too quickly for Jeremy to leave for his class. Everything tasted delicious. We thanked Dad for suggesting it. And, no dishes to wash.

"Here's the assignment for this evening's class," Jeremy said. "Try to get this done tonight and we'll work some more on emailing and the internet tomorrow morning if you have time. I'm off."

"Don't forget to come in for cake when you get home. I'll make some coffee."

I was still working on my assignment, making notes from the websites I'd visited researching the items Jeremy had given me, when I heard his VW pull through the gate. "Coffee," I said as it popped into my mind. I ran to the kitchen.

Dad sat on the couch, checking over his metal detector, to make sure it survived the trip down in the luggage compartment of the plane. Jet was content to lay in his bed a few feet away.

"Slow down," he said "Coffee's all done. I put it on about nine, thought Jeremy would be home earlier."

I was surprised to see it was after ten. "Class must have lasted longer than usual."

A few minutes later, Jeremy burst through the door, face pale, eyes wide. "Damn. Some idiot just ran me off the road into the brush."

"Are you all right?" I said, running over to check him out.

"I'm fine, just pretty well pissed off. He came out of the strip mall parking lot like a crazy man. A big four-wheel drive pickup. Would have run right over the top of me if I hadn't jerked the wheel to veer off the road in time. He was in one helluva big hurry to get somewhere. Never stopped . . . like he never even saw me. Just kept right on going."

I put my hand on his shoulder and squeezed, hoping I could calm him down. "Were you clear off the road? Why didn't you call? How'd you get back onto the road?"

"That's one thing about a Volkswagen. It's almost as good as a four-wheeler, extra traction with the engine weight in the back and all. It took me a few minutes to get my head back straight. I sat there in the middle of the creosote bushes, across the street from the parking lot. I had just turned from Oracle when he came out of that lot like a streak. Damned fool." Jet was at our feet, wondering what was going on.

"Well, we're happy you weren't hurt, son. Any damage to your car?" Dad asked.

"No sir, I don't think so." Jeremy reached down to give Jet a pat. "I checked it over when I pulled in under the yard light. I'll make sure tomorrow morning when I can see better in the daylight. And call my insurance if needed."

"Come on into the kitchen. Let's all have some cake and ice cream," I said, hoping to get everyone settled down, yet wondering if it had been just some irresponsible drinker, there's a bar in that strip mall . . . or?

"How did your class go?" I said, trying to change the subject.

"It's always good when we're working with the net. Everyone has so much fun. Of course, there are always a few that just don't quite get it. How'd you do?"

"You stinker. You gave me some great research to do. I can see why you guys are so interested in treasure hunting. Sounds like there's a lot of unclaimed and unfound loot around. I was still up to my ears in that when I heard you pull into the driveway. That's interesting stuff, sucks you right in. And fun. Dad was on top of things, or we wouldn't be having any coffee with our cake."

That started it. Once the subject of lost treasure was opened, we each had to fight for a chance to tell our stories, or ask our questions. And so, it went the rest of the evening, until we finally gave up around midnight with promises to do some more research tomorrow morning and Dad to give us a demo on his metal detector.

Too bad Bud wasn't here. He would have enjoyed tonight, I thought, as I put on my pajamas. I went into the office, grabbed my organizer and crossed off my last items—start sorting recipes, add security, and board horses. I smiled as I savored the now empty page, though my smile went south as I thought about Jeremy's encounter with the pickup tonight. I turned to the next page and wrote:

1. Call Bud - Jeremy

2. Set up Target Practice

3. Research Lazey Daisy Mine

It felt so much better to put it in writing. Sort of gets your worries off your chest, knowing you will make time to take care of them tomorrow. With that, I turned off the light.

26

The Watchers

The slender one looked through a night scope across the hood of the four-wheel drive pickup. The scope was mounted on a rifle, crouched in his right shoulder; his right eye peered through the lens as he zeroed in on one of the lights he had installed just today. "What are you doing?" the woman's hands were shaking so badly she nearly dropped her binoculars.

"Just checking my new scope from this distance. It's lit up like a rodeo ground down there. Those inside should feel safe for now."

"I wish you'd leave that thing at home. It makes me nervous, aiming it like that."

Just before midnight the student crossed from the house to the apartment above the garage. The lights began to go out one by one by one. Dennis whispered "Bam, bam, bam" in time to their disappearance. "That's how easy it would be to take them out, one by one if we have to." A smile spread across his face knowing this was getting to his partner. He hoped she wouldn't fall apart and screw up the whole thing.

He packaged the rifle back into its case and stowed it behind the seat. "Come on, let's get outa here."

27

Still excited about last night's discussion, I was all set to dig into more research about John March and his Lazey Daisy mine this morning. But, first things first: I called Bud's cell as soon as I got up. Wanted to run Jeremy's incident by him while everything was still fresh, but all I got was his voice mail. That bummed me a little. A little, hell . . . a lot. As I hung up the phone, Jet trotted in, his eyes searched the room.

"No one's here," I said. "Just me, talking on the phone. Come on, let's go find Dad."

I'd set up the coffee late last night while we were still chatting, and was all set to go for a few laps in the pool to clear the cobwebs hanging around in my head. Dad was nowhere in sight—must still be asleep— so I poured a cup on my way through to the pool. Caffeine was definitely calling . . . and that's not all. The phone rang as I passed the bar. Seeing Bud's number, I grabbed the extension to avoid any more rings. "Good morning."

"Morning, sunshine, what's up?"

"Well, I wish I could say just the wonderful Arizona sun. Something happened last night, Bud . . . and I wanted to run it by you. Jeremy was run off the road into that brush down at the corner on his way home from class. It might have been merely a random reckless or drunk driver, but thought I'd call our friendly detective to get his take on it."

"I hope he wasn't hurt?"

"No, thank God for that," I said, not able to contain my sigh.

"What do you guys think?"

"I didn't mention my suspicions to the guys; I was just happy Jeremy was okay other than shaken up a bit. He doesn't think there was any damage to his car—at least nothing he could see in the darkness. He was able to avoid an actual collision by pulling off the road into the desert. The pickup came out of the shopping center and raced away. It sure makes me wonder, though."

"I don't like the sound of it either. Especially a pickup. I'll come over and run through things with Jeremy, He and your dad both need alerted that it could possibly be the same people. If so, the danger level is escalating. Are you decent?"

"I will be by the time you get here; I'm on my way to the pool trying to shake off some of this restless energy. It's been pretty tense around here. If I'm not back in the kitchen when you get here, grab a cup of coffee and I'll be out in a second. Haven't seen Dad or Jeremy yet this morning. We were up kinda late last night spinning tales of treasure hunting after we got Jeremy settled down. Wish you had been here, it was great."

I had barely stepped out of the pool when Jet rushed to the gate to greet Bud. "That was quick. You must have been close by when we talked."

He let out a long wolf whistle. "I was already on my way over when I noticed your message light on my cell. I guess I was in the shower when you called, didn't see it when I put the phone in the car holder." His brows raised in a wide "V" as his eyes gave me a deliberate once over. "Ooo...eee... Sorry I didn't get here sooner."

"Down, boy," I said. Jet made a quick jump into his basket, laid his jaw flat on the cushion, big eyes looking up at me. "Oh, not you, Jet. I'm talking to this creature over here." I pointed at Bud and couldn't control the snicker that erupted with my words.

"Come on over here, Jet. I'm sorry," I patted his head and handed him a Milkbone biscuit from the cactus shaped cookie jar atop the bar. I was glad Bud and I were still able to joke around with each other and not be totally taken over by it all.

"Go get some clothes on. I'll go see if Jeremy is up," Bud said. "Got any of Rosa's churros or empanadas? I've got a feeling we may need something sweet to get through this morning."

Dad and I almost collided—he coming into the kitchen as I walked through the patio door. I grabbed some foil wrapped churros from the freezer and asked him to throw them in the oven. "Bud and Jeremy will be in soon," I added as I escaped down the hall.

We sat around the table as Jeremy once again described the details of his near-accident. He hadn't gotten a very good look at the pickup. Said it was all bright lights and tires—and headed straight for him in his little bug. He thought it might have been a Ford, but wasn't sure. It had all happened so fast. Bud took notes, then gathered up Jeremy to go down to the scene of the crime.

Once they were gone, I told Dad I suspected they'd find evidence of foul play.

Dad said, "I guess you definitely are a chip off the old block. I was thinking the same thing last night, but didn't want to shake Jeremy up any worse than he already was. I don't mind telling you, it crossed my mind when I first got here that Jeremy might be some way connected with this whole mess—the way he appeared about the same time as these strange happenings. But as scared as he was last night, if that was an act, he deserves an

Academy Award. His hands were shaking so badly. Hard to fake that stuff.”

“I had that same fleeting thought about him, but instinct tells me he’s too genuine—not to mention a gutsy guy—to join into this whole thing knowing what was going on. I tried to talk Bud out of it right from the start, but they both insisted. I trust Bud’s judgment. He’s had a lot of experience with people. All kinds.”

We chatted awhile. The intercom buzzer sounded, followed by “Mrs. Beale, Deputy McConnell here. I’ve got Rosa Flores here waiting at the ga . . .”

I ran to the control and poked the button, cutting him off. “Thanks, Deputy. I’m so sorry. It’s fine to let Rosa in. She’s part of the family here, comes in every Friday. I guess you haven’t seen her car before. I must have forgotten to put her name on your list. She has her own remote for the gate.”

“That’s all right, ma’am. Her name was here but not this pickup she’s driving today, so I needed to check with you. I’ll add this vehicle to our list, says it’s her husband’s truck. Any others we should know about?”

“No, I believe you have everyone now. Wait. Please add Manny’s name to the list, Rosa’s husband. He may be coming over sometime, as well.”

"Will do. You know how to call if you need us for anything. You have a good day."

Rosa's face was a little flushed when she came in, her eyes as big as her homemade tortillas. "I thought for a minute I was being arrested. The deputy . . . he stopped me before I could get out the opener for the gate, asked me over a loud speaker to get out of the peek-up. Manny needed the car today, so I brought his peek-up."

My eyes darted to Dad when she said pickup, he put his finger to his lips. I nodded my agreement that it was not a good idea to mention last night's incident to Rosa.

"I'm so sorry," I said. "The sheriff promised extra security patrols for us and they have been doing a very good job. I should have listed both your Camry and Manny's pick-up. I wasn't thinking. Come to think of it, I don't think I've ever seen you drive his pick-up before."

"Rosa, you remember my dad from our wedding," I said as Dad walked over to clasp her hand.

"Great to see you again, Rosa. My memory may be slipping these days, but there's no way I can forget you and that delicious meal you prepared for us following the wedding. I'm looking forward to sampling some more while I'm here."

The flush returned to her face along with her genuine ear-to-ear smile. "You are too kind, Seenyor Morgan. I am happy to see you here with Sam and hope you and Bud will soon catch these *cabrons* who cause her so much trouble."

"Me too, Rosa. Me too." Dad and I moved out to the patio to give Rosa free rein on the house.

Bud and Jeremy soon returned and joined us. They reported they'd found some big tire tracks following where Jeremy's Volkswagen swerved and skidded into the desert. Bud suggested it was the pickup coming back to check on him, hopefully a concerned citizen to see if he was hurt. That was doubtful, however, since Jeremy had—by his own account—sat there for some time while he gathered his wits, then pulled the VW out of the desert and drove on home. Bud had contacted Sheriff Schaeffer and they waited for his team to arrive to take plaster casts of the tracks and handle any further investigation.

Jeremy seemed to be taking things into stride this morning as we made plans for a trip back up to the Lazey Daisy Mine to do some target practice tomorrow. Bud said the mine's tailing piles would make a good backdrop for our targets, leaving no danger of bullets going astray. He would advise the sheriff of our plan so they wouldn't be alarmed if they heard shots from eleven to around two. It sounded like we were all set. Bud left for his office, promising to contact a friend to borrow another ATV.

Jeremy suggested we look for more information on the Lazey Daisy to see what we could learn before we went up tomorrow. We headed for the office and Dad for the kitchen to help Rosa make sandwiches to munch on while the three of us pored over anything we could find online. Rosa swished him into the office right behind us, saying she would be bringing in some sandwiches soon.

28

The Watchers

No one had noticed the blue Camaro sitting in the parking lot across Oracle Road at Fry's Market. It was sandwiched between a couple of SUVs, but the driver—masked behind tinted windows—had a clear view as the police team still canvassed the area, looking for clues, pouring plaster into the tracks. No one saw as she picked up her phone, dialed, and put it to her ear.

It had worked, the seed was replanted, ready to grow . . .

29

The afternoon sped by. We searched for anything we could find about the Lazey Daisy and found it wasn't the only claim John March had placed. Jeez . . . Dad and Jeremy were just like a couple of kids. Once we studied the internet info about March and his mining claims, the boys moved over to Jeremy's research notes and books on Arizona's old ghost towns and notable robberies and holdups to see what they could turn up there.

Dad was all ears. He'd always been a sucker for a good gold story and been known to spin quite a few of his own through the years. As kids we had never tired of hearing his stories over and over. Jeremy seemed to be just as taken with Dad's yarns and had forgotten all about his encounter of the night before.

I slipped out mid-afternoon and helped Rosa finish up the house. I don't think they even missed me. Rosa and I could hear their laughter and an occasional "hey, listen to this" as they played with the information they were finding.

The sheriff called to say they hadn't found any witnesses to Jeremy's incident the night before, but he had issued a BOLO (be on the lookout) for a vehicle of that description to all his men and other law enforcement agencies in the area. He would let us know of any progress, but cautioned us not to expect any miracles as the description was pretty sketchy.

"And, Arizona has no shortage of four-wheel drive pickups," I said and thanked the sheriff for his help and assured him Jeremy had pretty well settled down. We all had considered him very lucky not to have sustained any injuries or damage to his VW. It was probably just a careless or drunk driver. Nevertheless, we agreed to maintain a BOLO of our own. There had been too many probabilities and coincidences lately.

Rosa left us a Taco Salad for dinner. Dad and I had a quiet evening; Jeremy had gone out to work on some lesson plans. Dad checked and cleaned Trevor's guns we would be using for target practice and rounded up bullets, ear protectors, and targets. He packed up his metal detector and Gold Bug to take along. Tomorrow should be a busy day.

30

The house was quiet when I woke Saturday morning; the sun hadn't yet broken over Pusch Ridge, so I hunkered down under the covers for a few extra minutes. I scanned the notes Jeremy had typed from yesterday's research on the Lazey Daisy. It seemed John March was a pretty colorful character back in his mining days. The Lazey Daisy was one of four claims he had placed in this area from 1934 through 1936, looking for gold mostly, but taking anything he could find.

Jeremy thought March may have been looking for the loot from a stage coach holdup he and Dad had read about that happened shortly after Wells Fargo took over the Butterfield run, circa 1860s. A strongbox—said to contain about $5,000—had been taken when the stage was robbed ten miles or so from their last stop: presumably the stage station on our property.

The robbers had never been caught, no trace of the strongbox recovered. A reward of $500 had been offered for its return. Posses had been sent out to scour the hills, looking for a hideout, a cave, or newly turned dirt, but not a sign of even the empty strongbox had ever been found. No doubt others had gone out on their own. Who knows—maybe someone had discovered it but hadn't reported it for the reward, having kept the $5,000 instead. Or, better yet—maybe it was still out there?

Dad and Jeremy said they had a plan to search for clues to what March was digging for. I knew secretly they were hoping to find something that would lead to discovery of lost treasure of some kind—whether stolen or the work of sweat and toil.

Everyone had their assignment to get things ready. By the time Bud arrived shortly after ten, we had our lunch and supplies all loaded and ready to take off. Including Jet, it seemed. He wandered from Dad to Jeremy, over to Bud, blatantly avoiding me. I'd been the one who said he couldn't go last time, and he no doubt hoped one of the guys would take pity on him. Dad grabbed a couple of treats from the patio jar and settled him into his spot by the gate to wait for our return, and by 10:30 we were on our way. Jet was still watching us the last time I looked back.

31

The Watchers

Two sets of curious eyes watched through high powered binoculars as the four ATVs rumbled through the back gate of Rancho de Santiago. From the looks of the coolers and bags on the racks, they would surely be gone for a while.

Was a daylight visit worth the risk?

The man carefully scanned the surrounding desert. The woman, the road leading from the hilltop estate down toward the homes below. Both came to a stop when the Pima County Sheriff patrol car carrying two uniforms came into view at the bottom of the lane, and continued to the gate. The sheriff must have known the woman and her troops *would be gone and doubled the security. Must they wait for another time?*

32

Bud had been successful in borrowing another quad from his partner, Jim Murphy. His grin had not faded since he straddled the almost-new bright yellow Can Am 800. "This baby really hauls some ass," he said as we pulled into the mine. "I may have to get me one of these. Or, who knows, Murph might never get this one back."

Bud and Dad set up the targets and we were soon making wagers on who would get the best pattern of shots. It had been a long time since I'd done any practice shooting and I definitely needed it. By the time we called it quits, I was grouping them pretty well within the target's circles, but have to admit Dad and Bud were the only ones on the receiving end of the quarters we each put in for every round of shots.

I rolled my eyes toward Jeremy as we listened to their jeers. "Well, big winners. Guess who's buying dinner tonight?" I said, hoping to get them to give up on the teasing.

"Speaking of dinner, how about some lunch?" Dad said. "That piece of toast and Cheerios we had this morning is getting mighty thin." His hand roved over his waist.

Bud showed them where the old papers were hidden in the rocks by the claim post, while I unpacked our lunch. Jeremy was careful as he examined the claim, oohing and aahing as Dad pulled out his camera to take a close-up picture.

"Betsy will really be surprised we're out here in the desert finding authentic mining claim papers," he said. "This is hellish country to be doing the hard work miners had to go through to hit any pay dirt. She'll be wide-eyed when she prints these out."

Bud reached over to take the camera. "Here, hand me that. I'll take one of you and Jeremy by the marker, looking at the paper and that old bottle. Ya gotta have proof that you were actually here to go along with the paperwork." He snapped a couple of shots.

"Let me see." Dad looked at the little screen, and then handed it to Jeremy, their faces alive with excitement as each scanned the photos. "That'll show her," Dad said, with a nod of his head.

After lunch, we left the two of them to explore more of the area around the claim while Bud and I gathered and packed up the shooting gear and trash. It wasn't long before we could no longer hear the purring of the engines. We had barely finished up our chores and sat down with a Dos Equis when we heard the sound of a muffled shot and Jeremy's shout, "Bud. Sam. Over here quick."

"What the . . ." I said looking to Bud, my eyes probably wild. "Someone must be hurt." Bud holstered his .357 revolver and we raced over a small rise toward Jeremy's voice.

My heart jumped into my throat as I saw Jeremy standing on the edge of a hole going down into the mountain . . . straight down. "Oh shit. Is he all right? What happened? How did he fall?"

As I neared the brink I could hear Dad yelling, "God damn. Got that son of a bitch. And, we were right, son. Look here. It could be an old strongbox all right. Go get Sam. And, we're gonna need a shovel to dig this out. It's buried in a ton of sand."

My pulse was racing as I peered down into the black opening to see Dad standing about thirty feet down—at the bottom of the shaft, a fluorescent lantern lighting up the whole floor. He looked up with his best smile. He had a rope tied around his middle, holding what looked like the end of a bigger rope dangling in his hand. "Look at this . . . fourteen rattles on this big ol' boy."

I guess his grin was worth the race up the hill and the shock to my heart, but I slugged Jeremy in the shoulder as hard as I could and said, "Damn you. I can't believe you let him go down there."

Dad hollered, "Oh, he tried to get me to let him do it, but I knew he didn't have the sense to take care of himself, let alone any varmints that may be down here. He probably would have fainted when he saw this rattler. Now quit your fussin' and get me a shovel or something to help get this box up out of here. It's so buried in dirt and rocks I can't even tell for sure what it is, or how heavy it might be."

Bud went back for his ATV and the shovel and other tools he carried.

The shaft widened out as it progressed deeper into the ground. The rope made its way up and out of the shaft and led over to the hitch on the back of Trevor's ATV that Dad had been riding.

"I lowered him down a few feet at a time," Jeremy said. "He took that lantern from the box on the back of the quad. Said he found it and put new batteries in it last night when he was getting things ready to go. We went in intervals of a few feet to give him plenty of time to check for snakes or other problems as he went down. He was determined. Said he'd lower himself down hand over hand if I didn't do it this way. I tried to talk him out of it. Really, I did."

"I'm sorry I jumped to conclusions. I know how stubborn Dad can be, and should have known you wouldn't do anything foolish. But I was so scared." I massaged his shoulder where I had punched him.

"Don't worry about it. We were real careful. He's pretty savvy for an old guy."

"Just don't let him hear you say that," I said, winking.

Bud pulled up, got off his bike, and tied a GI shovel and small pick to the end of a rope. "Heads up, Hank." He lowered them hand over hand down to the bottom, then mounted his bike and inched it closer to the shaft's edge. He attached a sling to the end of the cable on the front-mounted winch and with his hand cupped at the corner of his mouth, called, "Okay, Hank. Jeremy's coming down."

Jeremy's eyes widened, his glance shot a question at Bud. Bud swung his arm toward the sling. "I need to stay up here to run you guys back up," he said. "Besides, you two are the treasure hunters here, not me. I'm not going down there." He chuckled.

Jeremy pulled on his gloves and stepped into the sling, pushing himself away from the wall as he made a slow descent into the cavern. It didn't take long for the two of them to shovel most of the sand and dirt from the wooden box and lift it enough to see that it was indeed an old strongbox—however, an empty strongbox. In fact, the weather and years had taken their toll to make it a not-so-strong box. Disappointed? I'm sure.

They slipped the sling under the box and looped one of the ropes around its sides to hold it together. I worked the controls while Bud did the best he could to keep it from bouncing against the rocky walls—working from the top, Jeremy from the bottom. We got it up with minimal damage and marveled at the trace of the Wells Fargo name burned into the top. Its leather handles were about gone—perhaps from the gnawing of critters looking for a meal or maybe just lost to the elements of nature's hardships.

Jeremy loaded Dad in the sling next, giving him the advice of his vast experience of the trip down. Then, after threatening to leave him down there if he ever listened to Dad again, we brought Jeremy and the tools up for the final load.

Dad and I found a canvas tarp in one of the quads, wrapped it around the box, and tied it onto the back rack on my quad for the trip home. Bud and Jeremy policed the area to make sure we hadn't missed anything, and we were on our way. It had been a long day and I hadn't even given a thought to what we were going to eat when we got back. I didn't think I could get away with a visit from the Colonel two nights in a row. We'd just go out to eat. It was almost five o'clock as we came over the last rise above the house.

I don't remember when our house had ever looked so good to me. I hoped it wasn't a mirage. I was beat and ready for a kick-back evening. Wait a minute. Was that movement on the patio? Maybe just the sun reflecting on a glass or something at the bar? There it was again. Not a flash of light, but yellow. Someone was at our house! I jammed my thumb on the throttle. What the hell was going on? Who could be at the house?

And where was Jet? Then I heard his bark as he ran out through the gate, dodging it as it swung open. How the hell did that happen? I hadn't taken a remote with me out on the trail since I'd lost one on a trip several years ago. As I sped through the gate, Manny stepped from behind the pool house, his arms held high in front of him, beaming his smile.

"*Bienvenido, mis amigos,*" he shouted. "Welcome home."

I switched off the bike and heard strains of trumpets and guitars as "*I... yi. . . yi. . . yi. Cie. . . .li-to-Lin-do*" drifted from the patio. "What's going on?" I said, but got the answer as I walked toward the music to see our tables covered with colorful serape cloths, a Dos Equis bottle in each center holding huge flowers made from crepe paper—red, purple, yellow, pink, teal—mirroring the colors in the serapes, the smell of spiced meat and piquant sauces wafting through the air.

"We are having a fiesta," a smiling Rosa announced as she walked from the kitchen door with a tray full of margaritas and chips and salsa clutched in her hands. "We thought you needed a party to cheer theengs up around here. Drinks are ready now. You will have plenty of time to freshen up before dinner is ready to serve. Seet down—all of you—and eenjoy."

Tears flooded my eyes as I turned to look at the faces of the guys, their eyes reflecting the red and green chili pepper lights Manny had just finished attaching to the corner of the pool house. "Oh Rosa . . . Manny. You can't imagine what a wonderful homecoming you've made for us. Come on guys, let's all have a drink. And sit down with us, you two. There'll be plenty of time for you to finish up while we make ourselves presentable—after we all have a margarita." I grabbed a glass and held it high.

33

We rattled on about our day in the mountains. The target practice, the old mine, Dad and Jeremy's discovery of the buried strongbox—which they carefully unloaded with much bravado to show Manny and Rosa.

Manny stroked the wood, pronounced it still sound with the addition of a few new screws to keep it together. He promised he could replace the disintegrated leather handles with some new ones; he could even make them look old and authentic to restore the historic piece to be as good as new. Well, an old-new.

"That's wonderful, Manny," Dad said. "But first we'd like to take it into Wells Fargo to see if they can determine if it's really one of theirs, and if so, if they can identify it with a particular incident. Maybe a robbery. Unfortunately, the loot, if any, was already gone from it when we found it. Only thing guarding it was an old rattler."

"Oh no. Seenyor Hank." Rosa's eyes went wild. "Nobody was harmed?"

"Not to worry, Rosa. Jeremy and I took care of that guy." He winked at Jeremy, pulled the rattles from his pocket and shook them between his thumb and finger. "He won't be bothering anyone anymore."

It was time to go shower and get on with the feast Rosa and Manny had prepared. Always a change of clothes in his truck, Bud used the shower in the pool house and we were all back within fifteen minutes to dig in. We gorged ourselves on tacos, enchiladas, refried beans, posole, homemade salsa, roasted peppers, and Rosa's special chocolate flan—and it wasn't even Sunday.

We were stuffed, but laughing and relaxing over a Kahlua and cream after dinner when the phone rang. "Let me get it," Bud said as he walked toward the bar for a refill.

"*Buenos Noches, amigo*," his voice boomed. His smile fell slack, his eyes steeled. "You miserable bastard. Get off this line and don't call back. I'm warning you. No more threats. No. More." He slammed the receiver back onto the base.

"What the hell was that?" Dad said, voicing the question on everyone's face, the fear in our eyes.

"Well, let's just say there's no more question about Jeremy's little friend who ran him off the road."

"But, Bud . . . what did they say?" I asked.

"It was him. I think they are watching us right now. I've got to call Sheriff Schaeffer."

Dad, Jeremy, and I cleaned up the dishes while Rosa and Manny packed up the things they had brought from home to prepare our dinner. They insisted we keep the leftovers and we didn't argue. Not one bit. By the time they were ready to go, Deputy Tim McConnell had arrived with an additional squad car to escort them home safely.

As soon as they were gone, Bud retrieved the tape and replayed it for all of us. It was only six words. "Next time we'll squash that bug."

"Son of a bitch," Dad said. "Real brave, aren't they?" He put his arm on Jeremy's shoulder and squeezed. "Don't you worry, son. We'll get 'em," he said, nodding with each word.

Bud shook his head and looked back to the deputy. "I'd like to take this tape in for analysis and comparison with the one we received after the rattlesnake incident. Please run that by Sheriff Schaeffer, A-sap. I can have a copy for him by morning. I'm off this weekend, but he has my cell number."

"Will do, Detective Holloway. I don't think there's any reason to bother him tonight. I'm sure he'll agree to hearing from you first thing in the morning. Go ahead and take it."

"That's great, Deputy, thanks again. And by the way, please call me Bud."

His thumb up, McConnell said, "And it's just Tim. I'm so sorry to see this thing hanging on, hoped it would be all over by now. I've authorized additional patrols in the area through the night. And, Mrs. Beale, please don't answer the phone once Bud is gone, unless you know who it is." He nodded and with a wave he was gone.

We all just looked to each other as the patrol car passed through the gate. None of us knew what to say, let alone what to do. We stared as the taillights faded into the night. Before we settled back onto the patio chairs, Bud convinced us to go to bed and try to get some sleep. He left to do the same—Pima was out there watching.

34

The Watchers

Not the only eyes on the patrol car, the binoculars followed as Bud's lights stopped at the gate, and then led their way down the lane. It had been a long day.

What would it take to get these people away from the house again? Attempts so far had only brought more people to the house—first the cop, then the college teacher, then the old man. And those infernal patrol cars.

What could they do to create a diversion that would take them all away? Time was getting short.

35

Sleep wouldn't come. I tossed and turned. Thinking about these past mysterious days and events, trying to figure out the haunting and bizarre things that were happening to me. To us. What possibly could have triggered such actions? I finally gave up; deciding sleep just wasn't going to happen. Got up, snuggled into my favorite robe—the one Trevor had given me last Christmas—went to my desk, and pulled out my journal.

Sunday morning, September 27, 2:30 am

Saturday night . . . can it be only a week since Jeremy was here installing my computer? I glanced at the desk calendar. It was exactly two weeks ago that I first heard the music! My God, it seems a month or more. We've all been on pins and needles. Pins and needles hell . . . scared half out of our wits most of the time but I'm trying very hard not to let it show. I need to write it all down. Can't believe I haven't already done this.

Friday pm/Sat am, Sept 11 - First time music was heard, at bedtime, dismiss it as teenagers parking, 6:30 am call, Bud comes
Saturday - 1am call, Bud comes to stay night.
Sunday - Bud and I go for ATV ride, discover mine.
Monday - Go to UA, meet Sandy Marks and Jeremy, see Blue Camaro at UA and Office Warehouse, Sheriff Schaeffer visits, Bud and I go through pictures, see mystery woman, Bud moves in temporarily
Tuesday - Visit Teri and Jon, Clint, no one recognizes the woman, CD comes in mail, my computer goes down, rattlesnake, 1st computer class. OMG, these were busy days. No wonder they flew by so fast!
Wednesday - Jeremy comes over, finds hard drive crashed.
Thursday - Computer class
Friday - work on recipes

Saturday - Jeremy and I shop for computer,
receive rattlesnake call, Jeremy to rent garage
Sunday - Rosa and Manny come over, clean
apartment, dinner
Monday - Jeremy moves in, package arrives (dead
flowers), Sheriff here, make plan and call Dad.
He's coming!
Tuesday - Jeremy to class, Bud and I dinner at
El Com, see Sandy Marks
Wednesday - Dad arrives, dinner Bud and Jeremy
Thursday - Move horses, Desert Security
Friday - pick-up runs Jeremy off the road
Saturday - Target practice, Fiesta, "squash that
bug"

Wow . . . let's look at this. 8 encounters
counting the blue Camaro and Jeremy's pick-up,
in 14 days. Sure seems like it's been longer
than that.

I still can't imagine who . . . or what .
. . could be behind this. The sheriff thinks
it's an enemy of mine or Trevor's. But why would
either of us have an enemy? Trevor would have

bent over backwards to make things right with anyone if ever questioned.

I was so against men in general after my experience with Drew . . . I hardly had a date after I moved to Tucson. That's how Bud and I became such good friends. He wasn't any more interested in romance than I was. Until I got acquainted with Trevor.

Could it be someone with a grudge against the investigative work I did for Colgan and Meredith? That's something to talk to Bud about, isn't it? Maybe we can shake something loose.

I looked at the clock above my desk. 5:18. Coffee should be clicking on any minute. I closed the journal, replaced it on the shelf. Almost three hours had gone by so quickly, but had certainly not been wasted.

My auto pilot must have been on again while I took a shower—didn't even remember dressing— but here I was, heading for the kitchen. How long can this crap go on? I grabbed a cup of coffee and called Bud. "Whatcha doing? Anything on your agenda for tonight?"

"Good morning," he said. "I guess I was trying to sleep in, took me a long time to settle down last night. How about you? Nothing new from our friends this morning, I hope?"

"No. Didn't get much sleep last night myself. Finally got up and wrote in my journal early this morning, rethinking everything that's been happening. I'm damned tired of this and ready to get it gone. Do you realize it's been two weeks since this stuff started? And we don't know any more now than we did then."

"The only thing I'm sure of is that you've been through hell, kid. What can I do? Any new leads come to mind?"

"No, but I thought maybe if we went through all the clues . . . sorta like they do on TV when they hit a roadblock in their investigations. You know. They tack it on a wall or big board. Map it out. Do you guys really do that?"

"Well, it makes for good TV shows, doesn't it? Of course, we have reviews of our cases, but if I told you exactly how we do it, I'd have to kill you."

He laughed. I didn't.

"Listen, I'm serious, Bud. Let's get Dad and Jeremy together and take a look at everything again. We've got to be missing something . . . somewhere. If nothing else, we can have some dinner and a few cold beers. Sound good?"

"Hey, I'm sorry. Just trying to lighten you up. I've been just as worried as you. In fact, I've been going over things again, myself. Yes, in the real world, we do that. And I think you have a good idea. Let's put all our cards on the table and get some new perspectives from the guys. Leave nothing unturned. My schedule is clear for tonight if that works for you."

"Should I call Rosa? She has known Trevor a lot longer than any of us. Maybe she will remember something that can help."

"I'm not so sure that's a good idea, Sam. Let's start with just the four of us. Rosa and Manny are both a little panicky. Might not be rational and clear thinking. You said she was pretty shaken up when the deputy stopped and questioned her the other day at the gate.

"I'll call the sheriff to see if there have been any other strange happenings out in your area," he added. "These guys might be doing the same to other people, not just you. We haven't had any reports in town, but we are a long way from your neighborhood. Schaeffer and I have talked about that before and he promised to let me know if any similar things turned up anywhere out here. I'm sure it's not as high on his priority list as ours, however. What time tonight?"

"Let's gather at five, plan to eat about 6:30. I think Dad and Jeremy are doing some more treasure hunting today, but they should be available by that time. I'll give you a call if we need to change anything. Okay?"

"I'll bring dessert. Or is that Jeremy's job these days?"

"No, Jeremy has been bragging about some specialty burger he came up with while working at Sand Witches. Hopefully we can persuade him to give us a sample tonight and you can pick up something to top it off for dessert."

"Good. Got it covered. See you at five."

Jeremy and Dad agreed it was a great idea. They did indeed have plans to go through some research at Jeremy's place today, looking for more on the lost treasures of this area, but promised not to go into the evening. Jeremy was delighted for a chance to show off his burger creation and gave me a list of his grocery needs. That settled, off they went to the garage with a quart of my homemade stew and a baguette of bread from the freezer for their lunch.

I was happy for a chance to have the house to myself to get things ready and maybe squeeze in a nap if I could settle down. It had definitely been a short night.

Sunday morning is my favorite time to shop, only a few cars in the Fry's lot. And no blue Camaros . . . or black pickups. A picture of Jeremy's burger popped into my head as I picked out ground chuck, Roquefort cheese, fresh mushrooms, red onion, avocados, and Kaiser buns for him; sun-dried tomatoes and artichoke hearts for my pasta salad. My stomach was growling just thinking about it and I stopped by the deli to add a pastrami sandwich to take home for my lunch.

After lunch, I picked some fresh cilantro from my herb planter, then threw my salad together, covered it, and set it in the fridge for the flavors to blend. Next, I stirred a jar of Tostitos Nacho Cheese with a can of refried beans into my small Crock Pot insert to keep in the refrigerator for heating up later.

Cooking always consumed my thoughts. Once my chores were finished, I found myself relaxing, the hot tub calling. Since I hadn't heard a word from the 'boys,' I assumed they were hard at it in their discovery of buried treasure. I pulled on my swimming suit, grabbed myself a margarita and headed for the hot tub about 1:30. The dip in the tub proved to be just what I needed before lying down for a nap. I didn't even remember my head hitting the pillow. Out like a light for two hours, I woke up refreshed and glad to have my part of the dinner ready for the final touches.

Dad showed up as I was cutting corn tortillas into wedges to make chips for the dip which was already heating alongside the fryer out on the patio bar. He showered while I quickly fried the chips, drained them on paper towels, and sprinkled them with a Mexican seasoned salt. Another little trick that Rosa had taught me. Then, under the heat lamp to keep the chips warm until dinnertime.

Bud popped through the door, munching on a chip he'd snagged from the patio. Jeremy was next, carrying a covered tray, his hair still wet from the shower. He looked a little like McGee from TV's NCIS. Handsome, clean-cut, but just a little on the nerdy side. I tossed him an apron, its front printed with a cartoon of Speedy Gonzales, sombrero and all, beside a barbecue grill with a spatula raised high. He laughed, tied it around his middle, and asked Bud to light the grill.

Jeremy uncovered his plate with eight thin patties he and Dad had pressed out at his place. What was going on with these two? They were like the kids I'd never had. Bud was back. The three of us spread around the kitchen island and watched in awe as Jeremy placed raisin-sized chunks of Roquefort between two patties at a time, sealing the edges to form four stuffed doubles. As the patties rested, Jeremy sautéed sliced onions he had separated into rings, adding freshly sliced mushrooms and crushed garlic about halfway through, then left them to simmer. He skillfully removed the pits and peels and sliced avocados, drizzled them with lime juice, and slipped them into the refrigerator.

The prep was done. We gathered up paper plates, silverware, and the remaining meal fixings and carried it all out to the patio. Dad volunteered for drink duty, which consisted of opening beer bottles and distributing them. Jeremy added the burgers to the grill then placed buttered buns to toast atop a griddle on the adjacent burner. He arranged guacamole slices on the toasted bottoms, then added the burger patties. A little melted Roquefort oozed from each burger's seam as he spooned the warm sautéed onion-mushroom-garlic mixture on top. My taste buds were cart wheeling as I added the bun tops, then speared the whole thing together with a plastic red pepper pick. Voila! A gourmet delight. I couldn't wait.

The burgers almost melted in our mouths . . . and were a mouthful. We all teased Jeremy about his hidden talents—for he had told us all along he didn't ever cook. My salad and spicy chips complemented the meal and Bud's Raspberry Cheesecake was the perfect dessert. He had actually made it himself that day—a favorite recipe from his sister—rich, but light. It was a meal full of goodness. And surprises. And fun. We had all but forgotten what we had gathered for. It had been a good release for each of us, but it was time to get to work.

36

Bud set up two easels: one with a large calendar attached, one with blank sheets, markers on the bottom rail of each. "I've filled in each day's highlights as I could remember them," he said, pointing to the giant calendar. "Let's take a look at each day, each event, and make as many notes as we can think of on the blank sheets. Anybody . . . please jump in at any time with comments or questions. Sam, compare my days with yours to see if I've forgotten anything. We want to get it all on this chart."

"I'll get my journal," I said and was back in a flash.

"Jeremy, will you take our notes onto that easel?" Bud pointed to the blank sheets.

"You got it." Jeremy jumped up and grabbed a marker.

"Sam, is there anything you haven't already told us about the first night you heard the music," Bud said his finger pointed to Friday, September 10th. "Anything unusual happen during the day or days before that you can remember? Any unfamiliar visitors or someone you bumped into? Anything at all out of the ordinary?”

“Phone hang ups?” Dad asked.

“Nothing I can think of. In fact, as I told Bud, it freaked me out a little. But I didn’t really think much about the music that first night—except that it was a damned big coincidence. Those kids out parking, that exact song on the radio outside my bedroom window. No, I didn’t think much about it at all—I was too busy feeling sorry for myself. Until the call came later that morning. Then, I mostly thought it was somebody’s idea of a sick, sick joke.”

“OK,” said Bud. “Now we’re at Saturday. You called me after receiving the call. We checked out the wash. Nothing else after I left for work?”

“Nothing but the longest day of my life. You told me not to answer the phone.” I shrugged. “But there were no calls, anyway—not one—except when you called after work. Good thing Jon did so well in the tournament. That kept me somewhat busy. Nothing that evening until after midnight when it happened again and I called you.”

“The rest of the night was quiet.” He pointed to Sunday. “We checked the wash the next morning. Same entry place, just more tracks. We tried taking casts both times, but nothing definitive. Too sandy out there to hold the pattern." Dad and Jeremy shook their heads.

"Nothing extraordinary about our ATV ride. That's when Sam and I found the mining claim. We talked about her plans, the U, computer classes. That about it, Sam?"

"Did you report anything to the police?" Dad asked, trying to get back on track. "Besides calling Bud, that is."

"Bud came right over, we went over everything I could remember, and he stayed in the guest room. He phoned the Sheriff the next day and brought him over that afternoon."

"Okay, we're at Monday," said Jeremy, anxious to get into the conversation. "That's the day I first met Sam—at the U."

"Oh, and I met Sandy Marks that same day at the U, when I registered with her. And the Camaro. I saw it twice that day. Did we ever come up with any more clues on that, Bud?"

"We checked the employees at the U and at Office Warehouse. No registered owners of a blue Camaro at either place, nor has security reported noticing any parked on campus since. We are looking for one between 2005 and 2011 based on Sam's description, T-top. She didn't see the license, but we're assuming it was registered in Arizona since there was no plate on the front. There are three-hundred-fifty-three blue Camaros in that age range in the state, eighty two of them in Pima County, most in Maricopa County. No wants or warrants on any of them."

"Have you had Sam look at the owners' list to see if anything rings a bell?" Dad asked.

"No, but that's not a bad idea, Hank. When I saw how many of them are in Tucson . . . well, I thought it was probably just a coincidence for her to see one at each of the places that day. I'll be glad to pull a list for you, Sam. But it's a lot of possibilities within less than a hundred miles."

"And, I'll be glad to check it, though I'm not sure what good it will do. I doubt I know anyone who drives one. Besides, I can't imagine anyone that I do know would be involved in this in any way."

"Still, I think it's worth looking at," said Bud. "Jeremy, put that as number one on the list. Sheriff Schaeffer checked the scene that afternoon, added extra patrols in the area. He didn't think it could have been a Camaro in the wash—too low-slung. I'm in agreement. That sand is pretty deep. In fact, also too loose and coarse for good tire prints. Looks like a truck tire to me. After the sheriff left, Sam and I went through photos from Trevor's funeral and saw the mystery woman standing off by that big oak. No one has been able to identify her."

"She looks vaguely familiar to me, but I still cannot place her," I said. "Here's her photo. We've also run it by Trevor's sister and her husband as well as Clint, our partner in the construction company." I passed it to Jeremy.

Jeremy studied it and said, "Ya know, she sorta looks familiar to me, too. Maybe I've seen her at school. Think she could be the one with the blue Camaro?"

"Hmm. No idea," said Bud. "Keep your eyes open. If she looks familiar, she may work somewhere you shop or at an office you frequent." He took the picture and gave it another look, handed it on to Dad. "You may want to look her over real good too, Hank. You never know when you might run into her if she's still around here or works nearby. Sam, you have a copier, don't you?"

"Yes. I'll make some copies. How many do we need?"

"One for each of us, please, and one for the sheriff. Let's take a quick break while she does that."

When I returned, Bud began again. "I'll have the sheriff distribute one to each of his patrol cars with instructions to keep on the lookout for her or the blue Camaro. Maybe we can get a license number to run. Or an ID if she is spotted somewhere.

"Sheriff Schaeffer asked Sam about any enemies she or Trevor might have had. As farfetched as it may seem, let's think a bit more about that one. Let's list some of the possibilities—no matter how remote."

I checked my journal list and jumped right in. "When I was with Meredith and Colgan Law Offices, I did some of their investigation work, but I don't believe any of the clients ever knew that. Mike preferred to let people believe we used investigators outside of the office."

"It would be good to talk to your old bosses," Bud said, "just to be sure. Some trouble may have surfaced after you left. I'll stop by tomorrow if you will give them a heads-up that I have your permission. Mike Colgan's a stickler . . . and rightly so."

"I'll call them tomorrow morning," I said. Jeremy added that to the list.

"Can you think of anything regarding Trevor's business?" asked Dad.

"I wasn't really involved in much there. I do know he always seemed to get along very well with his customers. If there was anything they weren't pleased with, Trevor always took care of it. It wouldn't hurt to call Clint just to ask for sure. I'll do that tomorrow. And I'll ask him again if he's thought any more about the mystery woman." Clint was added to the list.

"How about disgruntled employees?" Jeremy said, as he added that to Clint's list, as well.

"We might check with the homeowner's associations," Bud said. "There could have been a grievance filed that you didn't even hear about. Especially here at Santiago West."

"Homeowners here would certainly be familiar with our home location. I haven't been to a meeting lately, but I know most of the residents and can't imagine…."

"But there could have been a change of owners in the last few months," said Dad. "You've been pretty much out of touch. Let's talk to your partner about that, too." He looked up at Jeremy's list and pointed. "Clint."

We continued to go through each day, looking for leads, opportunities. The list grew. By the time we made it through the first week, we had all decided to call it a night. And our list was growing.

"Let's continue tomorrow evening," Bud said. "I've got an early call in the morning, and I agree we've all had enough for tonight. We've picked up some good ideas. Look . . . I know what you are going to say, but I want each of you to have one of these." He passed a small spiral notebook to each of us.

"When do you issue our badges?" Dad asked before Bud got any further. Jeremy and I busted out laughing. Bud tried to look serious, but couldn't help himself. A twitch began at the corner of his mouth and he soon joined our laughing jag.

"Okay . . . that's enough." He was back in control. "Don't let anything pass you by. If you notice anything—no matter how small or insignificant you think it may be—write it down. If you see a vehicle that looks out of place, someone who appears to be watching you, a wrong number on the phone. Write down the details. License number, description of the person, his clothes, glasses, identifying marks. Anything special about her voice, fragrance. There's nothing that isn't worth keeping. Even the smallest detail could help us solve this. Any questions?"

We shook our heads.

"Okay. And with that, I'll take my leave. See you all tomorrow."

"Just a sec, Bud. What's your email address? I'll type these notes into the computer and give everyone a copy tomorrow morning. I'll send yours to you." Jeremy took the pad from the easel as Bud handed him a card.

We all walked Bud out to his car: laughing, hugging, saying our goodbyes and thank-yous. It had been a good night. Somehow after talking it out, things didn't seem quite so dark, quite so dangerous. We were all in this together, the guys and me. I knew they would be here as long as I needed them. For the first time in two weeks, I felt we were moving forward rather than standing still—or maybe stepping backwards. We weren't home yet, but we were on our way.

37

I don't know if it was the dinner, talking through each day's events and what we could do to investigate further, or that I'd had maybe a couple of beers more than usual. Whatever, I had the best night's sleep I'd had since this thing started. It was going to be a busy day and I rolled out of bed to get going on my part of the plan.

Dad sat at the kitchen table reading a sheet of paper. "That kid's right on top of things," he said, nodding his head. "Here's your copy of our To Dos from last night. Want any help with your list? Mine's pretty skimpy. I'll be glad to go along to give you another set of eyes and ears."

"Sure. I'd love to have your company as well as your perspective on things. But I still have a hard time thinking either Trevor or I may have any enemies . . . let alone either of us knowing someone who would do these nasty things. What could their motive be?"

"I don't know, honey, but you can bet we'll get to the bottom of it. We should know more by the time we go see these folks. Jeremy's holding down the fort here this morning, checking out some things on the internet. Now grab your notebook and let's hit the trail."

"Not so fast, Sherlock. I've got to make some phone calls first, and it would be best if I put something on besides my pajamas. Get yourself ready and I'll buy our breakfast along the way."

"You're on."

I dressed in a casual Navajo print broomstick skirt and peasant blouse, chose soft leather Espadrilles, just a slight wedge in case our trip downtown included more walking than I had planned. It felt good to put on something besides shorts or jeans and to get out of the house for a change.

"Wow," Dad said as I stepped into the great room. "You clean up well, my dear." He offered his arm and I couldn't help but think he made a handsome escort in his Wranglers, Stetson, and western cut shirt. I noticed he wore the bolo tie I'd sent him for Christmas last year. It featured a Kokopelli idol handcrafted in sterling silver. Tucson is graced with many talented Native American silversmiths. This piece was made by our good friend, Raymond Quannie.

Our first stop was Mama's House in the Barrio District downtown and not too far from Clint's office. Mama's is a converted historic Spanish style home, and serves some of the best food in Tucson. Clint had a table waiting and met us at the door.

"Thanks for meeting us, Clint," Dad said as they shook hands. "It's good to see you again."

"Same here, Hank, but I wish it was under better circumstances. I thought this mess would be all straightened out by now. How can I help?"

"We'll catch you up on things once we get our order in," I said. "We don't want to hold you up too long, and besides that, I'm starved.

"Their food is great here, Dad. You can't go wrong ordering anything. I'm having the avocado, bacon and cheese omelet. Their Mexican hash browns are to die for. They put hot peppers, onions, and cheese in them. Or, you can specify jalapeno cheese bread for your toast."

"I'll have them both," Dad said. "With steak and eggs. I'm getting tired of yogurt and fruit." He winked at Clint. "My stomach thinks I've moved to one of them fancy spas down here."

"You poor thing. Maybe you'd better start doing your own cooking," I teased.

After the waitress had taken our order, and poured our coffee, we went right to work. We caught Clint up to date on the happenings of the last two weeks. He asked if Rob from Desert Security had taken care of the changes to our system and I explained about his accident and that we'd had another guy, whom I had checked out before letting him in.

We showed Clint the picture of the mystery woman again, and asked if he had any ideas about disgruntled customers or girlfriends that might have a grudge against Trevor—perhaps someone who didn't even know he died.

"I haven't come up with anything at all from the past," said Clint. "But just last Friday I received a call from the Industrial Accident Insurance people saying one of our ex-laborers had filed a disability claim against us. He'd suffered a simple injury several years ago that was taken care of at the time, but you know how some people are these days. They get a whiff of a big settlement from some attorney advertising on TV, and right away file for a permanent disability. The insurance people don't see it going anywhere from their side, since it had already been closed. They warned me that he may opt to file a lawsuit. I don't suppose it will amount to much—just a nuisance, but that's probably what he will be hoping for. A quick payoff to avoid the time and expense of a trial."

"Well, maybe these threats are his way of speeding things up," Dad said. "I hate the things some folks will do to get something for nothing these days. Lazy damned bastards. Will you send us the details on that, Clint? I'm sure Bud or the sheriff will want to check him out."

"You can e-mail it to us," I said. "My new address is SantiagoSam@gmail.com."

"Cute," said Clint, tilting his head. "And easy to remember. I'll send over a copy of the insurance file this afternoon. Name is Brett Hansen."

Dad pulled out his spiral notebook and began to write. "S-O-N or S-E-N?" My raised eyebrows and silent smirk left no reason for words. Detective Hank Morgan was reporting for duty.

"S-E-N," said Clint, who stifled a grin and winked at me as dad wrote it down.

Clint shook his head when I asked if he knew of any problems with homeowners, but promised to check with the management company for the HOAs for any unresolved grievance from the past or a recent incident that might be festering bad feelings.

Just then a busboy set up a rack beside the table and our waitress wrestled a fully loaded tray down upon it. Dad's eyes were big as last night's moon when he looked at the overflowing platter of cholesterol that now sat in front of him. Cheese, bits of avocado and bacon poked out from all sides of my omelet. Yum. We were ready to dig in.

Clint had already eaten breakfast by the time I phoned him this morning, so he just joined us for coffee. He stood up and grabbed a straw cowboy hat from the rack. Its brim was bent a little crooked in the back, but it went just fine with his faded Levis, khaki shirt, and scuffed-up Justin boots. He hadn't changed his work uniform since the early days when he was Santiago's foreman, not the full partner he is today.

"You two enjoy your breakfast. I've got to meet our architect on the new Marana West subdivision in about thirty minutes. I'll let you know how we come out on the permits when we meet with the county on that, Sam. It's been great to see you two. You be careful, now. And keep me in the loop. Let me know whatever I can do to help. I'd like to stop these SOBs from bothering you."

"Thanks, Clint. Glad you could join us this morning," I said as I stood and gave him a hug. "You take care."

Dad watched as the white Cadillac Escalade backed away from the curb. "Hmm, nice guy, Clint. He married?"

"Now Dad. Don't even think about it." I stuck my tongue out at him. "Eat your breakfast. We've got work to do."

I noticed the corners of his mouth curl up a little as he chewed his steak, the sparkle in his eye peering at me over his cup as he sipped his coffee, and how quickly he looked away when our eyes met. That old scoundrel was up to something.

We made small talk as we finished our breakfast. I showed him around the area a little, enjoying the colorful murals on the chipped and pitted stone walls of the centuries-old adobes.

Many of the buildings in this—one of Tucson's oldest areas—have been saved from a demolition crew by the Historical Society's intervention in the 1960s. The Barrio, originally established to house Mexican Americans in what was called a "free zone" in the 1800s, allowed its Mexican inhabitants freedom to more or less follow their own laws in the old days. Today's walls mostly surround private homes and offices which have been nicely restored to maintain the historical integrity of their adobe structures. Roofs made from saguaro ribs and packed dirt provide great insulation in the extreme Tucson climate.

Back at home, Jeremy, Dad, and I all scanned through the list of blue Camaros that Bud had e-mailed. We didn't recognize any of the names. Big surprise. Jeremy was bursting to tell us what he'd learned, but we convinced him to wait until Bud was here rather than have to go through it twice.

"Oh, I forgot to tell you," Jeremy said. "Bud called earlier. He's bringing pizza tonight around six. Said we could eat while we worked. And for you to make some cookies and chill the beer. I took care of the cookies, but must confess I cheated and used some refrigerated dough I keep on hand to satisfy my sweet tooth. The beer was already stocked."

Dad raised his hand. "That would be my job. Took care of it first thing this morning."

"I knew we were almost out of beer last night, but didn't give it a thought as we were on our way home today. How did you . . . ?" I shook my head.

"I picked up a couple of cases down at the store, long before you got up."

"Well, I guess that leaves nothing for me to do but take a nap. Thanks, guys. See ya around five o'clock."

Monday, September 26, 3:30 pm.

This is when a lot of folks would call in the cavalry. I'm lucky to have my own. What a team! What is it they say, "When the going gets tough, the tough get going?" Well, my guys are the toughest. I had to get out of there before I started to cry. Here we are in the midst of a crisis. I'm lucky to be thinking about the things

I set out to do this morning, hadn't even stopped long enough to give a thought to what we were going to eat tonight. And Bud thinks of pizza, Jeremy bakes the cookies, and Dad takes care of the beer. And they all take care of me.

How am I ever going to repay them? The best thing to do is keep my sanity and get to the bottom of this as soon as possible because I can tell they aren't going to stop, aren't going to get their own lives back until they've put mine where it belongs.

I didn't even know I was crying until a gigantic tear plopped down onto the page. I didn't need a nap. What I needed was a good soak in the hot tub. Soak out these chains that keep pulling us all down. Break them loose and start swinging them at blue Camaros and black pickups until we find the right ones. Find out who and what is behind it all. I peeled off my clothes, pulled on my swim suit, and headed for the patio.

38

"That doesn't look like a nap to me," Jeremy called, when he saw me step onto the patio. I rocked to one side as Jet bounded out behind me, almost knocking me down to get to Jeremy. They were sitting at a table, Dad with his head still down, running his finger along a page in a three-ring notebook.

"You should see this stuff, Sam," he called, his head never moving. "Ol' Jer here's got this whole book full of articles and photos about lost treasures. Some fifty years old, others maybe five or less, some older, some in between. We're going to start up a search on . . .." His head finally rose to look at me. His brows moved in to deepen the wrinkles that pointed down his nose. "Goo . . . Google? Is that what you call it? To see if we can find out which ones, if any, have been found and which ones we want to start looking for.

"Why, there's one here that's only ten years old. A guy embezzled over a million dollars from a local bank. Right here in

Tucson. He's in prison, but the loot was never recovered. I'd like to get my hands on that one."

"And he's still claiming his innocence," said Jeremy. "Caught shortly after the robbery, when he purchased a plane ticket to Mexico. Guy named Dallas, like in Texas. He was an employee at The Arizonian Bank, so he had the opportunity. But they had no real proof that he did it, and he had no way to prove he didn't. No alibi. I'm thinking maybe he's innocent and the money is long gone with the real crooks.

"I did a term paper on this and other unsolved robberies my first year at UA. That's actually how I became interested in Arizona's history and unfound treasures. Didn't take me long to get hooked.

"And I don't think Hank believed me about this lost loot just waiting out there to be found. I ran across my reference notebook when I packed things to move, so I drug it out when we got to talking about metal detecting and scavenging. With your dad's equipment, we may be on our way to finding buried treasure. Look how easy it was to find that old strongbox."

Jeremy's eyes mirrored the excitement I saw in Dad's— something I hadn't seen in years. Like suddenly Dad was twenty years younger. Oh, how I wished I could copy that look onto my own face.

"Now, I wouldn't get too excited, boys. You have no idea what— if anything—that strongbox may have been carrying before it went down in that hole. Might have only been someone's provisions. Or dirty laundry. It's obvious whatever it was, is no longer there." I chewed on my lower lip as my head swayed from Dad to Jeremy.

"Not too fast, there, girl." Dad's finger rose from the page and pointed at me. "Jeremy and I have been looking that box over and there's some numbers burned into the wood on the inside. He thinks it's like a serial number or code that may lead us to exactly what you're saying we don't have. We've already got a call in to a fellow who should be calling us back anytime now with that information. If it turns out to be a missing link, we may have to relinquish it over to the Wells Fargo people, but not until they give us the information we are entitled to as finders." He pulled his finger back down, shrugged his shoulders, and glanced at Jeremy.

"Well, that sounds good, Dad," I said, "but I still say don't hold your breath. You know as well as I do that these past bonanzas of yours haven't always 'panned out'—if you'll pardon the expression." I was glad to see them so interested in these old stories, and hoped they wouldn't get let down too heavily. "I'm going to the hot tub. Care to join me?"

Dad shook his head. "No, we don't want to miss our call. Some guy from Wells Fargo's main office in San Francisco that Jeremy found on the internet. Milt somebody."

"Milton D. Cramer, III to be exact," Jeremy said. "The third . . . sounds a bit stuffy, eh? I don't think I'd be calling him Milt if I were you, Hank. Somehow, Milton D. the third doesn't strike me as a Milt."

I was impressed. "Well, good luck with Mr. Cramer. You know where to find me."

They continued their banter back and forth while I lounged in the tub. What the heck—we were each enjoying our own style of relaxation.

Bud showed up right after six with the pizza. I had tossed a salad and gotten things set up right after I got out of the tub.

As we ate, we filled in Bud and Jeremy on what had happened with us today, and gave Bud a copy of the insurance file on Brett Hansen—the injured ex-employee—that Clint had sent over earlier. Other than that, Dad and I had drawn dead ends at every corner of our list.

We had eaten our way through the giant pizza, cleaned up everything but the grease spots on the box, and started in on Jeremy's cookies while he gave his report. He had visited with his friend who manages the Office Warehouse, and secured a copy of their video surveillance of the parking lot. It showed the blue Camaro was in fact parked there at the same time I pulled from the lot. Unfortunately, it was backed in with no license plate visible. Shortly after we watched my car pull out of the lot, the tape stopped.

"We lucked out to get that much on tape," said Jeremy. "Most of their parking lot cameras are synched to switch off after their busiest hours of the day. Their remaining focus being only on those in the areas of the front and back doors. The cutoff time is 2:30—about the time Sam left. They switch on again at five o'clock to catch the evening traffic and remain on all night. I wonder what efficiency expert came up with that one." Jeremy looked up, shaking his head from side to side and handed the DVD to Bud.

"Good work," Bud said. "I'm sure our department can come up with some identifying specifics under magnification. Those guys work wonders at times. At least we have a firm description of the vehicle and can pare our list down to only that model. Let's hope it's registered in Arizona."

"Too bad it's not in color," Dad said. "Oh, Bud . . . Jeremy talked to a Wells Fargo guy today, Milton Cramer from San Francisco, said he was a curator for them. He looked up that number we found inside the strongbox—well, he called it an express box—and found out it was lost in a hold-up on one of their old stages. He's meeting us tomorrow morning to authenticate it and give us more of the details so we can work with them to trace its history. Who knows? We may even get a reward for finding it."

"Where are you meeting him?"

"We arranged to meet him at ten at the branch office down here on Oracle Road. We didn't want to leave Sam here by herself any longer than necessary. He said he'd call us once he's in town to confirm his arrival."

"Good thinking. I'll drop by about 9:30. Planned to be out this way to meet with Sheriff Schaeffer. Suppose I can talk you into having the coffee pot on about that time, Sam?"

"I keep telling you I don't need a babysitter. With the new security and all, Jet and I will be fine while they're gone."

"No argument. It's either me or one of Schaeffer's men outside your gate. And I'm not singling you out, Sam. The same goes for the guys. No one goes out or stays alone for now."

I looked from Dad to Jeremy and could see neither wanted to tackle that one.

"I had a good visit at Colgan's law office today," Bud said. "Mike circulated the photo of our mystery woman among his office people. A few saw some familiarity in the photo, but even with enhancement, it's pretty grainy and unclear. Not sure how much we can count on an ID from it. I called the funeral home. They're checking to see if they have the originals on file to get a clearer enlargement. At any rate, Colgan will contact us immediately if they come up with a name.

"Mike doesn't think it could be a case you worked on, Sam, you weren't involved in any cases that went bad. But he will check, for anything that may jump out.

"Just like on TV," Dad said. "Sounds like we made some progress today. What do you think, Bud?"

"You're damned right. I also reviewed our latest tests to the envelopes and other items received in the mail. We'd sent them over to the state lab for more intensified testing—they have the most up-to-date equipment—but had nothing new to report. Still no fingerprints found. Used self-sealing envelopes, so no chance of a DNA match. Everything they used could be bought in any Wal-Mart. I guess our perps must watch TV too, Hank." He stifled his grin.

"Jeremy . . . Some good news on the tire tracks from your road hog the other night. We've matched them to a Japanese manufacturer, Toyo, called Monster Tread, not to be found on your run-of-the-mill street truck. These babies cost well over four hundred dollars each, and require a special order to get them in. We're checking the local tire stores to see what we can run down. But the farther we have to go with the search, the less chance we have for the right match. And, with people ordering just about anything from the internet these days, it widens the gap even more."

My eyes roved over the days on Bud's calendar. "Were they ever able to learn anything from the phone tapes the nights of the snake and Jeremy's incident?"

"I'm not sure how much help it is, but we did establish that it was an amateur job. Rather than a sophisticated voice distortion device as we thought at first, they simply made a tape recording and slowed it way down when they played it for your machine. Our people sped it up to establish what they considered a normal speed and recorded it for us." He turned his computer on and popped in a CD. "Let's check it out."

He clicked the mouse. "So, Samantha, did you enjoy yer visit with meester rattlesnake?"

"Play it again," I listened, willing my ears to pick up something—anything—that might sound familiar, give us a clue. Somehow it wasn't as threatening as it had been that night. That drawn out creepy-sounding voice and the thought that someone had intentionally put me in harm's way of that snake had really jolted me. Right to the core. But now, it was just a voice. Nothing creepy about it. There was no snake to deal with. No legs turning to jelly as Bud grabbed me up off the lounge. I was okay and we all needed to listen to the voice, to search for anything significant about it that we might recognize if we heard it again. Nothing seemed to ring any bells.

"Wait a minute. Let's hear it again," Dad said. "Sorry, Honey. I know you don't want to hear this over and over, but this guy reminds me of someone. It may sound strange—like maybe I think somebody I know from Idaho is down here causing your problems. Damn it, I could swear it's a voice I've heard not long ago."

"Do you think it could be someone you've talked to in the few days you've been here?" Bud said.

"Not likely. I haven't been many places, but if you'll let me stew on it a little, I may be able to figure something out. If you could leave that disk thing with me, maybe Jeremy or Sam will show me how to play it on a computer and I can spend a little more time on it."

"No problem," said Bud. "I can pick up another for myself tomorrow when I go in. In the meantime, please make a list of all the places you've been, people you may have heard speaking *around* you—not just *to* you.

"Now this second message was recorded with one of our recording devices we installed on Sam's phone, and is a little clearer than her answering machine. Our people say it's the same guy, but he's talking through something to muffle his voice on this one, like a towel. No hinted Hispanic accent like before. I guess they're trying to fool us into thinking there are more of them. Both of these are on the one CD that I'll leave with Jeremy. He can show you how to switch from one to the other so you can listen to either or both as much as you want, Hank." He shot a glance at Jeremy, eyebrows raised.

"Sure thing. I've got a portable CD player he can use."

We watched as Dad pulled out his notebook, turned a couple of pages, grabbed his pen, and began writing. Bud's eyes darted to mine, then to Jeremy. The three of us smiled and nodded to each other, shifted our eyes to concentrate on the calendar to keep from snickering. We didn't want Dad to be embarrassed by taking Bud's instructions to heart. We had ourselves under control as Dad again looked up, ready to go on. He never knew.

We went on through the other days. Nothing significant about the dried flowers. Real roses and violets, generic box, plain brown wrapping. The mailings had been sent from different post offices, so no pattern there.

I was beginning to think we might be dealing with someone a bit more criminal than Bud was letting on. How could I have gotten on the wrong side of someone so sinister? A real criminal? Or, as Dad said, maybe someone watching too much CSI and NCIS on TV. Whatever. Maybe we were getting somewhere, but still didn't know exactly where.

That was it. We had worked ourselves right up to and through today's calendar. Bud was meeting with Sheriff Schaeffer at eight o'clock tomorrow morning to go over the few new leads our discussions had uncovered. We promised to continue to keep our eyes and ears open and not to go anywhere alone. Jeremy balked a little at that, but in the end, he agreed. I think Dad's volunteering to ride shotgun for him was the clincher. They were developing quite a friendship. And we promised to alert Bud or the deputies if they would be leaving me alone at home. Well, I wasn't completely alone, was I? I had Jet. But I didn't feel badly about having a deputy nearby as well.

39

The Watchers

The man and the woman watched through night vision glasses as the cop's car slowly left the mountaintop estate. Time was running out. They had to be ready to move in just four days. If the Beale woman wasn't going to leave the house, they would have to do it while she was still there. She and the old man. And the teacher.

Maybe tomorrow's mail would get them out? If not, they must resort to the confrontation they had tried so hard to avoid. It was time to begin steps to put their final strike plan into action.

40

I'm so glad we took the time to go through each event, one day at a time. We are seeing things more clearly now. Well, at least I am. Maybe Bud is going through the motions to make us feel good, trying to focus us (or at least me) on something, so I won't sit around feeling sorry for myself, or scared, or batting my head against a wall. Whatever it is, it's working. I feel like we are on the downhill side. We're going to catch these guys, and put them behind bars if it's the last thing we do.

No, scratch that . . . it's not going to be the last thing WE do. Maybe them, but not us. They are not going to get the best of this family . . . and isn't that what we are, what we've become? It seems like we've known Jeremy forever. Can it be just a couple of weeks? He's in here slugging right alongside the rest of us, when most kids his age would be running as fast as they could . . . or causing the problems in the first place. He's amazing! So dedicated, so smart, so caring. That's right; he could be the son we never had. Maybe I'll adopt him.

Somehow, I always feel better when I write in my journal; don't know why I don't do it every day. Once I put things in writing, I can unload them off my mind. Just like that . . . Gone! Not there to trouble me all day.

I'll bet that's what has been dragging me down the last few months; I've been letting things eat at me. Maybe I should put <u>writing</u> on my To Do list each day and force myself to at least think about writing in my journal. I'll give it a try. It seems to be working well with the other things, and what a sense of accomplishment it gives when I can cross it off. Done!

I opened my organizer and turned to September 27. Grabbed a pen and put 'Write in Journal' on the first line, 'Work on Cook Book' on the next, then moved my pen up and crossed off the first line. Strangely enough, I felt better already. I turned that page and continued filling in line number one on each page this week. That should get me started on the daily writing. Unable to think of another thing that needed to be done today, I just left it blank. Maybe I'd work on the recipes for the cookbook all day. Maybe even search out something great for dinner. Uh-oh. Almost forgot I need to watch for Bud's emails in case he finds something more on the Camaro search. I added a third line to my list.

The phone jerked me from my thoughts; the small lighted screen read 'Mom.'

"Oh no, Mom . . . not now." What did she want? How can I hide this from her? She'd always known when I wasn't telling the truth while growing up. Oh, well . . . here goes. I put on my happy face as I pushed the ANSWER icon.

"Hi Mom. What's up?"

"Well, dear, it seems like we haven't talked for ages. Tom and I were chatting over coffee this morning and wondered if we could talk you into flying up for a visit? Get you out of the house for a while."

"Sorry I haven't called lately, Mom, but I've actually been a little busy."

"Oh . . . how so? Has something happened to Rosa?"

"No, no, nothing like that. I've enrolled in a couple of night classes through the university."

"Well, that *is* a surprise. What are you taking . . . some art classes . . . pottery?"

"No, Mom. Real classes. Computer classes. I decided I needed something to focus on and have started recording all the recipes Trevor and I collected. I'm going to make a cookbook."

"Wow, an author in the family . . . let's see . . . there's something I never thought about you doing. A book. A cookbook. What are you going to call it—*Beale's Meals*?"

"Oh, now, don't be silly. Actually, I haven't even thought about a name. Just typing the recipes has been all I can handle. What have you been up to?"

"Oh, you know Tom. He's always got something going. That's why I thought it would be fun if you came up for a few days. Besides, isn't Alabama one of your favorite groups? They will be here for a limited run starting next week. Well, Tom can always get tickets to the shows. Good seats, too. I thought we could make it a girls' night out."

"That does sound tempting, but right now, I can't miss these classes. I didn't realize how rusty I was—and how far I was behind the computer world until I started. My classes are Tuesday and Thursday nights, then with homework, it doesn't leave much time for fun. I am getting a lot of our recipes typed up, though, so that makes it all worthwhile."

"I don't know what got you started on this, but it sure sounds like you're enjoying it. A good project for you. Good for you, Honey. How long will you be taking the classes? I think Alabama will be here for several weeks. I'll check with Tom to see how long. Maybe you can still make it after your classes are over, at least for a couple of nights. Please think about it. I'll let you know how long we have."

"That does sound like fun, Mom. My classes are scheduled for nine weeks, and I've barely started. But, if Alabama is still there the last week of October, I'm in. I found out this week there's a break in our night classes for exam week on their regular curriculum. Have Tom reserve the tickets, and give him my thanks until I get there to do it myself. I'll put it on my calendar right now.

"Mom, I gotta run. Thanks for calling. And I'm really sorry for letting myself get so wrapped up in Chicken Cordon Bleu and Green Tamales that I haven't called you."

"Not to worry. I'm glad to know about your new project. I'm excited to let Tom know we have a budding author in the family! Goodbye, hon. Love you."

"Love you too, Mom."

Whew, was I glad to have dodged that bullet. At least, I didn't have to lie, just left out some of the truth. Now, where was I . . .?

Clipped to the top of my recipe file were the recipes we'd had for Sunday's dinner. I typed those first: Jeremy's Bleu 5 Layer Burgers, Sam's SW Pasta Salad, and Bud's Raspberry Cheesecake. I was off to a good start with three new categories now begun: SALADS, DESSERTS, and SANDWICHES. I picked up a batch of papers that were clipped together, identified with Salads on the attached Post-it. Soon I was lost in the world of lettuce, chicken, water chestnuts, slivered almonds, and exotic vinegars and oils.

"What the heck are you doing in here?" Dad asked, peeking around the door jamb. "I was beginning to think you were sleeping in for a change, and then I heard this faint clicking noise. At first, I thought it was Jet's feet tapping in the hallway, but decided it was too repetitive to be Jet. Then I heard talking. You must have been on the phone."

I nodded as he slipped through the door carrying in one hand a Thermos of coffee with two upside-down plastic cups perched on top and a plate of cinnamon rolls in the other.

"Girl, something must be wrong with your nose if you've been up and working in here all this time. My mouth has been watering for the last 15 minutes while these rolls were baking. I could hardly wait for the timer to go off. Want one?"

"You bet," I stood, stretched my arms above my head, then reached for the Thermos. "I got up early and stayed in here so I wouldn't wake you. I guess I got lost in these recipes and didn't even go out to make coffee. And then Mom called. What time is it anyway?"

"Damned near noon," he said, smiling. He set the plate on the coffee table and settled himself on the couch.

"Yeah, right." I eyed the clock. "Looks like 9:15 to me. Where'd you find those?" I pointed to the rolls.

"Hiding in the back of your refrigerator. So, I put the ol' Doughboy to work. I was getting hungry."

"Me too. Thinking about all this food I'm working on. But first, I've gotta have some coffee." I poured us each a cup while Dad dug into one of the rolls.

"They smell great, all right. Can you believe I've been up this long and haven't even had a sip of coffee?" I took a gulp and sat down next to him. "Thanks Dad." I gave him a quick hug, snagged a roll, and licked the frosting off my fingers in anticipation of that first bite. "Yum. Nice and gooey."

"You said your mom called. How'd that go? She isn't coming down, is she?"

"No. She wanted me to come up there for a few days. I told her about the computer classes and that took care of the rest of the conversation, but I did take a rain check. Hey, this hits the spot."

"I'm glad you didn't have to make up a story. Know how you feel about that—and mighty glad that you do. You know she'll be mad as hell once it's all over, especially when she finds out I was down here with you."

"Yeah, but she'll get over it."

"Humph. Glad it wasn't me that answered the phone. Not to change the subject," he said, reaching for another roll, "but Jeremy and I are leaving at 9:45 to take the strongbox to Wells Fargo . . ."

"Oh, shit," I said, a little too loud. I jumped up, slopping coffee down the front of my sweats. "Bud's supposed to be here at 9:30."

I sat my almost empty cup down as Dad mopped up a few drops that landed on the table. The rest of it was sinking into my sweatshirt. "I'd better get some clothes on. Keep those rolls warm, I'll be right back."

By the time I'd showered and dressed, Dad and Bud were sitting at the kitchen table, devouring the last of the cinnamon rolls. I looked at the empty plate. "Hey, I thought I said to save some for me."

"Hey yourself," said Dad. "I didn't say how many tubes I found, did I? There's some fresh ones keeping warm in the oven for you and Jeremy."

Jet jumped up from his basket, nose glued to the door. "Speak of the devil, it looks like Jeremy may be coming this way, eh Jet?" I opened the door. He darted outside, nearly upsetting Jeremy on his way.

"Come on in while there's still some coffee and cinnamon rolls left."

"Sounds awesome. Mr. Cramer just called me on the cell. His plane was a little late leaving San Fran this morning. He had just landed so we postponed the appointment until 10:15. Does that still work for you, Bud?"

"No problem. The sheriff and I had a good discussion this morning. He was agreeable to the no-one-here-alone rule. Said to call their office to have someone dispatched if needed. They'll continue their increased patrols of the area. I told him I would take the photo of our mystery woman and a generic picture of a blue Camaro around the neighborhood this morning to see if anyone has seen either of them.

"How about it, Sam? Wanna go along? Get out of the house while the guys are off gallivanting?"

"It's a hard choice." I rolled my eyes. "To slave over typing recipes or get out in the fresh air and sunshine to hang around with you for a while. Hmmm. I guess I can be your sidekick. "

Dad checked his watch and said, "Well, while you guys figure it out, it's time we get on the road. We may be late already."

"Good thing we loaded up the strongbox last night," Jeremy said, heading for the door. Dad followed, stepping aside as Jet slipped back in. He stopped at Dad's feet, head tilted up, as if asking if he could go.

"You take care of things around here, now," Dad said. He scratched between Jet's ears and was gone. Jet stepped into his basket, made a couple of turns and settled in, keeping his eyes on Bud and me all along.

"He needs to get out of this house, too," I said. "We haven't been thinking too much about his being cooped up at home lately. Let's take him with us. I'll get a blanket to put on your seat. The guys took my 4Runner."

"We can let him run alongside the car on the way home; he needs some good exercise. Come on, Jet, Let's go." Bud started toward the door.

Jet bounded up, knocked against a chair, almost upsetting it. He was ready. I realized I'd been neglecting him and felt guilty. With all the company around these days, I had been so preoccupied. We hadn't had our walks, our talks, or our simple quiet time together around the house in the evening, watching TV. Things had changed for him as much as for me lately and I needed to start thinking about that—and not take him for granted.

"Here." I threw Bud the quilt from the sofa and grabbed an extra photo of our mystery woman as I followed them out the door. As soon as we pulled through the gate, Jet made himself comfortable sitting up in the middle of the bench seat in the back of Bud's sedan, shuffling forward enough to rest his head between us on the seat back.

"I think we've made his day," I said, "but I wonder if we should have alerted the sheriff that we would all be gone. We don't have our trusty watchdog on duty."

As I spoke, a deputy patrol car turned from the subdivision at the foot of the hill, heading our way. Bud stopped and stepped out of the car. It was Tim, he pulled alongside and waved to me. He and Bud exchanged a few words and nods and Bud was back.

"He'll keep an eye on the road. I set the alarm on the way out, so if there is any break in the perimeter, we'll all know it. Now, let's get to work."

We knocked on doors and visited with those at various homes for a little over an hour. I was familiar with many of the residents from our work with their Homeowners Association but I hadn't seen much of them since Trevor first became ill. We asked if there had been any pranks or vandalism in the neighborhood and showed the photos around, including an internet provided shot of a blue Camaro.

They all expressed their sorrow over Trevor's passing: "He was such a treat to work with on the house." "We all loved him very much." "We're so sorry." It was hard, but also heartwarming. It confirmed how much he was loved and respected. I knew I'd better get used to people wanting to talk about Trevor—it was their way of grieving, too.

We found a man and a woman—at different homes—who felt our mystery woman in the photo was familiar, but like the others, couldn't put their finger on the who or where. It reassured us that it hadn't been a waste of time. Sooner or later, we would find a link to her identity. A link that could possibly lead to the threats we'd been receiving.

41

Bud stopped to let Jet out to run on the way home. He raced along beside us, barking, chasing a cottontail rabbit through the creosote brush scattered beside the roadway. We stopped about a half mile up the road to see if he wanted back in. He just looked at us, barked, then ran on ahead, turning his head to look back and bark as if to say: "Hey, what are you waiting for?"

"He's having a ball," I said. "Thanks for taking him. I'll get one of the guys to help me take him out more often. Maybe a quad ride."

"Just be sure you call the sheriff if only one or none of you will be left at home."

"Yes, sir. How about some lunch? You got time? I'll make a couple of tuna sandwiches and iced tea and we can clean up the pasta salad and nachos that were left over from Sunday."

"Sounds good, but looks like you'd better make it for four. Your car is back. Let's go see what they found out."

Jeremy and Dad were at the outside table by the pool, already swigging down some of the sun tea I had set out before we left. They were fully engaged in talking—fingers flying, laughing so hard they didn't even know we had gotten back until Jet's barking caught their attention to open the patio gate. One look and we knew they were bursting to tell us what had happened. I decided to pester them a little.

"Oh, hey guys. Glad you're back. Would you two go down to the garage and see if you can find the ice cream maker? I think it's on the shelf above the freezer. That and the rock salt, please. We thought we'd use some of those huckleberries Dad brought down and whip up some dessert for lunch. While you're down there, grab some ice from the freezer, too. There should be a bag of crushed. Sound good?"

"Oh, sure." The excitement had dropped from Jeremy's face, his shoulders slumped, his voice squeaked a little when he said, "Which freezer?"

"The upright just inside the door. The ice cream maker is wrapped in a white trash bag—should be easy to find. We have plenty of time to get it started before we sit down to lunch. Dad— you remember how to get it set up and going? I'll do the mixture for the inside. Bud's going to help me make some sandwiches."

The two of them took off, Jet nipping at their heels. Still rearing to go.

"Now that was bad," Bud said. "You know they were dying to tell us about their visit this morning."

"Oh, let them stew a little. We'll all have a good laugh about it while we're eating. Besides, I knew we wouldn't get dessert done in time to get you back to work by one o'clock if we waited. You wouldn't want to miss out on homemade ice cream."

"Well, in that case, you're forgiven. What can I do to start the sandwiches while you get the ice cream going? Huckleberry, huh? Can't say as I've ever had that. I do have to get back on the road to be downtown at a meeting shortly after lunch hour."

By the time we brought a plate of sandwiches, warmed nachos, and revitalized salad out to the table, the old ice cream machine was whining a bit as the cylinder spun in its blanket of ice and rock salt. Dad and Jeremy were sitting at the table, their tea glasses put away, drowning their excitement with a beer.

"Sounds like that could use a little TLC," said Dad, nodding at the churning machine. "Is that the same one we had when you were a kid?"

"Oh no," I said, pouring the purple ice cream mix into the container. "I picked this one up at a yard sale down here. I think most of the folks these days are using the new kind with the pre-frozen containers to put the mix into. It only takes a short time to get it from start to finish that way. You see a lot of this old-fashioned kind at yard sales."

"Old fashioned kind?" said Dad. "Plugging it into electricity is not the old-fashioned kind. Taking turns on the hand crank was half the fun of making the ice cream when I was a kid. I guess we were easily entertained. But we all knew it was worth it because whoever was last on the crank when it was finished got to eat the first bowl full, plus lick the paddle. We didn't make ice cream in those days except at family gatherings where there were enough people to eat it all in one sitting. That's when it was the best, just the right consistency for eating."

"I'll agree to that," I said.

"Making ice cream was how I first caught your mother's eye. We were having an ice cream social after church. They called on all us young bucks to turn the cranks while the ladies brought out their cakes and pies to go along. I was crankin' away and looked around and saw her staring at me from under an old oak. And she was a looker, don't cha know. I didn't even know who she was, found out later she had just moved to town. I guess my strength at turning that crank must have been what snagged her. Well, maybe the clincher was when I pulled out the paddle and took a couple of spoons over to where she was standing to share it with her. It was absolutely the best peach ice cream I ever ate."

His eyes just sorta stared right through me, looking across the pool.

"So that's why Mom's favorite ice cream was peach! How come I never heard that story before?"

"Well, I guess there's just some things we keep secret," he said. For a moment, his eyes betrayed that his mind was lost in the past. Suddenly, he snapped back with us. "But what happened at Wells Fargo this morning isn't one of them. Jeremy, tell 'em what happened with Mr. Cramer. I know you're about to bust wide open."

Jeremy kept us wrapped up in his story through lunch. Mr. Cramer had indeed attested to the authenticity of the express box, and verified the numbers. It was last seen by Wells Fargo officials when it was loaded on their stage in Tucson on April 19, 1860, bound for Yuma and San Francisco. The stage no doubt made a stop right here on this property that day for the passengers to have a break and the team to be changed. Somewhere between here and the next station, over by Picacho Peak, the stage was held up. The robbers didn't even stop long enough to blow the express box open, just loaded it on a mule and galloped away. The driver figured they already knew what was in the box and may have had some help from inside. The robbers had unhitched the team from the coach and scared the horses off so they could get a good head start. There was no hint of any trouble until the stage was late showing up at Picacho station at which time a rider was dispatched and found them stranded.

"Nothing was ever found," said Jeremy. "No sign of the loot or the rustlers. They had a good head start, and doubtless took the box somewhere they had access to tools considering the lack of damage to the box. It is believed an outlaw known as El Tejano and his gang may have been the culprits. They were blamed for a number of robberies in the 1850s era. El Tejano was found dead one day along the Santa Cruz River south of Tucson from gunshot wounds sustained in a robbery attempt on a stage in that area. His buried caches of stolen loot were reputed to be in the mountains near Picacho Pass to the north, and Cerro Del Gato, to the south of Tucson."

"Cramer thinks maybe the miner at the Lazey Daisy or other persons might have discovered El Tejano's buried loot and carried it down to the site of the mine where we found it," Dad added. "Another thought was that the robber's gang broke open the express box shortly after the hold-up, taking the spoils and discarding the box nearby to be later found by the miner, March. Maybe he carried it—empty—over to the site of the Lazey Daisy. Only thing we all agreed on is we'll never know for sure what happened."

"Mr. Cramer offered us a reward for finding the strongbox, promising it would be displayed prominently in one of the banks right here in Tucson," said Jeremy.

"That's great." I said. "How much is he giving you?"

"Ah, we turned him down," said Dad. "Jeremy and I agreed that box is a part of the history of the stage line and station, just as this ranch is, and this is where it ought to stay. Wells Fargo has a lot of artifacts from those days. Hell, I've seen completely restored old coaches at some of their locations up north. Once we explained how you've maintained the remnants of the stage stop here at the ranch, Cramer agreed with us. Said it was our choice and he was happy we felt it was the right one."

"I . . ." was all I got out. Tears spewed from my eyes.

"But," Jeremy said, grabbing my hand. "He said to tell you if you ever want to get rid of it, all you need to do is contact him. He's sending you an official letter relinquishing any right Wells Fargo has to the box, but asking you to return it to them at any time you no longer have use for it. That comes with his promise it will remain in a place of honor with you as donor."

"Wow, I can't believe it." I hugged and thanked them both and made a hasty retreat to gather the ice cream dishes and get a hold of my emotions.

Bud was pulling the paddle from the ice cream when I came back through the door. "You can have the honors," he said, handing the paddle and spoons to Jeremy and Dad. They slurped up the purple goop hanging from the paddle, then dove into their bowls.

"This is great," said Jeremy. "It's worth every bit of that $10,000 dollar reward Mr. Cramer offered, huh Hank?"

"Whaaaat . . . Are you crazy? . . .. Ten. Thousand. Dollars?" I was stunned. I hung my head a minute, then looked up to see their faces crumble as they burst into laughter.

"Gotcha," said Dad. "Guess that makes us even for your ignoring us when you first got back." He walked over and put his arm around my shoulders. "We know you will do something creative and useful with that box and retain its integrity at the same time. I'm just glad it isn't a big enough box for Jet to sleep in, or you might be lining it with sheep skin."

I stuck out my tongue, then hugged and said another thank you to them both.

"I've gotta go." Bud stood up, shaking his head. "This mush is gettin' to me. Thanks for the lunch. I'll see ya later."

Bud had no more headed for the gate when we were surprised to see his car backing up to the patio. "Incoming," he called as he stepped from his car. "There's an unfamiliar vehicle coming in, with the deputy right behind. Stay put until we identify who it is."

We all clustered behind the patio gate, watching as Bud walked toward the stopping vehicle. Deputy McConnell approached the SUV and called, "Step from the vehicle, please." The door opened and out stepped a man dressed casually in slacks and a golf shirt. He looked at the uniformed deputy, then to Bud.

"Hey, it's Mr. Cramer from the bank," shouted Jeremy, as he opened the back gate, waiting for all of us to step through.

"I hope he hasn't changed his mind about the strong box," Dad said, under his breath.

Bud dismissed the deputy and followed Cramer to meet us halfway to the patio. Dad made the introductions, with a brief apology about the police escort, explaining there'd been some vandalism in the area. "We didn't expect to see you again so soon, Milt. What brings you up here?"

"After hearing about this place and Mrs. Beale, I decided it would be a shame not to have a picture or two to take back to our regional office, plus I wanted to deliver our thanks in person." He pulled a camera from the case he carried.

"How nice of you," I said, stepping forward to shake his hand. "By the way, I'm Sam. Won't you come in and have a glass of iced tea with us?"

"No, I'm afraid I've got a plane to catch. I did want to meet you before I left, though, Sam. Looks like you've done a nice job of restoring the original flavor of the old station grounds. How about a quick tour? Then I'll be on my way."

Bud again said his goodbyes and left Cramer in our care. We gathered up the box and Milt took pictures of it by the loafing shed, then by the well, and the three of us by the loafing shed, then me by the well. Dad grabbed the camera and took one of Milt and me standing beside the well, the box between us. I took one of the three of them with the box by the shed.

"Thanks so much for your courtesy and thoughtfulness in bringing in the express box," Milt said as he shook hands with Dad and Jeremy and we walked him to his car. Wells Fargo goes back a long way here in Arizona and we're happy to find new stories and pictures to add to our archives.

"And, Sam, please accept our sincere thanks for your work to maintain another bit of Wells Fargo history here at your beautiful El Rancho de Santiago. I hope I can return someday to hear a little more of the story and perhaps take you guys up on that ATV tour of the area." He pulled an envelope from the visor and handed it to me, grabbing my hand at the same time "I'm going to dig a little deeper into our archives when I get back to San Francisco and will be happy to share anything more I learn about the stage station. And send you copies of my photos."

"That will be wonderful . . . and Milt, that invitation will be open anytime you can make it back to Tucson. Have a nice flight, now."

Jeremy opened the gate. Dad and I waved as the SUV drove down the lane.

"Nice guy," said Dad. "I wonder if he's married."

I rolled my eyes as I looked him straight in the face. "I can't believe you said that!"

42

Wednesday, September 28, 6:15 am

I can't believe the guys gave me the strongbox from the mine. I went to sleep last night wondering what I should do with it. Outside near the stable and corral since they were a part of its history? No, I don't want it to deteriorate any more. Plus no one would see it out there. I know. How about a holder for magazines and back-up towels in the guest bathroom? Right where the wall meets the tub, leave it open to provide good access to the magazines or towels. Oh. And put a little story in the open lid about how and where we found it. Perfect.

Dad will love it. Adjacent to his bedroom where he'll pass it all day long. Rosa will probably have a fit since it won't be easy to dust or keep clean. But . . . like everything else, it'll have its own place. It will belong. It doesn't have to bear the seal of easy cleaning to live in this house.

It's time to get back to my cookbook. Jeremy's coming over to work on recipes to make sure I'm using the program properly. Maybe he's got some hints or tricks to make it easier. I'm really enjoying the work. Work? I can hardly call it work. Each recipe brings with it memories of the first time Trev and I tried it. Or the restaurant where we discovered a favorite dish, then tried to duplicate it at home. Most of the time we came pretty close, but then there were the absolute disasters when neither of us could identify a particular flavor or an unusual spice. We'd experiment until we came up with a solution. Sometimes we'd go back to the restaurant more than once for another taste before we got it right. Sometimes we gave up and asked the chef, and sometimes they refused to help. Sometimes our version was even better than the restaurant's. And, sometimes it went in the garbage. We had fun making up new names for our creations, too.

I know, I'll include a description in the cookbook of where each recipe came from or who gave it to us. Or from whom we stole it. What fun Trevor would have had working together on this project. Too bad we didn't get it started.

Voices. Dad was talking to someone in the kitchen. I looked at my watch and was surprised to see I had been daydreaming. Jeremy was right on time. I closed my journal, ready to start my day.

"Busted," said Jeremy as I stepped into the kitchen. "I thought I had time to sneak a cup of coffee before reporting for work."

"You're safe, I need a refill myself." Jeremy already had his coffee and was sitting at the table next to Dad. I filled mine, topped off Dad's and joined them.

"Who's going to take Jet out for a session of catch this morning? Dad, we've been neglecting him lately."

"I can do that for sure. But Jet and I have a little secret. We've been going out each morning to walk the fence line so he's been getting more attention and exercise than you think. We make sure there are no strange footprints or anything out of place."

"Well, wear him out good, so he won't mind being on guard while I take you guys out for breakfast. I noticed a new place down at the corner when I went to Fry's the other day. Used to be a gourmet coffee shop, but now has new owners who've added breakfast and lunch. Thought we'd give it a try.

"That settled, I want to thank you guys again for giving me that express box. I thought about it after I went to bed last night and decided to use it in the guest bath for extra linens and magazines. At first, I thought about a planter or something to use near the corral, but I'm not sure how much more of Mother Nature that old box can stand."

"A terrific idea," Jeremy said. "If I can do anything to help you get it ready for house duty, let me know. We didn't do any cleanup on it before we took it into Wells Fargo. Wanted them to see it the way we found it—minus the snake! And we'd better get Manny started on that repair work he offered."

"Better spray it for bugs, too," Dad said. "No telling what might have been living in it down in that mine shaft. You may have some surprise visitors if you don't watch out."

"Good ideas, you guys. I'll call Manny, we can probably send it home with Rosa day after tomorrow when she comes. I'll write up a little story about its history and slip it in with the magazines in case anybody's interested."

"I'll bring it up on the patio and hose it off," said Dad. "Now, you two get busy on that computer work so we can go eat."

Jeremy did, in fact, find some shortcuts for working with the recipes. He showed me how to add graphics—suggested I take my own photos of the finished dishes to add to some or all of the pages. Wow. I imagined inserting a margarita or Corona here and there next to some of the Mexican recipes. Maybe I could find a photo of Trevor at the grill with his Melt-in-Your-Mouth Ribs. What a fun project this had turned out to be.

We called the sheriff's office to let them know we would be gone for brunch. As promised, the familiar patrol car was parked a short distance from the gate. Tim waved as we pulled out. We picked up a few things for tonight's dinner after a delightful brunch and pulled up our lane just in time to see the mailman pull away from the patrol car.

Deputy McConnell stepped out of his car, his hand up to stop us before we reached the mailbox. "I just put in a call to Detective Holloway," he said. "There's a manila envelope in your mail, same type as before, no return address, scratchy kid-like printing. Doesn't seem to be much in it, fairly thin and light weight. Here's the rest of your mail, why don't you all go up to the house. I'll wait here for the sheriff and Bud. They're on their way."

My eyes locked on the envelope. "Damn it." Why did they have to spoil such a wonderful morning? When would it stop?"

"Come on, Sam; let's do what the deputy says. Let the experts take care of this. We can't do anything here." Dad tugged at my arm. I gave him my wrinkle-up-your-nose frown, put the 4Runner in gear, and started through the gate.

Somehow, I snapped back to the realization of how rudely I'd just treated Tim McConnell and tromped on the brakes. Good thing we were belted in or I could have thrown Dad through the windshield.

Tim's eyes roved the area as I backed up. "Did you see something, Mrs. Beale?"

"No, just wanted to apologize. I was a bit of a bitch a moment ago. We had hoped we were done with malicious mail and phone calls. But it doesn't look that way. I'm sorry, Tim, and so thankful you were here."

"Apology accepted, but none needed. It's been one shock after another for you all. We're glad to be here to buffer those as much as we can. If there is anything I can do, give me a shout. I'll be right here."

43

Putting the groceries away did not do away with my butterflies. Dad and Jeremy kept watch out the great room window until Bud pulled up to the gate. He swished them right back inside as quickly as they started out the front door, telling them to wait inside with me, then turned to join the others as Hazmat arrived.

Waiting is never easy. Especially when you're afraid that what you're waiting for could turn out to be a loud blast. Somebody could get hurt. Our eyes skipped from one to the other. We finally sat down, tried to make conversation, each no doubt willing the door to open with every second that dragged on. We all jumped as Jet let out a yip, followed by the clanging of the patio gate latch.

The dead stare of Bud's eyes as he came through the door shouted to us that it was not good news. Dad, Jeremy, and I stood as he walked into the kitchen. My heart thundered in my chest. Jet ran over to touch his nose on Bud's hand, baleful eyes looking upward. He backed away when he received no returning pet, not a word, not a smile from Bud.

"We were able to open the envelope after the HAZMAT people got here. Their scanners revealed nothing but paper on the inside." I guessed Bud was giving us his professional tone. He sounded just like the TV detectives talking to strangers, talking to victims.

"What's in it? Another pieced together note?" My mind raced to conjure up what it might say this time.

"It's photos, Sam. Photos of each of us. In your yard. On the patio. Even one of you in the pool."

"Oh my God," Dad choked the words out. "If . . . if they can get close enough to take photos . . ."

"That's right." Bud eyes sought out mine. They looked just like Jet's when he looked up at me, waiting for me to say something. But my brain—though spinning—wasn't synching with my mouth. I couldn't spit out a word.

"Was there a note?" Jeremy stepped in.

"Yes. On the bottom of each page of photos. Which are on their way to the sheriff's lab to see what they might turn up. Basically, the envelope looks the same as the others, only this one's full size—9 X 12. The pictures appear to be taken with a digital camera and printed on an inexpensive home printer. Regular paper. There is probably no way to trace the photos unless they were careless with fingerprints. We can only hope to find something they missed. A hair, a skin particle, a thread. Maybe we'll get lucky under magnification. It's easy to miss something out there in the bright sunshine."

"You're not going to tell us what it said, are you?" I asked but I didn't really want to know. Maybe it didn't matter what it said. Maybe it said nothing. The photos say it all. We were being watched. That we weren't safe anywhere. Certainly not at home, not outside, anyway. I supposed we were all thinking the same things.

Dad broke the silence. "What do we do now, Bud?"

"Sheriff Schaeffer will be here around five. He had some things to check on and will meet with us to decide our next plan of action. It's obvious our current precautions haven't kept them at bay. The sheriff will bring copies of the photos so we can try to identify when each was taken. He wants to take a look at our board with the notes we've just gone over, to see if anything new pops out from our discussions.

"I've tried to keep him up to date, but with these golf tournaments and other events going on out here in his neck of the woods, he and his men have been spread pretty thin. We've been damned lucky to get as much coverage from them as we have. They've all been putting in plenty of overtime.

"I've got to take off now to get things updated from my end. Any of you need to go somewhere? I'd like you all to stay put the rest of the afternoon. And, please stay in the buildings until we see what we may be up against. Are we all okay with that?"

Nods from around the table—solemn faces, no one cracked a smile, just slowly nodded, each lost in his own thoughts.

Dad and Jeremy had shuffled around ever since Bud left. None of us really knew what to think, what to do. It was hard to keep my thoughts focused on the recipes, but I was in the office—hacking away at them. Today's mail had taken away this morning's sunshine and I was about ready to give up when I smelled popcorn.

Popcorn?

Jeremy poked his head in the doorway. "Hank says time to wrap it up and come out to help us work on the puzzle."

Oh . . . my . . . God. We've been going over and over this for the last three days. What else can we do? I decided I might as well join them; they were only trying to help. I closed down the computer and put the files away.

As I entered the great room, the load I was carrying on my shoulders floated to the floor when I saw Jeremy turning over the pieces to a jigsaw puzzle at the table by the window. "Whoa. I didn't know you meant a jigsaw puzzle," I said. "What a great idea. I haven't put one of these together in ages."

"I found this one in the cupboard over there," Dad called from across the kitchen counter, pointing to the entertainment center. "Betsy and I put a lot of these together during the winter once the snow starts flying. She's crazy about 'em, has one going at her house most of the time. I use it as an excuse to have popcorn, but I'm getting pretty good at finding the pieces, too.

"As I remember, you used to have a knack for these when you were growing up. You and your mom argued about which one to do next. You'd want the horses, she the scene of Paris, Waikiki or some other exotic place. It sounds like we'd better get used to staying inside for a while, so Jeremy and I thought this might help pass the time."

"A super idea. I'll get some napkins and bowls and help Jeremy get these pieces turned over while you finish popping the corn, Dad."

The puzzle worked its magic. Or, maybe it was the popcorn. Maybe it was both. What mattered was that the magic was there, like a bolt of electricity that crackled around the table as we reached in front of each other, gathering up pieces to complete the sections of the border closest to us. Finally, the outside was done. We were ready to start on the middle.

We celebrated with a beer. Dad was good at finding things—excuses—to celebrate with a beer. One turned into two, the inside of the puzzle began to grow and, before we knew it, the clock struck four. The afternoon was gone. Time to start thinking about dinner and get ready for Bud and the sheriff to arrive.

We had played too long with the puzzle for any elaborate plans in the dinner department, so opted for Chinese delivery from the Brass Monkey down on the highway. They have the absolute best Moo Goo Gai Pan and Mu Shu Pork I had ever eaten. There would be time to stir up a cake to go with the leftover huckleberry ice cream . . . that should take care of us all.

The Monkey's card was always handy on the bulletin board by the kitchen phone. I called to make sure of their delivery hours. Mai, the owner herself, answered—no doubt there to get dishes prepped for their supper business. Between the two of us, we put a menu together to take care of my hungry crew, including the sheriff if we could talk him into staying. I needed to call thirty minutes before we planned to eat and Mai promised to have it here on time.

I poured spice cake batter into muffin tins lined with those crinkled multi-colored papers, thinking cupcakes would be much easier to send home with Bud and the sheriff. And handy for munching while working on the puzzle. Not to mention no dishes to fool with.

Bud walked in just as I pulled the cakes from the oven. "Mm . . . something smells delicious. That probably answers my next question. Anything I can do for dinner?"

"All taken care of, thank you. Once I get these cupcakes cooled and frosted, thanks to the Brass Monkey, everything else will be delivered at the time we decide."

"What? No fortune cookies?" He nodded toward the cupcakes.

"There's always room for fortune cookies. And I'm ready for a good one. One that says: you will soon be done with this madness."

"Amen," Bud said. "I do have some news. Mike Colgan called just before I left the office. One of his gals—in fact, Janet, who was hired to take your place when you left—identified our mystery woman. It's Susan Duncan. The daughter of Hiram Duncan who sold this property to Trevor."

"I don't remember ever meeting Duncan's daughter." I was puzzled. "I helped with the transaction. Actually, it was me that discovered the owner's name. That's what brought Trevor and me together. It was the son who was pitching a fit about the sale. He had a buyer for a higher price, but the stage station would have been destroyed. His dad put a stop to that."

"Yes," Bud said. "I remember that story, but this still leaves us with the question. Why was she at Trevor's funeral?"

"And one more," I said. "Does this take away one of the possible suspects to our stalker?"

44

Sheriff Schaeffer showed up at a little after five. He brought copies of the mail photos for us to study as we talked. He explained he had ordered law enforcement helicopters and small planes airborne to scout the hills and desert surroundings and report any suspicious looking activity. His pilots were to fly low enough to get license numbers and/or aerial photos of anyone close to our ranch, regardless of what they were doing.

He gave us maps of the area with our property boundaries outlined in red; a circle in blue identified the boundaries for an average personal type camera shot. His experts were studying the photos to verify if the angle proved they had been taken from the air, and with instructions to draw a larger search boundary in green if the photos proved to have been snapped with a professional type camera. Seems he had covered all possibilities.

Bud went over our boards and notes outlining all of the events, plus updated everyone on his news of the mystery woman. "I haven't had a chance to check out Susan Duncan, I was at

Mike's office when I got the deputy's call. But that's the first thing on my agenda in the morning. I would be surprised if it's connected to the case in any way, but at least maybe we can eliminate her from our list, allowing more time to concentrate on the rest."

"I'll check our files on the Duncans, too," the sheriff said. "We may have something we can add. As far as I know, her father still lives over in Marana. He's been a big benefactor in some of Tucson's historic preservation projects, and in Marana and Oro Valley of late. I can't imagine his family would be involved in something like this."

Bud said, "Probably wouldn't hurt to run the brother, as well. David is his name."

A chill streaked up the middle of my back, ending in a shudder that ripped across my shoulders as I glanced at the photos. One of me on the lounge—that had to be the same day the rattlesnake showed up. It was a close-up. It seemed he . . . or she . . . had to have been really close. Close enough to turn a snake loose?

Jeremy was pictured in his VW, driving down our lane. It could have been taken from almost anywhere since the desert is pretty wide open out here, a few scattered prickly pear and creosote bushes, but nothing too tall to get in the way.

Another showed Dad standing by a saguaro the day he and I went riding. It could have been the same shot I took on Dad's camera.

There was a group photo of us all having dinner Saturday night when we came back from target practice, as well as one zoomed in on Rosa with her tray of margaritas, one with Manny putting up the lights. There was no single photo of Bud. What was the significance of that?

Thoughts raced through my brain. What had I done to put my friends—my family—in harm's way? That was the message here, wasn't it? It wasn't just me anymore. First me, then Jeremy. Now they were threatening us all.

Bud added the date and place to each photo on the sheriff's pages as well as the copies he tacked to our calendar board. They hoped studying this information would allow them to pinpoint a common location from which the photos were taken, eventually to lead to the identities and capture of the culprits.

We discussed Rosa and Manny. What to do with them? We decided to encourage them to visit some of their family south of the border to ensure their safety. We agreed it might be easier said than done, but we would do our best to convince them.

Of course, Sheriff Schaeffer suggested we vacate the premises. Once again, we refused. All agreed to stay inside as much as possible and to take every precaution to keep out of sight.

We studied the premises and sketched a route between the garage and the front door of the house least likely to be seen through the lens of a camera. Since Jeremy mostly used the front door, the sheriff thought that was probably why the photo of Jeremy was the only one taken outside our gate—they'd had no opportunity to catch him inside the perimeter for a photo.

Bud warned, "Make sure you all use this front route between the garage and the house. And Jeremy, announce yourself coming over so Hank or Sam can unlock the front door for you so there will be no waiting outside. Keep all doors locked at all times. Yours too, Jeremy. And don't use the patio. Consider yourselves under house arrest." His eyes circled the table as he nodded and smiled.

I didn't see anything different about house arrest. It seemed like I had already been under house arrest for some time. And wasn't I the person who had decided to get out of her rut? This was just not working.

We ordered our dinner and the sheriff turned down our invitation. Said he was allergic to something in oriental foods so he just stayed away from it all. Somehow, I couldn't imagine this bear of a man could be daunted by any Chinese vegetable or spice.

The Moo Goo Gai Pan was as crisp and delicious as I remembered, the Mu Shu Pork always a delight for making our own "Chinese tacos." I am quite sure my father had never experienced most of the dishes Mai presented to us that evening; one or two was new to me as well. My experience with Chinese foods while growing up was the simple combination plate offered by most Boise restaurants: Chow Mein, Egg Foo Yung, and Sweet and Sours—tiny pork ribs in sauce. I could thank Trevor for introducing me to many of the specialty dishes featured these days. He loved Chinese and I was soon hooked on the new found delicacies.

Wednesday, September 28, 10:15 pm

We received the worst threat of all today. Photos of us. Right here on the property. This expands the danger circle to include us all. Rosa and Manny, Dad, Jeremy, Bud, and me. Damn it. What if something happens to one of them? Jeremy came close. How can I protect them? I'm thinking maybe we should just leave. That's what the sheriff wants. Probably what the stalkers want.

Maybe they aren't after me at all? Could be they are after something . . . some thing, rather than a person? But what?

Susan Duncan. She continues to be a mystery. Why would she or her family want me off this property? Surely not revenge for buying the land. That was six or seven years ago. A long time to carry a grudge. Seems like they would have started sooner, caused problems at our home while it was still under construction . . . and while Trevor was still here, still working on it. Why wait until Trevor died? It seems he would have been the target, not me. What could have triggered it now?

Or, was she smitten with Trevor, hence her appearance at his funeral? Definitely a long shot . . . but, that certainly ties her to the song. I can't just dismiss her, can I . . . ? Or could she have been there merely paying the family's respects?

45

The Watchers

The watchers crouched under the camouflage webbing that had been carefully stretched between a series of boulders on the hillside, their ATVs disguised under more of the same on the back side of the boulders. They knew they couldn't be seen by the Piper Cubs of the Civil Air Patrol and Pima County's helicopters. Desert camo was invisible in this country, matching the tans and drab greens of the slopes of the Tortolita and Catalina Mountain ranges.

They would be leaving soon, their night vision goggles lighting the familiar primitive roadway enough to make headlights unnecessary on this, their last trip back down to their pickup. They knew *if today's photos didn't chase the Beale woman and her friends away, their next trip would be a direct assault on the ranch.*

46

Thursday, September 29, 8 am

I couldn't get to sleep last night after writing. I don't think I can blame the Chinese food. Other than a trip to the kitchen for a cold bottle of water, it was sitting just fine. But I was upset. Wondering. Worrying. What to do next?

I dreamed I was talking to Trevor, asking him what the Duncan woman had to do with him or how could she be mixed in with our troubles? Had she been involved in the property sale in any way?

Sitting at my desk, staring off into space. Looking for answers, yet nothing came. An urge arose to visit Trevor's grave. I hadn't been there for a couple of months. At first, I went out regularly, placing fresh flowers, thinking I needed to go there to feel close. But one day realized that I felt closest to him right here at home. The home we built together, the home where we spent our last months and moments together. But now, I had to go. Had to make sure all was well at his gravesite at Saguaro Gardens. That there hadn't been any desecration there like we'd had at El Rancho de Santiago.

I pulled the drapes across the slider to check the weather before I showered. The news had reported a cool front on its way, and it wasn't as bright as usual in the bedroom this morning. Sure enough, clouds had moved in and it looked like we might get some rain today. I found black jeans and a lightweight multi-striped sweater to wear over a white blouse for today's trip to the cemetery. It was best to use layers this time of year. Fall can bring surprises even in Arizona.

"Good morning, Dad." I sauntered through the great room at 9:05. There he was, head bent over the puzzle, coffee in his left hand, his right index finger slowly drifting over the scattered pieces, searching for that one perfect fit.

"Aha." He'd found his piece. "Morning, Hon. Grab some coffee and come on in, I'm making some pretty good progress this morning. Figured I might as well get started early. It's about all the excitement we can look forward to while we're under

Bud's house arrest." He held up his hands, each with two fingers bending to feign quotation marks as he said 'house arrest.'

I poured me a cup, snatched a raspberry yogurt from the fridge. "Do you want some toast? Yogurt?"

"I already had some toast. That's good sourdough, tastes like homemade. No yogurt for me. I think they should revise that quiche saying to: Real Men Don't Eat *Yogurt*. Quiche isn't at all that bad—at least Betsy's. It's delicious. I just can't understand why they don't call it egg pie."

I snickered to myself as I sawed a thick slice off the hefty loaf, and pushed it into the toaster. Egg pie? He's still the same old Dad. Not afraid to say whatever he thinks. His comments and antics have always amazed me. I'd only seen him a half a dozen times or less since he and Mom divorced, but those years have melted away these last few days. Boy, we need to spend more time together.

"So, how're things going for your mom? She still enthused about living in Las Vegas?" he asked as I set down my plate.

Jeez, Louise. Could he possibly know I'd just been thinking about him and Mom?

"We . . . ah. We talk at least once or twice a month. It sounds like she is still enamored with the bright lights and fast pace of Vegas. They have a fabulous view of the Strip and the downtown area from their apartment windows and terrace. I think they keep busy with Tom's social calendar that comes along with the job. You know Mom—always the entertainer."

"Well, it sounds like she's got what she always wanted. She deserves it after putting up with me all those years. Can't blame her because she wasn't ready to be put out to pasture when I was, I guess. We had some great years together, but they were done. You just know." Nodding, he pulled his eyes away from mine and refocused on the puzzle.

"Hand me that piece right there in front of you, will you, Babe? With a corner of the horse's nose. I swear I've been looking for that one for an hour."

"This one?" I passed it over. "Dad." I closed my hand over his as he took the piece. "I'm glad you and Mom both have a life you love and someone to share it with who makes you happy."

"Anybody up in there?" Jeremy's voice blasted from the intercom by the doorway. And his timing was perfect. I made a hasty retreat from the table. Jet raced me to the door, his tail wagging.

"Present and accounted for. Coming over? Want a piece of sourdough toast and yogurt?"

"No thanks, I've already had my breakfast long ago. Had research to do. I've been reviewing some of the old treasures your dad and I have been discussing and have some updated information. Can I get you to open up the door for me?”

“Already here,” I said. A quick knock and Jeremy stepped in, tucked some papers under his arm, locked the door behind him, and gave Jet a two-handed scratch along his back. “How’s Jet today?”

He barked and wiggled under Jeremy’s touch, wanting more. They wrestled along the entryway and into the great room. Jet was excited to have Jeremy rough-housing with him. Just like he and Trevor used to do. He settled down once we reached the jigsaw table, and went back to his basket by the fireplace, his eyes glued on us as Jeremy settled himself across from Dad.

“You guys are still under house arrest.” I didn’t sit. “Deputy McConnell is taking me on an errand this morning.”

“What? What’s up?” Dad asked.

“I’d like to keep this private. I’ll give you a report when I get back. Let’s just say, I’m following up a clue that surfaced yesterday. The deputy should be here any minute.”

They both stared at me, eyebrows raised, Jeremy chewing on his lower lip, Dad biting a fingernail. I gathered up my dishes and headed for the kitchen.

The intercom buzzed from the gate just as I closed the door on the dishwasher. “Mrs. Beale. Deputy McConnell here.”

The deputy's face grinned from the little screen as I clicked the gate switch. "Come on in, Tim. I'll meet you at the front courtyard gate."

The trip from home to the cemetery sped by. I was glad Tim McConnell had been on duty today, and felt safe and comfortable since he had been the one to investigate most of our incidents. We chit-chatted along the way, me giving directions to Trevor's grave as the patrol car cruised through the main gate of Saguaro Gardens. He circled the gravesite area checking for anyone who might look suspicious, but we saw no one at all. He walked with me to the back side of Trevor's grave, then stepped back toward a big cottonwood tree to give me some privacy.

I turned around the end of the large double stone and saw black roses—in a black vase with a black ribbon—sitting directly beneath my name chiseled into the stone beside Trevor's. Below my name was inscribed: *born: April 21, 1989*. Directly across from *Laid to Rest* was a taped-on paper reading: *Soon*. I recognized that scrawl.

"TIM . . ." I shouted. Tears flooded down my face.

McConnell ran to me, his gun in his right hand. He pulled me close with his left, his head rotating to survey the cemetery. Satisfied there was no one in sight, he let go and keyed the microphone on his shoulder radio: "This is McConnell at Saguaro

Gardens with Mrs. Beale. Request back-up and a Crime Scene Unit. Mr. Beale's gravesite in the Oracle section. No perps in sight, no injury."

Within minutes two more patrol cars slid to a stop on the otherwise deserted roadside. McConnell dispatched a Deputy Brooks to take me home, and sent the other new arrivals to comb the surrounding area while he stayed at the gravesite to wait for the CSU.

"Well, that didn't take long . . . Holy Jesus!" Dad had discovered my hair in disarray, the ugly mascara tracks left behind by tears trailing down my cheeks as I unlocked and entered through the front door. Jigsaw pieces scattered to the floor as he and Jeremy jumped up and rushed to the door where Deputy Brooks and I stood.

Dad: "What's happened?"

Jeremy: "Where's McConnell?"

Me: "Everyone is okay. I'll grab a washcloth and be right back out, while you guys all sit down. Dad, Jeremy, meet Deputy Brooks. He and I will explain in a minute."

Once refreshed and seated, I described the scene we'd encountered at the cemetery adding that Tim McConnell had radioed us on the way home to report that no one had been found at or in the vicinity of the cemetery site, and the crime scene people were at work. Deputy Brooks added he had been assigned to bring me home and station himself at our gate until Bud or other replacements arrived.

"Can we do anything, Sam?" Jeremy asked. "Why don't you go lie down awhile?"

"You ought to know me better than that by now," I said. "I'm much better off to stay busy. Besides, it's about lunch time and I'm sure you guys haven't strayed away from that puzzle while I was gone."

"Guilty," said Dad.

"Deputy," I said, "please join us for some lunch. It sounds like you are going to be under house arrest along with rest of us for the remainder of your shift and that won't include a lunch break."

"That sounds great, ma'am, but I'd better get outside where I'm supposed to be."

"Then we'll bring lunch to you as soon as it's ready," I said. "Lemonade or Iced Tea? You like Reuben Sandwiches?"

"Either is fine to drink, ma'am. It all sounds just great. You can call me Doug, if it's all right with you." He nodded and smiled. "I'm sorry I haven't been assigned to this duty earlier, if you don't mind my saying. Thanks so much."

"It's us who thanks you," I said, as he headed for the door. "You can move that little table and chair in the courtyard over to give you a clear view of the road and gate. Dad will bring your lunch out, probably in fifteen or twenty minutes."

We munched on our sandwiches at the puzzle table, sipping lemonade, searching for that next piece. Though I doubt too many pieces were actually added.

Jeremy broke the silence. "I didn't have a chance to tell you what I found on the internet this morning, Sam. Remember when Hank and I talked about that Tucson bank embezzlement money that was never recovered? They announced on the news today that James Dallas, the guy who was convicted of that crime, is set to be released on parole this Friday—tomorrow. Said he'd been a model prisoner in the state prison over at Picacho, and has been approved for early release, probably partly due to the overcrowded conditions at most of the prisons these days."

"Isn't that something?" said Dad. "And just when we were ready to start lookin' for clues for that bank loot that was never found. What do you think, Sam . . . we ought to tail him?

"I think you'd better find another treasure story to follow and leave this guy alone. If he did it, he's probably dangerous and will no doubt be laying low for a while anyway. If he didn't, he's probably had enough notoriety for a lifetime."

47

Bud showed up at 2:30. We were all sitting around the puzzle table, all quiet, still not much progress being made on the jigsaw.

Bud had been to the cemetery, handed photos of the black roses to Jeremy and Dad and brought a chair over to sit beside me. He leaned over and put his arm around my shoulders. The second time today I was pulled into the protective embrace of a strong and handsome man, yet I was unable to think past the danger I had put them in. The danger I faced myself. A danger I couldn't explain, nor justify with neither reason nor blame.

"You've had about enough of this," Bud said. The tenderness of his words chased away my thoughts. "I think we need to get you out of here, into a different atmosphere, away from the nastiness of it, and do something constructive, maybe even fun.

"Wait a minute. I've told you all along . . ."

"Simmer down, now. This isn't the sheriff talking or the detective. This is Bud—your friend. There's a fund raiser auction at the University tomorrow night, and it just so happens I have an invitation to attend. I've already talked to Sheriff Schaeffer, and he agrees. Now that the Dove Mountain golf tournament is over, he's got plenty of help and will have his men strategically placed to cover everything here at the house while you're gone. And a police escort on the way home. We can all have a night out on the town. How does that sound?"

My head was reeling. "You have no idea how wonderful that sounds. This house arrest and the whole business have given me the heebie-jeebies. So much time on our hands and we can't seem to make any headway. I'm ready to say to hell with it all. Let's go out and howl. Tell me more about it. How did you manage to get an invitation to the University, anyway?"

"Well now, I guess it's time to fess up," he said. "Actually . . . Sandy asked me to go to the auction a few days ago. But at the time, I didn't have any idea what our situation here would be. The way things have been go . . ."

"Wait a minute. Sandy, is it? Are you speaking of my new friend Sandy Marks? As in the Dean of Women at the U? The Sandy that you just met down at the Conquistador the other night?"

I watched as Bud kinda rolled his eyes and shrugged his shoulders at the same time. A sly grin creased his face.

"Why you old smoothie. What have you been up to?"

"Well . . . I didn't want to say anything, but Sandy and I have gotten together a couple of times since you introduced us. I didn't mention it. Didn't want you to start thinking it was going somewhere that it wasn't."

"You can better believe that I'm thinking it's going somewhere. Already two dates in less than a couple of weeks? And now she's inviting you out to where she works? My God, Bud, unless you've been keeping secrets all these years, you're not the average Joe Macho, out there searching *Matchmakers R Us* for dates on the internet. By the way, when have you managed to fit all this in?"

"I guess my low profile has been working. Got you buffaloed anyway. No, it's nothing like that, not what you'd call real dates. Sandy and I have discovered we're a good fit, though. Lots in common, easy conversation. Neither looking for anything serious but we definitely enjoy each other's company for a lunch or dinner. Seems to work so far.

"She's got a table reserved at this fund raiser on Saturday and we thought it might be a good opportunity to get all of you out of the house. How about it?"

Jeremy jumped in. "You and Mrs. Marks, huh, Bud? Wow. Mrs. Marks. How cool is that? I'm available for a night out if Sam will do me the honor of being her escort, sharing that honor with Hank, of course."

"You can count me out. That'll be too late for the likes of this old geezer. I've been up late working this damned puzzle and I need to catch up on my sleep. Besides, I told Betsy that I'd borrow your cell phone and take advantage of those unlimited minutes everyone keeps bragging about. Thought I'd give her a call to catch up on what's happening on the ranch."

"Oh, come on Dad. Don't try to fool us with that *tired* business. Hell, you could walk circles around most of us the way you work at home. Plus, all you do to help Betsy out at her place. I'm thinking you're just missing Betsy more than you'd like to admit."

"Well, maybe so, but I'm still not going out with you youngsters." He rolled his eyes from me to Jeremy. "It sounds pretty boring to me. Jet and I will hold down the fort here, won't we, Jet?"

When he heard his name, Jet raised his head to look up at Dad, then hopped from his bed and trotted over to plop his butt right on top of Dad's foot.

"You and I have a job to do, Jet, while the rest of 'em go out. Think we can handle it?" Jet's tail swished in an arc along the tile. He leaned his head against Dad's leg. Dad scratched between his ears, pulling his hand down almost to Jet's nose to ruffle the smooth hair on the dog's face. Jet pulled his head back and shook it. Dad laughed.

"You trying to say you don't like that, eh, Jet?" Jet reached up to rake his paw across the Levis covering Dad's thigh. "Oh sure, now you want to play, is that it? Come on, I'll take you outside while these guys make their plans."

They jumped up and bounded out the door together.

"So, tell me more about this fund raiser," I said to Bud. "And, by the way. Did I hear Jeremy to say Mrs. Marks?"

"That's right. Another thing we have in common. She's divorced, too. We're legal.

"And now, about the party. The girls' basketball team has been invited to participate in a tournament in Hawaii, an unbudgeted trip. Sandy is their faculty advisor, and she's been out gathering sports equipment, golf games, dinner packages, and resort stays from the locals to be auctioned off to the highest bidder. It sounds like a lot of fun. She's even convinced the guys' basketball team to auction themselves off for various odd jobs to support the girls. And, I might add, a few of Tucson's finest are lined up to be auctioned off for a date with the highest lady bidders."

"And, is your name at the top of that list of volunteers?" I asked.

"Not at the top, but I've been drumming up some of my friends to join me in helping out the cause."

"Sounds like tough duty to me," said Jeremy, his lips turned down to form a frown as he slowly shook his head. "You cops have all the fun."

Bud called Sandy to let her know Jeremy and I would be attending. He filled us in on the details: "casual cocktail" dress, hors d'oeuvres prepared by the culinary department of the UA and served by the girls' basketball team members, no-host cocktails catered by Sportsman's Grill and several of the wineries from the Patagonia area. All proceeds would go to the Athletic Department, Girls' Basketball. Bud and Sandy would meet us there around six for cocktails; auction would begin at seven. Sandy's table was number thirty-six. We were to give that to the doorman who would check off our names and show us in.

Jeremy looked at his watch, jumped up and said, "I'm out of here. Gotta get ready for my class. I'll drop the lesson by on my way out."

"Now that that's settled," I said to Bud, when we were alone, "any clues or news about the cemetery scene?"

"I'm afraid we drew another blank there. We're checking the florists and hobby and craft shops for the black roses. Hell, we're even checking Wal-Mart and places like that, but I doubt we'll have any luck unless we can tie them to a credit card purchase. Even though black roses aren't that common, artificial flowers are too accessible at too many places. Would you believe even the dollar stores? Besides, we have no idea when they were placed there, other than the groundskeeper says it could be any time since their last mowing 12 days ago. So far, we've found Hobby Lobby and a couple of other shops who carry black silk roses. They're checking their inventory and sales people to see if they can tell us anything. We should know something—one way or the other—by tomorrow. But don't get your hopes up that we'll get anything out of it."

"As much as I hate to say it, I'm beginning to wonder if we'll ever solve who's doing this, and, when—or if—it will stop. It really got to me this morning. Being there by Trevor's grave, seeing my name on that tombstone and the rest . . ." I let the words fall, shaking my head.

Bud, once again, pulled me into him. "Don't you worry. We'll get them. Maybe not today. Maybe not tomorrow, but sooner or later they'll screw up. They'll get careless."

"You'd better watch out," I said, lifting his arm off my shoulder and pushing him away. "I don't want to make your new girlfriend jealous. Now let's hear the details about these two dates."

Bud had called Sandy the day after we ran into her at the El Commodore. They met for lunch at the University. He showed her the photo of the mystery woman, asked her about the blue Camaro that I had first encountered in the campus parking lot. She couldn't remember seeing the woman or the car, but confessed that unless it was parked right next to her, she probably wouldn't have noticed it anyway. Said she was an early-to-work gal and usually one of the last out after school.

He had been very comfortable with Sandy right from the start, much as I had when I signed up for my classes. Confessed he'd told her more than he intended, even asked her what she could tell him about Jeremy. She had nothing but good things to say, was glad to know he was staying at the ranch, and offered any assistance she could. Bud left his card with her, just in case she thought of anything, hoping he would hear from her.

And he did. She called Bud a few days later and invited them all to the auction, asking what he thought about the cop/date idea for the fund raiser. Though he couldn't guarantee to be there, he had promised to try to drum up some date candidates for her auction.

They met for cocktails at the Sportsman's Grill near the campus, one day after work. Cocktails turned into nonstop conversation; dinner turned into grazing Sportsman's superb appetizer menu. They made final plans for the auction—with or without him.

"That's quite a story," I said. "Good for you. Good for you both. I'm excited to see Sandy again, but who thought it would be under these circumstances. I'm not sure how I feel about an almost-stranger knowing so much about my personal challenges, but it sounds like she may be more than that someday."

"Whoa…slow down. I told you. Sandy and I aren't looking for anything other than friendship for now. Who knows where this may or may not go? I don't want you trying to play cupid from her side or mine. Are we clear?"

"Crystal," I said, and wrinkled my nose at him. "Now get out of here. You probably have someone to call. Or see. Or something."

He reached over and gave me a swat on the butt, pointed his finger at me, and said, "I told you . . ." And he was gone.

48

Wow, almost a new month, new things to think about. I haven't decided just what I think about Bud and Sandy. Who would have thought my trip to UA that day could have affected the changes we've seen? First meeting Jeremy, then Sandy. Now, Jeremy living here, a part of our family. And last night I learned that Sandy has become . . . what has she become? Should I listen to Bud and not try to encourage them? Do I want to "lose" Bud's companionship I've learned to rely on? I'm torn. I can't be selfish, but, if any good thing can come from this trouble we've had, I guess it could be that I've gotten used to leaning on him, to calling him, to looking forward to his smiling face coming through the door.

Enough of that stuff. I should be thinking how happy I am for Bud, how happy I am for both of them. Get over this jealous streak and wish them any happiness that may come their way. And listen to Bud's advice to buzz off. If it's meant to happen, it will be. Get over it. Bud's a big boy.

I can't wait for tonight. Actually, going to a party. Going anywhere will be a treat, but I hate to see Dad staying home alone. Uh oh. Here I go again. Trying to be everyone's everything. Dad's just looking for a little peace and quiet and private time to talk to Betsy.

If Trevor was here, he'd be saying "Butt out, Sam!" He was always the smart one. The one with the clear head to see things as they really are . . . how they should be, anyway.

Better go see what I have to wear to the party tonight. But first, I'll call Sandy to get

her interpretation of what 'cocktail casual'
really is.

No one in the kitchen. Where is Dad? Eight-thirty and he's nowhere to be found? He was still working on the puzzle when I gave up and went to bed. Probably waited up for Jeremy to get home from class—they've gotten pretty close these days. I zonked out while the news was still on.

Sandy's cell went straight to voice mail when I dialed the number Bud had given me. I checked my watch to be sure I hadn't misread the clock and called too early. At the beep I asked her to call me, turned and noticed Jet wasn't in his box by the door. Where was everybody?

Just then, the front door opened and I heard Jet's toenails ticking along the hallway toward me, Dad shushing him until I yelled, "So, what have you two been up to?"

"We've been over havin' toast and coffee with Jeremy." He hung the front door key back by the intercom. "Didn't seem like anyone was ever gonna get up around here. You been up long?"

"Up . . . but not moving too fast. A little time to catch up in my journal and think about that party tonight. I'm not sure what cocktail casual means. Tried to call Sandy, but had to leave a voice mail. Maybe Jeremy knows, sounds like a university thing to me."

"I asked Jeremy," Dad said. "He's still trying to talk me into going. He said cocktail casual in Arizona means anything made out of denim as long as it's accompanied by a sport coat and no tie. Oh . . . and boots. I told him I'd have to remember that. Would suit me just fine."

"So, you're going?"

"No, I'm leaving that to you kids, like I told you last night. I've got some sleep to catch up on and Jeremy doesn't figure you will be home until after midnight."

"Well, I'm looking forward to it, midnight or not."

Sandy called and said she was so anxious to see us, and find out more about what's been going on with us. She said Bud wasn't very talkative about it, and asked me if he was always that way. I said I was sworn to secrecy when it came to Bud. We both laughed and said goodbye.

Jeremy pulled the 4Runner around to the front door at 5:15 following his call to let us know he was on his way. Dad walked me out to the car. Jet followed directly in his footsteps.

As he opened the car door, Dad whistled and said, "Woo-ee, you kids clean up pretty well. She's all yours, son. Have a good time, now."

Jeremy was dressed just as he had described: a raspberry-colored polo tucked into faded blue denim jeans and cowboy boots. A tan corduroy jacket—leather patches at the elbows—lay carefully folded on the back seat. No tie in sight.

I had chosen an indigo jumpsuit. Embroidered white arrows accented the pockets, sequined red, white, and blue stars dotted the front and back yokes. White Justin boots and a petite white fringed leather shoulder bag completed the outfit. I slipped a credit card and some cash into my bag in case I got carried away at the auction.

Dad closed the door, gave a couple of pats on the top of the car and turned back to the house. I hated to leave him alone, but knew he would enjoy the time to himself. And I had left him my cell with Jeremy's and Bud's numbers on speed dial. We waved to Deputy Brooks as we drove from our lane onto Santiago Way.

"Thanks for being my escort tonight, Jeremy. Let's just forget about everything else and have fun. I'm anxious to see Sandy again and get better acquainted with her."

"She's really well liked at school. I've got to admit, though, I never expected to be spending an evening at the same table with her."

"You'll do fine; she certainly has a way to put people at ease. And, by the way, Dad was right. You do look pretty spiffy tonight."

"We'll knock 'em dead." Jeremy meant it as a joke, but I knew he regretted his use of words as soon as they rolled out. "Uh oh…sorry."

The party was in the Student Union Building. Jeremy found a parking spot on a side street off Speedway, much closer than the on-campus parking garage. It pays to have a student for your escort.

I felt the stress drain from my body stair by stair, lifting my spirits to soar as the happy notes of Toby Keith's popular *Red Solo Cup* led us to UA's South Ballroom. Jeremy helped the doorman search his list for our names. I scanned the already sizeable crowd. Red bandanna and straw-hatted coed servers—their trays filled with red plastic cups full of unknown concoctions—wound their way through the tables. Red basketball-sized balloons hung from the ceiling like bunches of giant grapes; a red sequined netted hoop filled with mini basketballs provided a centerpiece for each table. This already had the makings of a night to remember. The doorman pointed us to our table occupied only by Sandy, a pitcher of margaritas, and four—you guessed it—red Solo cups.

Sandy jumped up and hugged us both. She was dressed in a blue denim skirt, white and blue striped western shirt, natural leather vest and boots and a tan Stetson. "So glad you came tonight, Sam, . .Jeremy. How are you? Sorry to hear about your trouble."

"We're darned glad to get out of the house. Thanks for asking us! It looks like it's going to be a fun night," I said, taking the seat Sandy pointed to on her left. "Where's Bud?"

"He's backstage checking on his police buddies who are in the show. He'll join us once they're all here. Shouldn't be long now." She looked at her watch. "They were due by six. Ready for a margarita? Or would you prefer something else? The margaritas were Bud's idea."

"I'll do the honors," said Jeremy grabbing a cup with his left, the pitcher in the right.

"It's about time you two showed up." Bud's voice boomed across the floor. He leaned to kiss my cheek, and said to Sandy, "They're all here, rearing to go. I bought them a drink to settle 'em down. His fingers slid across Jeremy's shoulder as he passed behind to sit at Sandy's right."

His western tailored suit looked a bit fancy for Bud. I wondered if it was for Sandy, or if he was actually dressed up to be a part of the auction. Time would tell.

And tell it did. Seven o'clock arrived too soon, and it was time for Sandy and Bud to go to work. Sandy proved to be just as well poised with a microphone in her hand as she was behind her desk. After she welcomed the crowd, the familiar notes of *Red Solo Cup* once again blasted from the speakers. The curtains parted and Toby himself stepped to the mike with his red Solo cup held high.

"Hey, I heard there was a party goin' on here tonight."

Did I say this had the makings of a fun night? You have no idea. Well, at least it looked and sounded like Toby himself. Everyone was on their feet holding their cups high as they all joined in to sing along. Our look-alike Toby stepped into the role of MC and auctioneer. His wit and tenacity persuaded us all to reach deep into our pockets to send the girls' basketball team to Hawaii. Bud, who was in fact auctioned off along with eight of his Tucson Police Department friends, brought the highest bid. By the end of the auction, Sandy and Toby were proud to announce they had way surpassed their goal of $30,000 and—thanks to the generous merchants and bidders—the girls' team would soon be saying "aloha" to join the competition in the Islands.

At ten o'clock, the band kicked it up a notch and the crowd was ready to dance. Toby joined our table and I don't believe Sandy or I sat out more than a couple of dances. Jeremy taught me a few new moves, and even convinced Sandy to try a number or two with him. Thank God the band took a break on the hour. We gals needed it.

Though not the real thing, our Toby was besieged with autograph seekers; he managed to sneak in more than one dance with each of us. I don't know about Sandy, but I was awestruck as he twirled me across the floor in the Texas-two-step. It was as if we'd been dancing together for years. I felt like Cinderella in the arms of yet another handsome man and hoped the co-eds were envious as the frustrations of the last weeks drained out of me, and were forgotten. It was a night I will always remember.

Then the band announced the last dance. And it was time to pack up and head for home. I had been the winning bidder for a date with Bud, also a dinner certificate at Marriott's Starr Pass Resort & Spa. As we said our goodbyes and thanks for the evening of fun, I presented both the winning tickets to Bud and Sandy with wishes for a wonderful date.

Bud and Sandy escorted us home, handing us over to the deputy at the bottom of the hill. When we approached our gate, Deputy Brooks advised us he would be off duty for the remainder of the night, and McConnell would be on watch for the rest of the night at the start of our lane below. It was seven minutes to one when Jeremy pulled the car through the gate. He dropped me and waited until I was safely inside the front door. Jet toddled along the hall to meet me. He looked a little droopy-eyed. I guessed he was as tired as the rest of us at this hour. I couldn't remember how long it had been since I'd stayed up until one a.m. I peeked in Dad's room, found him with his mouth open, snoring in the recliner. I let him be. No need to disturb him; he deserved a good night's sleep. And I felt I could do the same after such a great evening.

49

The Watchers

There were three of them now, and the Watchers were getting restless. They'd waited since right after dark . . . waiting for the lights to go out, signaling the all clear. But something was different about tonight: a sheriff's deputy had been parked right outside the gate, another stationed at the bottom of the hill where their lane meets Santiago Drive. What the hell was happening? There had been no cars in or out while they'd maintained their vigil since sundown. It seemed everyone was there, but was no one ever going to bed?

"Heads up." The newest member broke the silence. "There's a car approaching from the

highway. No. Two cars. Both stopped at the deputy below the hill."

"One's coming up the lane," said the shorter one. They watched the other car turn back toward the highway. "That's her car coming through the gate. The kid's driving."

They watched as the woman went into the house, the kid closed and checked the gate, then pulled into the garage. Lights went out in the garage, flashed on in the upper story. Her bedroom light came on. Soon, the garage apartment was dark, only the glow of a TV in her bedroom . . . and so they must wait. One deputy was gone, but one stayed at the bottom of the hill.

"Let's have another beer . . . she'll watch TV for a while before she goes to sleep. We'll be waiting at least another hour to make sure they're all out. There will be no trouble from the dog, but we want to avoid any confrontation if possible.

The newest member and the shorter one returned to their chairs out of sight on the side of the truck away from the house. The tall skinny one pulled the cooler over next to them, passed out beers, and sat on down on top of the cooler, leaning

back against the truck to wait.

50

We'd left lights on in the house and yard while we were gone. I flipped them off on my way to bed and it hit me I was tired too . . . although still reeling a little to the music and excitement of the evening out. A whole night without any thought of dangerous threats and crazy happenings. What a welcome feeling.

I'd set the DVR to record the late news before I left, grabbed the remote and clicked it on as I went after my pajamas. Yes, I'd traded Trev's old T-shirt for jammies these days, so one of the guys didn't catch me wandering around the house half dressed.

Commercials finally over, the familiar voice of anchorman, Ted Danvers, rang out as I pulled back the bedspread: "Good evening, folks. Breaking news. Convicted felon George James Dallas was released from Picacho State Correctional Facility today after serving seven years of a . ,.fifteen-year sentence for embezzlement of over one million dollars from the

Arizonian Bank on Skyline Road. Attorney for Dallas, Leonard Pace, spoke to us early this week . . ."

A gaunt and sober face appeared on the screen leaning into a microphone. "James has been a model prisoner. As you know, the missing funds were never recovered. We've always maintained that the real culprit and the money were probably long gone across the border way before James was ever charged and came to trial. I don't believe the authorities ever really looked once they had him in jail. Thank God he's been released."

"Thank you, Mr. Pace. And now we go to Channel 8's Rick Montez, reporting onsite at Picacho."

"Rick Montez here in front of the Arizona Correctional Facility as James Dallas is about to be released after serving seven years of his sentence which many believed was unjustly based on circumstantial evidence."

"And here he comes . . . Mr. Dallas, Channel 8 news. Can you give us a state . . .?" The camera followed Dallas shoving and cursing his way through the crowd that had gathered.

"I'm sorry folks. James Dallas has refused to comment on his way through to his waiting vehicle."

My heart took a giant leap into my throat. "It's the blue Camaro!" I was shaking so badly I could hardly hit the button to rewind the whole newscast to see what I may have missed. I watched it again as the camera followed Dallas, then pulled in for a close up as he jumped into the open-top Camaro, then zeroed in on the driver as they pulled from the lot. Oh my God! It was Susan Duncan—our Mystery Woman.

Thoughts spun through my mind. The blue Camaro. Susan Duncan, Property, previously owned by the Duncan family. We'd dismissed them as suspects for the harassment and threats, thinking there was no reason for them to want this property back. Maybe they didn't want the property back . . . maybe just access to it. . . The missing money! Money that was missing before Trevor bought the property from Hiram Duncan. There was nothing here but the remains of old buildings and a few graves. Graves. Could they . . . would they have dug up a grave? Jesus! No. Remains of the old loafing shed . . . part of the station walls . . . the well. The old well. How deep is the well? Didn't they throw bodies down wells in the old west days? And, no digging . . . it's already done? Trevor had closed the well off with a shelf, down about a foot from the top. Is it possible something had been hidden in the bottom without his noticing? Would he have even checked? The stolen funds must have been buried somewhere on this property.

I threw on some old jeans and ran to wake Dad. He wasn't too hot on getting out of bed but as soon as he understood that I said buried money he perked right up. He grabbed his metal detecting gear and away we went. We thought about calling Bud, but didn't want to disturb plans that he and Sandy may have. Jeremy's lights were out before I had even turned ours out.

"Where's Jet, Dad asked.

"Sound asleep. About like you were when I got home. As a matter of fact, he was even snoring a little when I walked by just now. You must have really given him a workout tonight."

"He should be. We went for a romp down the lane to talk a little shop with Deputy McConnell. Jet barked and raced after rabbits or prairie dogs the whole time. Let's let him sleep."

"Well pilgrim, I guess it's up to the two of us rustle up that money."

It's quiet at two o'clock in the morning. Arizona's clear skies full of stars and about a three-quarter moon allowed us to use no artificial light to keep our caper under wraps as much as possible. It didn't take long for the beep of Dad's metal detector to lead us toward the well. Something metal was down there for sure.

I gave him a high five and helped him remove Trevor's wooden feeding trough. Dad looked down into the well, reported nothing to see but bare brick walls. He shook his head and said, "It looks like another wild goose chase, hon."

I grabbed an LED flashlight from the tack room at the end of the loafing shed, leaned as far as I could down into the well and kicked it up to full power. "There's a shadow or something dark . . . looks like it's coming right out of the bricks." I moved around to the other side of the well until the light confirmed that it wasn't a shadow, but a dark cord coming through the bricks five or six feet down, then disappearing down into the blackness. Back to the tack room for the hay hook we used to pull bales down from the stack. Dad held my belt while I leaned down into the well. After a few misses, I hooked the cord with the gaff, then Dad took over. He put on his leather gloves and worked hand over hand to pull up an awkward bundle wrapped and tied in a black garbage bag to the edge.

"Just like havin' a big halibut on the hook up in Alaska," Dad laughed, as he flopped it over the side. Another high five ended in a bear hug.

"By God, girl, you were right on this one. Let's get this in the house and keep it for Bud or the sheriff in the morning. We got no business handlin' this any more than we have to."

"Besides, I'm pooped."

51

A hand grasped my shoulder, shaking me. I opened my eyes to a gun pointed at my face. I was looking at three intruders wearing nylon hosiery over their faces. The closest one moved back a step but still held the gun pointed right at me. The others stood at the foot of my bed and near the bedroom door. I didn't recognize them. Hell, how could I? They all looked Asian with the nylon pulling their lips and eyes toward the tops of their heads.

"Who are you?" I shouted. I sat up in the bed, pulled the covers up over my pajama top as far as I could, burying my hands in the silk binding to hide their shaking. I looked from one to the other, not really expecting them to tell me anything, but what else does one say with a gun pointed at them?

They didn't actually look like Asians, but that's what their scrunched-up faces made me think of. The toe and heel of the panty hose sticking up at the top of their heads reminded me of Japanese Ninjas with their little braids. They all wore black pants and black T-shirts. One was on the short side, one taller and a little more muscular, and the gunman medium height but skinny.

"Don't worry about who we are," said the skinny one with the gun. "What did you do with our money?"

"Your money? What the hell are you talking about?" Untangling myself from the blanket, I leaped up to face them squarely. I steadied myself, stalling for time, trying to think of some way to get out of this mess.

"Don't be cute with me, Saaa . . maan . . th. .tha. You know damned well what I'm talking about. Since Meester Snake didn't run you off to make it easy, we have to take it directly from you . . . at whatever cost."

My heart took a pole vault right into my throat. So, these were the guys behind all the trouble. What did I ever do to piss off a bunch of Ninjas? More importantly, what was I going to do right now? Where was Bud when I needed him?

"How'd you get in here?" I managed to spit it out, trying to act tough. I looked around, noticed my bedroom door was wide open. "What have you done with Jet?"

"If you're talking about your watch dog, he's taking a little nap."

"You son of a bitch. I'll kill you if you've hurt him."

"I don't believe you're in any position to kill anything, much less the three of us." The skinny one did all of the talking.

"Now hand over the money and we'll get out of here. It's as easy as that." He shrugged his shoulders, waving the gun back and forth in front of my chest.

"I have no idea what you're talking about. There's no money here. I have maybe a little over a hundred dollars in my purse. You're welcome to that if it will get you out of here."

"Don't play cute. We know you found the bag in the well. It was still there last week." It was the taller one talking now. "Now show us where you've hidden it and we'll be out of here."

"Shut your trap," said the skinny one. He shot a quick look at the one who spoke, then brought his attention back on me.

There was something familiar about that other voice, the taller one. He definitely sounded like someone I should recognize. If only he would talk a little more. Here last week? And then, I knew. It was Dennis. The security guy.

"You were here last week. You worked on my alarm system."

"Smart lady. But you're a little too late." He pulled a small black box from his back pocket. It was a remote, a twin to the one he'd left for us when he completed his work. "This got us in with no trouble, but the money wasn't where we left it. Where it was last week. So just tell us . . ."

"Is this what you're looking for?"

All eyes turned to the doorway. It was Dad. He held the dirty bag in one hand, his .357 revolver in the other. He lobbed the black bag directly at the security guy who scrambled to avoid it.

The gunman lunged to grab me. I sidestepped, leaving my left foot in his path, throwing my weight into his side. The element of surprise worked. He went down hard to the floor; his gun clattered across the tile. He wiggled his body like a snake across the squares toward the gun. But there was nothing slow about this snake. It was a race to get there first. His fingers were a scant inch from the grip when my bare foot kicked it away. Those same fingers closed around my ankle and he pulled me down on top of him. I grabbed the stocking from his head, then grasp a handful of his hair and yanked as hard as I could.

"You bitch," he said. Twisting his body from under me, he poked me in the midsection. I coughed and released my grasp; he wrestled himself over to straddle me, his hands suddenly around my throat. "Stay right there, old man," he said. Dad held the others at bay, but they stood between us. "Or I'll snap her neck right now." It was a standoff.

Even skinny as he was, I was no match for his strength. I gasped for breath as his thumbs tightened on my neck. I clawed at his hands, knowing my consciousness would soon slip away if I didn't do something. As he looked at Dad, I drew my right arm back and jabbed my fist into his Adam's apple with everything I had left. His hands went slack. I sucked in a quick breath.

Now it was him doing the gasping. He slumped to the floor, not moving. My God, had I killed him? Bud had said that move could actually do that.

"Sam? You okay?" Dad's voice sounded shaky, betraying his fright. "I was about ready to shoot that son of a bitch just as you threw that punch. Good work, girl. You really whupped his ass."

Savoring a deep breath this time, I turned my head and nodded to Dad. His gun was still trained on the other two.

"We make a pretty darn good team, Dad." I eased my already aching bones up off the floor, walked over to pick up the gun, and pointed it directly at Skinny's contorted face, but could see he was in no shape to go anywhere.

"Where in hell did you learn that little trick?" asked Dad.

"Our friendly neighborhood detective."

We heard the welcome sound of sirens coming up our lane. "Here comes the posse," Dad snickered. "I called Bud when the shouting woke me up. Go on out and open the gate, Honey. It'll be my pleasure to keep these guys covered. And check on Jet. He was just layin' there in his bed when I came by. Not like him at all."

"Oh my God. That son of a bitch did something to him. I hope I killed the bastard."

"Don't worry. That damned dog'll be awake before morning," Dennis said. "Just ate a little meat with some sleeping pills."

The Pima County patrol car raced through the gate as Jeremy ran from the garage door. Seeing me, he called out, "What's going on? Is everyone okay?" Under other circumstances I would have probably broken out in laughter. His hair spiked in all directions, he wore only a pair of cut-offs, his face pinched in pain. He ran across the driveway, threw his arms around me and said, "Sam, are you all right? Where's Hank?"

Deputy McConnell jumped from his car, turned to see Bud's Victoria sliding to a halt next to him. Bud threw himself out the door while it was still moving. Dad was right. It was the posse. I could see two or more sets of spinning red and blue lights streaming up the lane.

"Let's get inside," I shouted. "Dad's got them covered in the bedroom."

Dad had the three of them down on the floor, their hoods removed when we all rushed into the bedroom. The smaller one faced away from us, fussing over the skinny one I jabbed in the throat. He was still flat out. I recognized the third. He was indeed Dennis from Desert Security.

Bud and McConnell stepped inside and took control, cautioning the three not to move or talk as Dad and I related the story.

The deputies from the other two cars and two EMTs from an ambulance announced themselves from the front door and joined us. The skinny one pulled himself up, his upper lip curled in a sneer. "I paid for that money," he croaked, barely able to whisper. "With seven years of my life."

"That's him," Jeremy squeezed through the doorway, pointing. "It's that Dallas guy. The one that stole the bank money we've been researching."

"Yeah . . . and hid it in the old stage well. Sam saw him on TV tonight after you two got home and figured it all out after seeing our Mystery Woman here and her blue Camaro at the prison to pick him up this afternoon." Dad said as he nodded toward the woman still fussing over Dallas.

"Sam grabbed me and the metal detector and we went prospecting. The signals were coming through pretty faint at first, but got stronger closer to the well. We took the feeding trough clear out and shone a good light down there. That bag there was at the end of a rope buried inside the mortar in the shadows.

"We decided to hold it until morning rather than waking everyone in the middle of the night and we went to bed. I heard Sam shouting. I grabbed my gun and came running.

"And not a moment too soon," I said.

"You guys should have seen Sam. She knocked the shit out of that guy."

"Looks like she did that, all right," said Bud. "Dallas has been out less than one day and he's on his way back already. Along with his friends. Now, let's get these guys loaded into the patrol cars and into the station for booking."

I looked at Dallas as two of the deputies helped him up and cuffed him, wondering if he would ever be able to talk again. I guess maybe even feeling a little bit sorry for him until I remembered how viciously he had attacked me, how threatening he'd been with that gun in his hand.

For the first time, his smaller companion's face turned toward mine.

"Why the hell couldn't you have just gone away?" she said. "That's all we wanted. No one needed to get hurt." Our mystery woman. The one we'd been trying to identify for weeks, only this week to merely dismiss her as a person of interest when we realized she was Mr. Duncan's daughter. Now I knew only time would reveal the real story about these three. And I was happy to say goodbye to all of them.

Bud stayed behind as the Pima County boys loaded up and drove off with the bad guys. The EMTs checked Jet before they left, assuring us that his vitals were just fine and he was in fact only sleeping it off.

"Look at the way his front paw is jerking," said Dad. "I'll bet he knows he's missing out on something and is trying to wake himself up."

"You're partly right," I said, smiling as I knelt down and stroked his neck. "He'd really be sorry if he could understand what went on here tonight and he wasn't able to come to my rescue. He's quite a dog."

"Are you guys going to be all right?" Bud asked. "I want to be at the station when these guys are questioned."

"I think we'll be fine, now, Bud," Dad said. He grabbed my hand and pulled me to him, circled his arm around my shoulders, drawing me even closer as I wrapped both arms tightly around his middle. "I think we're going to be just fine."

Bud nodded and smiled. "I hear that."

"I'll come over in the morning to bring you up to date on everything. Try to get some sleep and call if you need me. I'll be close by, over at the county jail." He gave us his classic salute and was gone.

"He didn't even tell us to lock the door." I said.

"I think those days are over," Jeremy said. "At least I hope so."

"Amen," Dad and I blurted our agreement at the same time.

"Now, who's up for a good strong Baileys Irish Cream and coffee to settle us down so we can get back to bed?" I asked, heading for the kitchen.

"Okay if we work on the puzzle? Jeremy said.

"Baileys and puzzles . . ." Dad said, his palms seemingly weighing the two in his hands. "Probably take both of them to settle us down after this. You've got my vote."

52

We stayed up until almost time to get up. We worked the jigsaw and each had a couple of coffees with Baileys. Guess the caffeine was working against the alcohol and the lure of the puzzle kept our attention until we all finally said: "Enough."

Before we went to bed, we had agreed to do a champagne brunch to celebrate. After all, tomorrow was Sunday morning. And this celebration called for quiche—now that Dad had proclaimed himself a quiche man—and biscuits and gravy. Nothing like a good healthy egg dish combined with a load of carbs from buttermilk biscuits and cream gravy.

It was a short night. I woke up hungry and finally hauled my butt out of bed a little after nine. I showered, dressed and found Dad in the kitchen, up to his elbows in flour.

"What in the world are you making?"

"Well, well, well. Look who's up. I was about ready to see if you had skipped out. Since no one else was worrying about that brunch we discussed last night, I thought I'd better get busy. Called Betsy for her biscuit recipe. Hope that goes along with what you're planning 'cause it's too late to change. I'm past the point of no return, just about ready to start cutting 'em out. Bets said we could keep them in the fridge until we got half an hour from baking time but they'll be like Rooster Cogburn's corn dodgers if we get carried away with the champagne and leave 'em in there too long."

"That's perfect. Just what we need to go with the seafood quiche I'm going to make. Are you any good at making gravy?"

"Already got you covered. I thawed out some Jimmy Dean's sausage for gravy starter. The way I look at it, there's nothing that won't go with some good ol' country biscuits and gravy."

"And, from the looks of that mess you're making, you'll end up with enough leftover flour on that breadboard to have plenty for your gravy."

"Picky, picky, picky. But, damned nice to hear you joking again. Things were getting pretty tense around here. Have you heard anything from Bud this morning?"

"I gave him a call a few minutes ago. Told him we have a bottle of champagne on ice and plan to pop it at 11:30. He's going to pick up some more on his way over, agrees we've got some real celebrating to do."

I took two bags of shrimp from the freezer and a can of lump crab meat from the pantry, and stuck the shrimp in cold water to thaw. I chopped some green onions, cilantro, and a couple of jalapenos, and then sliced fresh mushrooms. When the shrimp was just right to peel off the outer shell, I deveined and cut it into bite-sized pieces. Then, sautéed the veggies and mushrooms, tossed in the shrimp until it turned pink, and set it all aside while I mixed up the rest of the quiche ingredients in a large bowl. I folded in the shrimp and crab mixture, then divided it into two greased fluted quiche dishes. Into the refrigerator they went, beside the awaiting biscuits. It was time for the festivities to begin.

"How's the party going?" Bud's voice boomed from the kitchen. "From the looks of this empty Baileys bottle on the cupboard and the iced open bottle of champagne, I'd say you guys are off to a good start without me."

"We're in the great room," Dad called. "And, you're damned right. We were ready to celebrate. Where you been?"

"I spent what was left of the night with our perps. Would you believe Susan Duncan is secretly married to Dallas? She was the first to spill. She convinced Dallas to stash the money in the well, knowing it was a safe place since her father had vowed to keep the historic property intact as long as he was alive. Dallas was convicted long before Trevor purchased this property. As his release neared, Susan and Dennis—he turns out to be Dallas's step-brother—have been following the plan the three of them worked out over the last few months to chase Sam off the property, so they could rescue the money once Dallas was again free.

"Dennis took the job with Desert Security to get access to the plans for your system, Sam, in case it was needed. Your call to increase the service was a bonus. Though he hasn't admitted it yet, we think he was probably behind the regular serviceman's hit and run accident. And, I checked our Camaro list and guess whose name is on it? George J. Dallas. James is his middle name. We had all the pieces. Just couldn't put them together."

Bud grabbed a glass of bubbles and joined us at the jigsaw. "Scoot over, Jeremy. Make room for the master." He raised his hands, rubbing palms together. "I haven't worked one of these for years, but I used to be pretty darned good at it. Especially when I'm the only sober one at the table."

"Don't knock over your glass patting yourself on the back," I said, holding up my champagne. "This is only our first glass. We emptied the Baileys last night. Now that we're all here, who's ready for a toast? Here's to our kick ass team . . . many thanks to you all."

Bud jumped up, glass in the air. "Here's to Sam's quick thinking and Hank's metal detecting to wrap this whole thing up."

"Well, let me tell ya, pilgrims," Dad casually stood, tipped his head a little downward, pushed back the brim of a faked hat, then rested his hand on his hip as if ready to draw. "I was ready to shoot them bastards if it hadn't been for the little Missy here a beatin' me to the punch. Literally."

We all burst into laughter. A hearty "Here, here," resounded around the table as the guys stood, their glasses raised to me.

"And," said Jeremy, trying to clear the catch in his throat, "here's to my new found family and to quieter days ahead."

All eyes turned a little glassy as together we nodded and took a long drink of our bubbles.

As the guys rambled on, each with their own thoughts on the recent happenings, I sneaked into the kitchen to check on the "Egg Pies" already in the oven. It was time to add the big tray of Betsy's biscuits and stir Dad's Sausage Gravy in the Crock Pot. Listening to their laughter, ribbing each other a little, able to let go of the tension and really get to know each other, I got a little teary and I took a few minutes to compose myself as Jet padded over from his bed beside the kitchen door. I gave him a treat and rubbed his back. "I think it's going to be all right now, boy. It's all over."

I stole an orange slice from my fruit salad waiting in the refrigerator. Everything was ready to serve, thanks to Jeremy the table was already set. And as if on cue, here they came—empty glasses in hand ready to pop another bottle of champagne. "What a team!"

Epilogue

It was over, all over. And, we were damned glad of it. Dallas was back at Picacho State Prison, his accomplices were in the county jail awaiting trial, and things were settling back down. Dad had gone back home; Mom made a quick trip down to Tucson to "help me get things back to normal." It only took a couple of weeks for her to learn that I didn't want to get back to the way things were before all the bad things began. I had decided to change my life, to live out Trevor's wishes as I promised, to live for myself and for him. What that might bring I didn't know, but it wasn't going to go back to where I'd been for the last nine months. I wouldn't do that to myself, to him, or to his memory.

Maybe it took the bad things to make me realize what I needed to do, what I had to do. To make some drastic changes, to get back to my journal, to sort things out, and to understand the meaning of living as Trevor wanted. So be it.

Christmas had been a special time for Trevor and me. We chose tree ornaments as we traveled, picking up little mementos all year long to commemorate important events in our life together. We relived those memories as we hung each on the tree to share throughout each holiday season. It was an eclectic tree, like our home had become over the few short years we had together.

I'd seen trees so painstakingly decorated in matching blue bulbs, blue lights, even blue snowflakes and blue tinsel. Ours had been a simple freshly cut green tree, the unmatched ornaments ranged from a ceramic totem pole from Vancouver Island to a plastic surfboarding Santa from Maui, a miniature sombrero from Cancun, and a Voodoo mask from Haiti. A cracked and faded angel I'd made for my grandmother using flour and water dough when I was little. Gram had hung it on her tree every Christmas from that time. And it had decorated mine since she passed. Those are the true ornaments for the holidays, the things to celebrate. To go over memories as we hung each bobble. To laugh at times, cry at others; to share those memories with our friends and family . . . and ourselves over and over again.

And that's what happened Thanksgiving weekend. El Rancho de Santiago became alive again: alive with laughter and love among family and friends.

Dad was back, with Betsy this time, to announce to the world that they are, in fact, in love. And loving their little piece of the world in the mountains. Both happy to be away from home, here in the sunshine rather than the snow that is already piling up in Elk City, Idaho. And, Betsy's already taken Amber, Jeremy's new friend, under her wing while he attends to the drink orders.

Rosa and Manny had prepared the table of Mexican delicacies—in miniature so we can each enjoy a taste of everything. Including the little red and green foil cups filled with their chocolate flan and a few pitchers of—what else—red and green margaritas.

Bud and Jeremy had charge of the bar; and Dad the coats (though sweaters or a light jacket or two was all he collected thanks to our gorgeous fall weather). Sheriff Schaeffer and Deputy McConnell brought their wives along but the boys navigated directly to the bar to catch up on the latest news in the "Dallas Caper."

Mom and Tom arrived yesterday, taking time from their busy schedule to see how the other half lives without the bright lights and busy streets of Las Vegas. She's right in her element, though, flitting from group to group to welcome everyone, especially those she's never met.

The Morrisons are all here—Teri and Jon mixing, already acquainted with the new faces, Jon now trying to convince the wives of the sheriff and deputy to enroll in his free golf clinic for the families of Pima County peace officers. And what's a holiday party without kids? Josh and Sara were already stretched out on the leather sectional sipping Shirley Temples, watching yet another showing of *Miracle on 34th Street*. An annual tradition at the Beales.

Debbie and I had finally met for that promised lunch, and I'd heard all about her new cowboy, Will Engle. He was easy to pick out of tonight's crowd . . . western cut jeans and shirt, the ever-present Stetson. And just as good looking as she'd said. I melted when he shook my hand. His "nice to finally get to meet you, Sam," delivered with the slightest hint of drawl, his smile as big as all of Texas from which he hails.

Sandy Marks and Debbie seem to have struck up quite a friendship since arriving. I knew they would hit it off, as Sandy and I did when we met that first day at the U. The dean is quite a remarkable woman. Now sitting at Trevor's piano, she's collected a crowd around her for a sing-along. Didn't I tell you she was a take-charge person? I waited to see the look on her face when she hears Debbie's beautiful voice.

I tinge of jealousy rippled through my chest, quickly replaced by thoughts of Trevor and my promise to him. Will I make it through this evening . . . this weekend? This season of joy? My family, my friends are here . . . yet I can't shake the feeling of being alone. And, yes . . . they will be gone in a few days. Then what? I glanced again at the bar, the myriad of chili pepper lights once again lighting up the patio. Bud looked at me now, his wink triggered my smile, my nod. Warmth streamed through my heart and in that moment, I knew I was not alone.

As the beginning chords of *White Christmas* rolled from the baby grand, Jet sprang from his bed and headed toward the door just as the doorbell rang. Bud met me at the front door, reached across me to open it. Still the protector.

The handsome face wore a familiar wide grin; the voice boomed a "Happy Thanksgiving, Sam. Special Delivery from Montana," as the weathered hand of another cowboy pointed to the Christmas tree perched beside him on the walk, then swept the Stetson from his head.

"It's Clay Harding. Trevor's longtime friend." I cried. "What a surprise. Come in, Clay." I grabbed his hand. "What brings you to Arizona? Snow getting too deep for you up around Kalispell?

"Well, it's started already, but not so deep that I couldn't cut you a tree to bring along. I promised Trevor I'd deliver this and a package from him for your Christmas this year. He said you liked to trim your tree right after Thanksgiving. We received a flight forecast yesterday showing clear skies all the way down, so here I am. But it looks like I'm intruding . . . guess I shoulda called."

"No way!" I said, but beyond that, I was speechless.

Bud stepped in, his hand out to shake Clay's and help with the tree. "Don't know if you remember me, Clay. I'm Bud . . . Bud Holloway. Your timing couldn't have been better. Sam's having a little holiday kick-off this weekend and you have saved the rest of us from going tree shopping tomorrow." That drew laughter from the crowd. "I'm probably not the only one here who's heard Trevor's stories about you two through the years— you guys did have some adventures."

"Yes, we did," Clay smiled and nodded his head. "That we did."

I made his official introduction to the whole group who in return welcomed him all at once with a boisterous, "Welcome, Clay!" Sandy and the carolers finished their *White Christmas*, there was a lot of laughing, getting better acquainted, and reminiscing as the guys rallied to bring in my holiday storage containers from the garage and everyone joined in to decorate the tree. Each had tales of Trevor that were shared through the evening. Yes, there were tears, but they were the good kind. The kind that helps you remember, not forget. The kind that cleanse and ease your heart. The kind that you want and need to share.

"I know you and Trevor found new ornaments for your Christmas tree each year to commemorate important moments in your life, Sam," Bud said as we all gathered around the bedazzled and twinkling tree. He stepped toward me holding out a tiny package wrapped in silver foil, the loops of the red and green bow hanging over its edges like of a weeping willow. "I think this is a good time for you to open this."

All eyes were on me as I pulled off the bow, careful not to tear the wrap. Inside the tissue-lined box nestled a sterling silver globe, a little bigger than a golf ball. I pulled it from the box and dangled it from its red ribbon as I read aloud: "Today is the First Day of the Rest of Your Life" scrolled into the shining surface. I noted the RQ—initials of my friend and Native American artist, Raymond Quannie—along the bottom.

"It's exquisite," I said, blinking back tears, wrapping Bud in a hug. "Thank you."

"Merry Christmas, a bit early," he said and held me in his arms as everyone applauded. "And, Raymond sends his love."

We found the perfect spot to hang it between two lights that reflected tiny beams from the etched message of the slowly rotating ball. It *was* stunning.

We talked Clay into staying for Thanksgiving dinner with us at the El Commodore the next day. Another Beale tradition. Their famous annual never-ending buffet literally stretches from the front door clear across the resort lobby and down the long, wide hallway bordering their shops and restaurants. My stepdad, Tom was so impressed that he promised to add a similar buffet to the

Monte Bello's holiday fare, inviting us all to do this again in Las Vegas the following year. Of course, we all pledged to do just that.

Clay dropped off a package for me on Friday on his way to the private airport in Marana to fly back home to Montana. It was a leather shoulder pouch that I recognized to be Trevor's.

"He sent this to me about a year ago," Clay said. "There's a letter inside addressed to you, with his journals."

"Journals?" I said, "I never knew Trevor to keep a journal."

"I'm not sure when he started, but know he wrote during college and through our Navy years. Maybe he kept them at his office. At any rate he wanted you to have them after he was gone."

"I can't thank you enough for bringing them. And the beautiful tree. What a wonderful surprise. I wasn't sure how I was going to get through the tree thing, wasn't sure that I could. You made it a night to remember, Clay . . . a night of fun and sharing. Just the way it should be—and will be from now on. You know you're always welcome here. Please don't be a stranger."

He circled me in his arms, whispered, "God, I know how you miss him, as I do, Sam. I'm so sorry for the trouble you've had. But glad that's behind you now. If I can ever do anything, you just call."

He swiped at the tears that were clouding his eyes, nodded, and turned down the walkway. "Let me know if you want the same size tree next year . . . and the same delivery date. I put my address and phone in the pocket on the outside of that pouch, just to make sure it's handy. Please use it—anytime."

The End

Recipes featured in Sonoran Shadows

Sam's Southwest Pasta Salad

8 oz Bowtie Pasta
1 Tbsp Cilantro, fresh
4 Green Onions
1 small jalapeno, seeded, chopped
1 small can Sun Dried Tomatoes, reserve 1 tbsp oil
1 small jar Artichoke Hearts
1/3 cup EVOO
1 tsp Lemon Juice, fresh
Mrs. Dash seasoning to taste
Black Pepper

Cook pasta and cool. Wash and chop cilantro, green onions, and jalapeno. Mix oils, lemon juice, Mrs. Dash, and pepper; set aside. Drain tomatoes and artichokes. Cut into bite size pieces. Combine all ingredients, increase seasonings as needed. Chill at least 2 hours for flavors to blend.

Jeremy's Five Layer Burgers

1 ½ pound Ground Chuck
½ cup Roquefort Cheese
8 oz. Fresh Mushrooms
1 Red Onion
1 Garlic Clove
Butter
2 Avocados
Lemon or lime juice
4 Kaiser Buns
Poppy seed dressing

Divide beef into 8 portions, make into bun sized patties. Spoon Roquefort on four patties, cover with second patty and press edges together to seal. Loosely cover and hold in refrigerator. Clean and slice mushrooms, slice onion, separate into rings. Mince garlic. Sauté onions in butter, add mushrooms and garlic about halfway through. Peel and slice avocados, drizzle with lemon or lime juice to prevent browning. Toast buttered buns on griddle. Place slices of avocado on bun bottom, top with burger, spoon mushroom/onion mixture over top of burger, spread bun tops with dressing, place on top of burger and insert pick to hold.

Bud's Raspberry Cheese Cake

8 oz Cream Cheese, room temperature
14 oz can Sweetened Condensed Milk
21 oz can Raspberry Pie Filling
1 tsp. Vanilla
8 oz Whipped Topping, thawed
1/3 cup Lemon Juice
1 Graham Cracker Pie crust

Thoroughly blend cream cheese and milk, stir in filling and vanilla, add whipped topping and lemon juice. Pour into crust and chill to set.

Sam's Crustless Seafood Quiche (6 servings)

4 eggs
1 c. sour cream
1 c. small curd cottage cheese
½ c. grated parmesan cheese
¼ c. flour
1 tsp. onion powder
½ tsp. salt
2 c. shredded Pepper Jack cheese
½ pound fresh mushrooms, sliced
2 tbsp. butter
1/4 c. chopped green onions
16 oz. deveined shrimp, cut in bite-size pieces
2 tbsp. fresh cilantro, chopped
8-12 oz. crab meat, bite-size pieces

Sauté mushrooms, onions, and shrimp in butter. When shrimp is pink, stir in crab and cilantro, remove from heat and drain. Combine eggs, sour cream, cottage cheese, parmesan cheese, flour, onion powder and salt in a large bowl and blend with a hand-held blender until smooth (or use blender or food processor). Fold in jack cheese and drained cooked mixture.

Spray 9" deep-dish pie plate or 10" quiche dish with cooking spray. Bake at 350 for 45-60 min. Top will brown, knife comes out clean. Let stand about 5 min before cutting and serving.

Note: This recipe works well to double the basic egg mixture part to split between two different meat fillings. I usually make one with the seafood, the other with sautéed bacon and/or sausage, mushrooms, and green onions to serve a larger group.